THE
OBITUARY
PAGE

Also by David Ackley

Mystery
The Opinion Page

Magical Realism
Prospero's Staff

Historical Fiction
The Patent Clerk's Violin
The Language of Equals

THE
OBITUARY
PAGE

DAVID ACKLEY

RAIN AND BREEZE BOOKS

MOSCOW, IDAHO

David Ackley/Rain and Breeze Books, LLC
P.O. Box 9874
Moscow, ID 83843
www.rainandbreeze.com

Publisher's Note: This is a work of fiction. Any references to historical events, real people, or real places are used fictitiously. Other names, characters, places, and incidents are a product of the author's imagination and any resemblance of these to actual people, living or dead, businesses, companies, events, institutions or locales is purely coincidental. Locales and public names are sometimes used for atmospheric purposes.

Book Layout © 2014 BookDesignTemplates.com
Cover photo: istockphoto.com/TonyBaggett. Lettering by author

The Obituary Page/ David Ackley. -- 1st ed.
Library of Congress Control Number: 2021924110
ISBN 978-1-950631-02-5 (Paperback)
ISBN 978-1-950631-03-2 (Ebook)

Rain . . . rain . . . rain . . . we are buried in rain,
It will rain forever, the swift wheels hiss through water,
Pale sheets of water gleam in the windy street.
The pealing of bells is lost in a drive of rain-drops.
Remote and hurried the great bells beat.

— From: The House of Dust by Conrad Aiken

CHAPTER 1.

THE DECIBEL levels were off the chart, and Galen dug at the pain in his left ear as an iron bar hit the floor while pneumatic wrenches hammered and whined in the background. The busy garage had cars jacked up at five stations for tire changes. Strangely, he appreciated the noise, since it covered up much of Mike Carlson's continuing harangue. "... couldn't find your ass if it was welded on..." came through as Galen motioned once again that they should retreat into the Butler Tire Center's office space so they could possibly hear each other.

Carlson yelled something to his employees on the floor and then led Galen back into a minimally quieter, and much messier room. When Mike yanked two plugs out of his ears as the door shut, the detective understood how he could bear the daily aural onslaught. The distraught garage owner sank into a swivel chair near a desk and seemed to deflate at the same time.

"I know it's frustrating," said Galen, leaning against the nearest wall, "but we really have nothing much more to go on. We have all-points bulletins out across the city for her or her car, and the Bureau is dedicating its resources to locating your wife." He neglected to mention that the Portland Police Bureau was so overworked at the current time that Detective Galen Young was pretty much the extent of the resources available. And his plate was full.

"She wouldn't just walk away," Carlson muttered. "Something must have happened to her. You've checked all the hospitals? The fucking morgue? I'm just dreading that call...," he tapered off.

"Yes, of course, we've checked. There's no reason to expect that anything untoward has happened to Erin. Maybe she just needed a break or had some other reason for spending time by herself. You said that there were no problems with your marriage?"

Carlson shook his head adamantly. "No. Like I told you, everything has been fine."

"Well, then as I've said previously, it would help us immensely if we could have access to her phone rec..."

"No way!" Carlson jumped in. "I told you before. I'm not having the goddamned government digging around in our personal information! Once you have that, God knows what else you'll do with it!"

Galen could see that Carlson was winding up again, and so instead of saying, "But that is exactly the information we need to help find your wife," he said calmly, "Well, even without it, we have a very good chance of locating your wife, so I'll keep you apprised as soon as anything develops," without mentioning that, as with all missing persons cases, the odds were equally good that she may never be found.

"Everything OK in here? Any news?" asked Glenn Knowles as he entered, awash in a wave of sound until the door shut behind him. "Hi, Detective," he said as he passed by him and took a seat.

"Hello, Mr. Knowles."

"Yeah, Glenn, it's all good, and no. No news," replied Carlson. Knowles was Carlson's brother-in-law and was equally concerned about the whereabouts of his sister-in-law as Galen knew based on previous interviews with the man.

Carlson immediately started ranting to Knowles about the lack of progress in the case and unceremoniously waved Galen out of his office while he piled on his complaints. Galen's last image of the pair was of Carlson sinking his head into his hands as he himself walked through cacophony and outside to the quiet of his waiting car. This was the fourth time in the past two weeks that Carlson had demanded an in-person update on the status of his missing wife and he'd received much the same answer with each visit.

The detective removed his mask and put his key into the ignition, but instead of twisting it, let his hand drop into his lap. The afternoon sun glared off the opened white envelope he'd thrown on the dash that morning, and he closed his eyes to avoid it, levering his head back against the headrest. *Just a moment of ...* he thought.

He was sure it was only seconds later when he was startled awake by the creaking of the tire center's huge garage door being opened for another customer. Galen rubbed his face, reached for the envelope, and was rereading the notice that his upcoming mandatory retirement date was in less than a year, when he looked up as a thought came to him.

What is that quote about protesting too much? he wondered, realizing that the same could be said of Portland lately. *I think I need to take a closer look into Mike Carlson and his actions around the time that Erin disappeared. He seems genuinely concerned, but won't give us the information we need to find his wife. I think I'd better dig around a bit more, just to be on the safe side.*

He wadded up the letter and tossed it on the floor mat, extracted himself from his sedan, redonned his mask, and spent the remainder of the late afternoon interviewing each of the busy garage employees about Mike Carlson and his wife Erin under the watchful gaze of the Butler Tire Center's related co-owners.

On the drive back to headquarters, he found that he'd already mentally filed his report on this, one of the least productive cases in his current workload.

Chapter 2.

I HOPE Robert Armlin is still alive, but I wish this damn case would just die, thought Galen the next morning as, for the umpteenth time, he stepped up to the familiar brick walkway leading to the Armlin house. He was emotionally drained by the whole affair, and he was sure that Armlin's wife, Emma, was even more wrung out by it.

The high-profile case, which had seemed to grow cold over the past three months, was still not without a few smoldering embers of hope and frustration. Emma was deluged daily with emails that ranged from quirky to threatening, but since her husband's disappearance, three seemingly solid ransom demands had sparked interest. The first was the most credible of the three and had been received by Emma a month after Armlin had vanished. An envelope included in her normal mail had contained a short lock of Armlin's gray hair along with the picture of a bewildered-looking man staged against a blank white background. The photo of the missing newspaper editor had been optimistically taken as proof of life and had both surprised and energized the Portland Police Bureau since the consensus among the detectives up to that point had been that Armlin had long since met a bad end. The postmark on the envelope had been from Longview, Washington, a town located further west from Portland down the Columbia River toward the Pacific Ocean.

Galen had been part of the all-out effort to discover and nab the ransomer, but Forensics had found no match to the DNA discovered on the typed letter and nothing had turned up in Longview. It was difficult to say whether anyone had approached the arranged money drop at an Albertsons grocery store parking lot on the SW Beaverton Hillsdale Hwy in southwest Portland—a location very near to where Armlin had disappeared in the first place. The drop site itself had shown nothing but normal shopping traffic at the prearranged exchange time, but a nearby episode had raised some eyebrows. Detective Jenkins had been stationed on the periphery, slumped against the far end of the store near a small adjoining recycle center. Dressed as a homeless person, he'd been ignored by shoppers during the scheduled drop-off. However, as things were wrapping up after forty-five minutes with no show by the ransomers, a car had pulled up to the recycle center. Jenkins had thought the driver was acting strangely—dumping some papers, pulling some back out and sifting through them while eyeing the far end of the grocery store the entire time. Jenkins had risen to confront the COVID-masked man when the jittery suspect had jumped into his car and peeled out of the parking lot into honking traffic. No positive identifications had been made of the driver, and the license plates had been removed from the older model car, so it was impossible to discover whether he was connected with the kidnapping or not.

The second ransom note was more mundane and had also been typewritten and received by the Managing Editor of the Portland Sentinel where Armlin had been employed as the Opinion Page editor. However, the muddled and vague copycat attempt had been easily traced, resulting in serious charges against the misguided sender.

Now, a third ransom note in as many months had arrived—remarkably similar to the first and discovered by Emma on her doorstep that morning. Forensics had already visited the scene and taken the hand-addressed envelope along with the typewritten demand folded inside it for processing.

Emma lived in an older Craftsman-style house in the long-established Goose Hollow neighborhood of the city, nestled under the steep wooded hill that stretched up toward the Oregon Zoo, the International Rose Test Garden, and the Hoyt Arboretum beyond. Galen had visited the house on Myrtle St. so frequently over the past months that it had become almost like a second home to him. "Hello, Emma," he said as the door swung open soon after his knock. "I understand there's been another note."

"Hello, Galen, good to see you," Emma replied, and Galen could easily picture her welcoming smile beneath her blue oriental-themed mask. "Yes, and this one could just be the sorriest of the three. It's nearly identical to the first one, but with nothing to show that Robert is still alive. Could it be real? I'm sure it's just been planted here to torture me for some reason—just like those online trolls."

Galen nodded as he made certain that his own mask was secure. "Do you mind if I have a look at it?" Adjusting the mask had brought on a terrible itching to his left jaw, and he fought off the insistent urge to scratch.

"Sure. Care for some lemonade in the back garden?"

Although he'd often been inside her house, he'd never visited the backyard, and on such a warm, sunny autumn day this sounded perfect. "Sure," he echoed back.

Emma led him through her home, and Galen was reassured to see that it was tidy and well-kept. During the worst days of Emma's dealing with her missing husband, the house had been in a total state of disarray. Her sister, Maureen, had come to the rescue, and Emma had shown the physical and mental benefits of the visit during that trying time.

"How is Maureen?" asked Galen once he had been seated in a peaceful pergola just off the back wall of the house. They'd both agreed that it was fine to lower their masks once outside, and it was good to see Emma's face which was so like that of her sister.

"Stuck in New Jersey because of the virus, but otherwise doing OK. Well, maybe not. That legislature there is driving her absolutely nuts—they're even worse than COVID!"

Galen lowered his head and sipped at his tall lemonade glass, hoping that this visit wouldn't turn into a political rant. *Well, it would be a rant to me, simply because I don't usually agree with her point of view,* he thought.

"Oh, now, don't worry, I know your leanings," said Emma, reading Galen's mind as she often did.

"Nah, this pandemic has us all coming and going," said Galen. "Not to worry. So, forensics has the original?"

"Yes, they're going to check for fingerprints and DNA, but they gave me a copy. Here, have a look."

Emma consulted her phone and passed him a scanned image showing the dark folds that had been made to fit the page into an envelope. The message and wording closely matched the first ransom demand.

We have your husband, and I promise you things will become worst for him if you dont do what I say. I'm serios. Dont call the police and come by yourself to George Park in the St. Johns part of town. Drop a plastik bag with $20,000 in the trash near the northeast corner at noon sharp this Friday. This will be your last chance.

"Wow, that is very similar to the first—even the misspellings, like the word 'serious' if I recall," said Galen.

"Yes, I confirmed with your colleagues that the only changes were the details about the drop-off spot." She glanced at him with the same sad-eyed expression that he'd seen so often. "It's just more fluff and stuff... isn't it, Galen? Should I do it? Leave the money like they said?"

Galen nodded. "We'll follow the same procedure as before—flood the scene with undercover cops who no one will ever pick out—maybe even disguised as old ladies with grandkids..." Emma gave him back a grin. "And we'll arrest whoever shows up to claim the prize. If they show up this time."

"I'm numb, Galen, absolutely numb. All of that hope I built up with the first demand—only to have it all lead to absolutely nothing. And that only added to the misery and confusion of the days just after he disappeared—first Robert is missing, then he's accused of being an adulterer, then suspected of being a kidnapper himself, then..."

Galen understood and was a little embarrassed at the same time. Robert Armlin had disappeared, and the first clues had convinced the detective that the 70-plus-year-old editor was off having a fling. The available information had then pointed to Armlin being the kidnapper of a four-year-old girl. And the final outcome had been that he'd tried to rescue the girl from the actual kidnapper, but had disappeared in the process. Now ransom notes kept popping up and reanimating the tired case. No wonder Emma was skeptical about this most recent development and unimpressed with the Bureau's flailing efforts in discovering Robert's fate.

He reexamined the image. *And the envelope didn't even include a picture or any proof that the ransomer has Armlin. Just another lame attempt at some money?* he wondered as he handed back the phone.

"Did you ever get that home security video system installed like we suggested?" he asked hopefully.

Emma wiped the sweat off her tall glass and took a long drink of the tart version of lemonade she'd served. Meeting Galen's eyes, she said, "No, and truthfully, I probably never will. This is a good neighborhood, and I don't want to add any more distrust into my life right now. Anyway, at my age..."

Galen hid his mild frustration. They'd disagreed on this before, and so he decided to change the subject. "Great lemonade by the way, and not too sweet at all—what's your secret?"

"We learned this in Nepal—lemons, a bit of sugar, and some salt. It quenches your thirst and gives you back the salt your body needs on a hot day."

"Thanks, it hits the spot," said the detective as he felt his phone vibrate in his pocket. "I'd better go, Emma, but I just wanted to make sure you were doing OK. We'll coordinate the Friday drop off and I'll drive you there myself, so don't worry. Are you staying connected with the world?"

"Oh, heck yes," Emma reassured him. "Zoom civic meetings, the Grant's stop by to play socially distant Rummy here in the pergola, and Maureen is going to move here once this pandemic cools down. Even if we find Robert, she wants to come. The house is plenty big for all of us either way. She says that with people moving out of the city, she can make a killing on her place in Maple Grove, and that it's getting too crowded there anyway."

They said their goodbyes, and Galen found himself wishing that hugs were once again acceptable. Emma's had always been great.

CHAPTER 3.

GALEN STARTED his car and put it in gear, but then remembered the missed call. He shifted to park and rolled down the side windows to get some air into the musty sedan. He suspected that he had a leak where water entered somewhere, because the smell of mildew was getting stronger, especially on the wet days. The number that came up was that of Jodi Knowles, Erin Carlson's sister, and he tapped the icon on his phone to return her call.

"Hi, Detective Young," said Jodi, obviously having stored his number as well.

"Hello, Ms. Knowles, you called me a minute ago?"

"Um, yes, and thanks for calling back." There was a long pause, and Galen was patient. "Um, I just wanted to let you know that Erin is safe, and that she's with me."

"What?!" Galen couldn't help but exclaim. "Why, that's great news—she's at your house right now?" asked Galen.

"Yeah. She didn't want you involved, but I said it was sorta too late for that. Anyhow, she's willing to talk with you."

Galen let out a slow breath and found that his main relief was that he wouldn't need to report in with Mike Carlson anymore. "Good. That's good because I need to speak with her, too. Has she called her husband yet?"

"No, and that's what she wants to talk to you about. She'll be here at my house every late morning and all afternoon for a few days."

"Tell you what. I have an appointment after lunch, but I can make it there by mid-afternoon. Does that work for both of you?"

"Yeah, we'll be here."

"Great, see you then," said Galen as he switched off and put the car in drive, wondering at the same time where Erin had been and why she was hesitant to make contact with her husband.

On his way downhill toward the river and his office, Galen was initially thinking about the now concluded Erin Carlson case—a wife who'd gone missing more than two weeks earlier, leaving behind a worried sister, Jodi Knowles, and her husband, Mike Carlson. But then, as they often did, his thoughts switched to a replay of the Robert Armlin disappearance—a mental six-track tape stuck in a never-ending loop, leaving him searching for a segment of any sort that he might have missed. Four-year-old Melissa Davidson had been shopping with her mother in a local mall when she'd been abducted by Gary Rockney. It had been by mere coincidence that Armlin had been unexpectedly ensnared in the case. Armlin had stopped by the house of a new friend and, quite by chance, he'd glanced in the neighbor's window only to recognize Davidson as the kidnapped girl whose face had been plastered all over local newspapers and television broadcasts for weeks. He had noticed an open window and had coaxed the girl out of the house and into his car in a valiant rescue attempt. Unfortunately for the pair of them, Gary Rockney had discovered Davidson's escape, given chase by car, and retaken the girl while scuffling with Armlin near Fanno Creek, a local stream near where both cars had come to a stop. There had been scant physical evidence at the scene, and other than the recollections of four-year-old Melissa Davidson, there was nothing more than the firm conviction of all those involved in the case that Gary Rockney had killed and disposed of Robert Armlin. Melissa Davidson was now home and safe, but only after an interstate manhunt which had resulted in Gary Rockney's arrest.

Galen was diverted for a few blocks by barriers meant either for construction or crowd control—it was becoming difficult to distinguish which—and was finally back on course to the office once again carrying the whisper of hope for a missing, but possibly still living, Robert Armlin.

Downtown Portland had changed. During a normal sunny September day, the streets and parks would be busy with shoppers, tourists, and Portlandians, keeping it weird and taking advantage of the clear skies before the weather rained its way toward winter. As he drove along S. Naito Parkway and approached headquarters, it was obvious that Waterfront Park between him and the Willamette River was much less festive than on any similar day in previous years. The city had been rocked by both the COVID-19 pandemic and the George Floyd protests.

The virus had closed businesses up and the demonstrations had brought people out. What had once been a bustling central business district was now a sterile corridor where shopfronts were either dark or boarded up and a daily ebb and flow of protesters washed between Frontier Square during the day and the Multnomah County Justice Center, his place of work, each evening. The faint scent of wood smoke and tear gas greeted him through his open windows as he neared the Portland Police Bureau headquarters, and he knew that the smell must be even stronger on the side of the building facing away from the river and fronting the embattled parks behind.

He nosed into the underbuilding parking garage, locked his car, and then, noting the time, quickened his steps to make his appointment.

He always preferred taking his daughter Beth's calls from his office where they could speak undisturbed. He settled into his chair and at precisely 1:15, the phone rang. "Hi, Beth, how are you doing?" he asked.

"Hi Dad," said Beth. "I'm good, so far. But things are starting to get a little crazy around here. There have been two more cases in the last three days, and ten ladies have been checked by the medical center for fevers just today."

Beth was allowed two five-minute phone calls each week from the Coffee Creek Correctional Facility south of Portland. Galen's allotted time slot was 1:15 each Tuesday, and she called her two sons at the same time every Saturday. The facility had entered a COVID lockdown in early summer, and in-person visits had been terminated. The lack of contact had been especially hard on Monty and Ryan, Galen's two grandsons now under his and his wife's care while their mother served out the remainder of her sentence.

Beth had been a handful for him and Jan when she was growing up, and she'd managed to kick up a ruckus even in sleepy Pendleton. Despite her father being one of the two local detectives in town, she'd been in and out of brushes with the local police and had finally been arrested and convicted for cooking and dealing meth after she'd graduated from high school and moved out of her parent's house, away from their influence.

"That sounds serious, Beth. Is everyone following protocols? Are they sanitizing?"

"Dad, this place is like a Clorox commercial. Everything is wiped down many times a day, we wear masks, scrub hands like mad people, try to keep our distances, change our clothes… but what do we expect, being crammed in here like hamsters?"

Galen could now hear the frustration in her voice. *Or was there a hint of desperation?* he wondered. He couldn't imagine being confined in one place, watching the virus creep its way toward you. "I know they're doing their best there, Hon, and I've heard that with such a young population, it won't have much effect."

"Yeah, I've heard that too, but my very, very close friend, Ashley, said she woke up this morning and couldn't smell anything. Isn't that one of the symptoms?"

Galen was wondering what 'very, very close' meant while he answered, "Oh. Yeah, Beth, that is one of the symptoms. Is she being monitored?"

"Yeah, she got tested, but so far no fever or anything else. I'm so worried about her."

And I'm worried about you if she has it, thought Galen.

"Anyway, how are the boys doing?" asked Beth.

"Well, school's started up, and so that at least gives them something to do. I try and take a walk with Monty every evening that I can to loosen up his hip, and his physical therapy is still going well. Ryan apparently has a new girlfriend, which I think is doing him some good."

"Yeah, he told me about Amelia, and she sounds like a nice girl. I can't believe that one of my sons is already dating. What do you think of her?"

"To tell you the truth, I haven't had a chance to meet her yet, but Jan says that Ryan is completely smitten."

"You should check her out for me and let me know your impression, since Mom obviously won't. Tell Ryan I said that he had to introduce you to Amelia."

"You know him. But I'll start insisting and see where that goes."

"OK, Dad. And Monty?"

Galen hesitated. He was having trouble keeping up with his grandsons. Angels to devils to angels again. In addition to puberty, things had not been easy for either of them. They were living with their grandparents, the pandemic meant not seeing their friends, their mother was in jail with some time left to serve, and Ryan had shot Monty earlier this year. It'd been an accident, caused by his wife's negligence in leaving her handgun out for the boys to find, and they were all still feeling the effects, including legal and emotional issues for Ryan and healing and emotional issues for Monty. The answer to Beth's question seemed to change from week to week.

"Well, to be honest, Beth, I'm starting to worry about him. It's probably just normal hormones kicking in, but he's not always the chipper Monty that we know and love. I can't tell you how impressed I was by how he took that accident in stride. It was like nothing fazed him, and he had that... What is it? Indomitable? I can hardly pronounce it. Indomitable spirit. Now he's like Ryan at this age—a mess. And moody as hell."

"Oh, God, I wish I was there for them. See? You just told me something I had no clue about. I think they're telling me everything, but they still hide stuff."

"Now, I might be just a little too close to the situation. Monty's really doing fine, but entering that... introspective phase... I guess."

There was a beep on the line indicating their time was up. "Oops, I gotta go, but thanks for all you're doing, Dad. I'll try and ask Monty what's up when I call him on Saturday. And tell Mom not to be so hard on Ryan."

"Will do, Sweetheart, and I hope your friend tests negative."

"Thanks, Dad, I'll tell her. Bye," and the connection was terminated.

CHAPTER 4.

GALEN WAS glad to be able to put the Carlson's case behind him, since he was feeling somewhat guilty that he hadn't given it his full attention in the first place. This and all of his other cases had been demoted into the same second-level tier while dribs and drabs of tips or leads kept elevating the Portland Police Bureau's attention back to discovering what had become of Robert Armlin - the prominent missing person who had absorbed so much of the Bureau's and his own efforts over the last four months. His inattention to the other cases was due to either that, he thought, or else he finally had to admit to himself that he was simply running out of the energy required for this line of work. He was now, officially, the oldest working member of the Bureau, and was staring with trepidation at the mandatory retirement age which was approaching him like a lumbering bear. It was getting near time to either stand his ground to the bitter end, or flee into an uncertain retirement. The recent riots and lack of manpower in the Bureau made any thoughts of leaving fraught with serious misgivings and thus not as attractive a choice as it might once have been.

It was another clear September day, but recent forecasts had projected that this fine weather wouldn't last. Galen enjoyed the afternoon sunshine as he headed south in light traffic toward Tualatin, a small town just to the south of Portland.

He needed to interview Erin Carlson at her sister's house, and this required a courtesy check-in with the Tualatin Police Department before he did so.

He glanced at a sign on the roadside as he drove along SW Durham Road on his way into Tualatin and saw that he was crossing Fanno Creek. *Fanno Creek – way down here?* he was mildly amazed he hadn't noticed it before. It was along this very creek to the north near Beaverton where they'd discovered the last evidence of Robert Armlin's existence - crumpled foliage from a struggle and bits of duct tape with Armlin's hairs on them. And, it was also near Fanno Creek a little further south from Beaverton where Miracle Furnishings was located—the place the kidnapper of Melissa Davidson had been employed. Galen checked his GPS location at the next stoplight and saw on the map that Fanno Creek was finally finished and done with a short way downstream where it emptied into the Tualatin River. *And good riddance,* thought the detective.

Tualatin Police Chief George Daniels was accommodating as usual, and thanked Galen for checking in with him before interviewing members of a household under his jurisdiction.

Galen hoped the little terror slept; the one that had strewn the neon plastic shapes about the cluttered yard like they were playthings. He'd parked in front of the beleaguered house and was just pushing his car door open when his phone chimed.

Glancing at the screen he saw that it was his grandson as he swiped up to answer.

"Hi, Gramp!" said Monty in a hurried voice. "Hey, do you know where the stain remover is? Can it get out permanent marker?"

Uh oh, thought Galen. "Monty, it's called a permanent marker for a reason," he said calmly. "What exactly got marked?" He took the phone away from his face to rub at his itching ear, but could still hear the boy on the other end of the line.

"Oh, duh," his grandson was saying, and then, "Oh, herk!"

"What happened, Bud?"

"Well, I was making a poster for the assignment about Black Lives Matter, and I looked down and saw my Timbers tee had some red smears on it. What should I do? Is it ruined?"

"Um, yeah, it sounds like it," said Galen. He heard a groan on the other end of the line. "Hey, but everybody has a sloppy shirt, don't they? And that's usually a guy's favorite one. Right?"

"Sure," came a defeated voice.

"Yeah, I bet it's not even noticeable, Bud."

"Not after I toss it," Monty whispered, but knowing that his grandfather wouldn't be happy with that solution, he followed with, "Just kidding. I'll figure something out."

"OK, Monty," said Galen. "I know this seemed like an emergency, but remember, I said not to call me at work unless it really is one."

"OK, sorry Gramp," Galen heard as the connection ended, but the words, "I thought it was…" were also captured.

Galen emerged from the battered sedan, slowly stretched, and then made his way up the front walk, skirting several large plastic cars in the process. His knock on the door was answered by a high-pitched, "I get it!" *Nope, the terror's not asleep,* he thought and watched the handle twist back and forth a few times before the door was finally swung open by a grinning three-year-old boy who craned his head up to take in the full height of the detective and then shout, "That big man, Mommy!" And that was it. The toddler just stood there staring up at him while Galen heard the final words of a hushed conversation in the background, and then Jodi Knowles finally came to the door. The detective wished he could remember the boy's name as Jodi pulled her son and the door away to make plenty of space for Galen to enter. "Hello, Ms. Knowles, I'm glad you got in touch. It's a relief that your sister is safe, and I'd like a few words with her if that's all right."

"Sure, that's why I called you," said Jodi. "Come on in, Detective Young."

Now that he'd identified himself, Galen brought the black mask up to cover his lower face. "And I'd like to speak with you at the same time," began Galen with Jodi immediately cutting in.

"Yeah. I expected that, too," she said with resignation.

"How long has she been here?" he asked as they walked along a short hallway to the living room situated off to the left.

"She's been dropping by for several days—and before you read me the riot act, we both thought it was for the best if she took some time for herself."

Galen stifled the reprimand that struggled to part his lips for keeping this information from him for so long.

On the worn sofa sat Jodi's sister, Erin, who gave a little smile when the toddler ran full tilt to the couch and planted himself into the cushion next to her. She gathered the squirming boy up and held him in her lap.

"It's good to finally meet you, Ms. Carlson," said Galen. "We were becoming more than worried about you and have had some trouble tracking you down." He sat on the offered straight-back chair that had been situated the now-customary six feet away from all the others in the room which, he now noticed, closely resembled the state of the front yard. Neither Jodi nor Erin had donned a mask, nor was one in sight.

Erin kept her attention focused on her nephew, but answered, "Yeah." She gave the boy a hug and then continued, "I guess I'm sorry about that. I didn't even know you were looking for me until I finally came to Jodi's, and she said that you'd been by to see her a couple of times."

Galen leaned forward with his hands on his knees, "Yes, your husband reported you missing three weeks ago. He's been genuinely concerned that something serious might have happened to you. He didn't think you'd just run off."

These last words brought unexpected tears to Erin's eyes, and after taking a moment to wipe them away and compose herself, she began to tell her story. She'd been unhappy in her marriage to Mike Carlson and had started exploring online dating sites for some possible male companionship. She stressed that she wasn't necessarily looking for an affair—she was seeking affection. She'd hit it off with a liquor distributor in Salem, and he'd convinced her to leave Mike and come live with him. That had lasted two weeks. "He was nice enough at first, but after a few days it was sports this and sports that, and he began to get rougher and rougher—in general, and, um, in bed. After ten days, I couldn't take it anymore, but when I made that I was going to leave, he got even worse." Erin pulled up a sleeve to reveal some fading bruises on her upper arm, "and there's more where that came from," she said, shaking her head. She'd finally fled while he was at work, and she'd driven up to her sister's house on Seminole Trail in Tualatin.

She told Galen that Jodi had arranged for her to stay with a mutual friend during the evenings and only visit during the days, so that Jodi's husband, Glenn, wouldn't know that she'd returned and inadvertently tell Mike before she herself was ready. "I was simply too ashamed to face Mike right away, so I came here for a few days to heal," she ended her explanation. "If he'll take me back, that is."

Galen rubbed fiercely at his chin under the mask and then turned to Jodi. "It would have saved us a lot of time and effort if you'd let us know as soon as your sister showed up, Ms. Knowles."

"I know, but like I said, she needed some time to herself. You should see the other bruises."

Galen shifted again to face Erin. "Would you like to initiate any assault charges against the man, Ms. Carlson? Oh, and what's his name by the way?"

"No!" She was adamant. "No charges, and I won't tell you his name. I just want to forget the whole stupid thing as a huge mistake and get back to Mike." She shook her head. "Jesus. Mike really isn't that bad after all. I'd rather have boring than a brute like that man any day."

"OK," said Galen as he winced and briefly pressed his knuckles against his left jaw. "I'll have to write this up, since your husband filed the missing persons claim, but I'm just guessing you'd like your whereabouts before you showed up at your sister's house to be kept as vague as possible."

This was met with strong affirmatives from both women. "Is something wrong with your chin, Detective? It must be that mask, huh?" asked Jodi. "I hate the things."

"Just a little itch," said Galen.

"Oh. Well, you might want to think twice about needing to wear that crap anyway. I hear the whole pandemic is nothing more than a big hoax," she began adamantly, but Erin cut in.

"Hey, Sis, I don't think he wants to hear one of your tirades about the Chinese virus right now."

Jodi was about to retort, but then softened and turned back to Galen. "Thanks so much for not digging too deep into Erin's little... experiment, Detective," she said. "I urged her to file a complaint against the guy, but like she told you, she just wants the whole thing to stay buried," as Erin nodded in agreement.

"I understand. The..." he was going to say 'affair' but quickly made another choice, "encounter was, after all, between two consenting adults," he said as he rose to leave. "And do you want to contact your husband, or would you rather have me drop by and talk to him, Ms. Carlson?"

"Sit here, Bobby," said Erin as she set the boy on the couch next to her.

Bobby, that's his name, thought Galen.

She rose and was about to reach out to shake Galen's hand when she suddenly pulled back, remembering the distancing rules. "I'm going to call him this afternoon and tell him I've been with a girlfriend all along. I would have gone back sooner, but I just needed time for these damn bruises to settle down first. Thank you though, Detective."

Galen said his goodbyes and then saw himself out. This sort of spontaneous affair was nothing new to him, and he knew that it was up to the spouses, and not the police, to work things out in the aftermath. He was aware of the facts that would need to be included in the report, as well as those items that could be phrased more delicately.

CHAPTER 5.

GALEN LEANED over to open the glovebox and rummaged around inside until he came up with a nearly empty bottle of extra-strength Tylenol. Downing two caplets with the dregs of his cold coffee, he put the car in gear and headed for the freeway and back into the city.

His jaw felt as if he'd been punched, and he grimaced at a sudden stabbing pain in his ear. "Damned viruses!" he cursed quietly as he eased into the northbound traffic on I-5. He'd been impacted by three bugs at about the same time. Just at the outbreak of the COVID-19 pandemic the wounds in his marriage had begun to fester, and, possibly due to the stress from the other two, he'd been hit with a bad case of the shingles.

He'd had the shingles once before as a rash that had spread in a line across the right half of his ribcage. It had been mildly irritating at the time—itching with small blisters and some minor twinges, but the symptoms had soon disappeared. Thinking himself immune from another flare-up, he hadn't bothered to get vaccinated even though his doctor had highly recommended him doing so. He should have listened to his doctor.

It had struck him again with a vengeance two months before—he'd been standing in the cafeteria talking to his fellow detective Stan Jenkins when he suddenly had the impression that someone had jabbed him in the ear with an icepick. The pain hadn't abated by quitting time, so he'd driven to the nearest Urgent Care to get his ear checked out. Unfortunately, this was when the coronavirus hit, and the hospitals and clinics were focused solely on detecting the disease. The masked Urgent Care doctor had given him a cursory examination and had suggested that it was probably a sinus infection, prescribing a course of antibiotics to treat it. He'd been suspicious two days later when blisters had formed on his lower left lip and on his scalp next to his left ear. The next doctor to see him had correctly diagnosed shingles and given him a course of antiviral medication along with steroids to help with the blistering. The two-day stretch between doctor visits had meant that the antiviral medication wasn't as effective as it would have been if administered right away, and he was now paying for the consequences of that delay. Although unbearable at first, he now felt like he was on a perpetual camping trip—hit in the jaw by a tree limb, stung in the left lower lip by a bee, and besieged on the left side of his face by no-see-ums that crawled about and bit randomly to their heart's content. And the bad news was that this condition could last for up to a year or more.

He was glad when his phone rang to take his mind away from his brooding. It was his captain. "Hey, Tom. What's up?" he asked as he thought again about how good it was to have Tom Weston back.

"Hi, Galen," said Tom. "I just wanted to let you know that I'm done with self-quarantine and will be back in the office tomorrow."

Tom had taken a vacation to visit his aging parents in New York City just as the pandemic hit and the two-week stay had extended to seven weeks while New York was under lockdown in an attempt to control the spread of the virus. When he'd finally been able to return to Portland, he'd still faced two weeks of self-quarantine to guarantee he hadn't brought the virus back with him.

"That's great!" said Galen. "And your parents are still doing OK?"

"They're fine, just fine," said Tom. "Thank God they weren't in assisted living yet. A nearby nursing home was ravaged, but the outbreak was eventually contained. It's funny—one of the reasons I went back there was to help them scout out a facility just like that one, since Mom's dementia is getting to the point that Dad has a hard time keeping up the house and tending to her at the same time. Who knows how long this thing will go on? I guess moving them will have to wait till it's over."

"Yeah, like everything else," said Galen. "Glad you're out of quarantine though."

"Thanks, Galen. I gather that nothing has come in from forensics on the note Emma Armlin received this morning?"

"Nope. Too early. I'm sure you'll see a copy, but it looks like it's an exact match to the first one. Only the location for the drop-off was different. It's pretty obvious that someone has this letter stored on their computer or phone somewhere."

"OK. I'll go through my emails and see if I've received it. Another dead end, you think?"

"Yeah, I hate to admit it, but I think so, Tom." Galen paused a moment. "But, I think we still need to set up for the ransom drop-off as if this is the real deal. Again."

"Yeah, unfortunately, I agree," said Tom. "And how about the Carlson case?"

"I'm going to file on it when I get back to the office. She's... Erin Carlson has turned up and has been staying with a friend over nights and at her sister's during the days this past week. Apparently, she had an affair that went sour, and showed up at her sister's house to lick her wounds. She said she's going to go back to her husband in the next day or two, so that's at least one case that we won't have to worry about."

"Ah, good," said Tom. "Listen, I'm encouraging all of my detectives to work from home as much as possible for the time being. I'm going to stick with Zoom meetings for a while yet for those who do work remotely. The George Floyd protests are taking place mainly on the side of Headquarters fronting the parks, so they don't really impact us that much, especially if we use the parking garage entrance, but we want to keep foot traffic in and out of the building to a minimum. Our PR is in the tank right now, and we don't need any chance encounters turning bad and setting things off even more. By the way, there are two more protestors who've been reported as missing, and I've left their files in your inbox—your email inbox. It's hard to know if the damn Feds have grabbed them, or if they truly are missing. I'm having Pembrook and Cushing pay attention to those cases and want you involved, too."

"OK, thanks, Tom," said Galen. "Will do."

"Say, I keep forgetting to ask about the case of shingles you had before I left. Are they gone?"

"Not hardly," said Galen, trying to keep a positive tone to his voice. "They might be with me for a while yet." He was glad the Tylenol was beginning to take effect.

"Sorry to hear that, Galen."

"It's manageable. Hey, say hi to Carol for me."

"How can I? I've hardly seen her since I got back." Galen should have guessed the reason why as Tom continued, "She's been involved in the George Floyd protests since they started, and she leaves early in the afternoon, gets home late, and sleeps till noon. What is this, the sixties?"

Galen thought that for Tom's wife, Carol, it probably always was. Her tarot booth had needed to cease operations due to health restrictions, but she'd been conducting card-reading sessions via Zoom before the Floyd death had again changed Portland's landscape. He found himself once more wondering how two completely opposite personalities could have fallen in love and stayed together for all this time. *Then again,* he thought, *Jan and I seemed to be so much alike – and look at us now.* "Yeah, her hours sound like the retirement kind of sixties," joked Galen as he was starting into that very decade himself. "See you, Captain," and they rang off.

As he neared his neighborhood, the phone vibrated, and he caught the name on the display. Monty again. This time Galen jumped in before his grandson could speak. "Monty! Goddamnit, I told you not to call me at work!" he snapped, already regretting his outburst.

The line was silent for a moment, and then Monty sheepishly said, "I just wanted to remind you about the pizza…"

Galen had completely forgotten, but said, "Yeah, I'll pick it up on the way home. But please, Monty, only call me in emergencies. OK?"

"Yes, Detective," said Monty in the mildly sarcastic tone that Galen was hearing more frequently from his youngest grandson.

CHAPTER 6.

GALEN PARKED in front of the house where Monty sat, undoubtedly playing video games, waiting on his pizza, and annoyed with his grandfather. The house looked cheery—kitchen and living room lights becoming more prominent as dusk enveloped Portland. But this wasn't his home, and it wasn't his kitchen. He and Monty lived downstairs in the basement. It had been just a month since he'd separated from Jan, his wife of... *jeez, was it forty-two years now?* thought Galen, shaking his head at the memories. The former couple had agreed to a trial separation, and now he lived in this rental property eight blocks from his home.

When had it gone sour? wondered Galen as he sat in the car aware that the pizza was growing colder by the minute. Of course, he knew when it had. He and Jan had been keeping it together—moving from Pendleton to Portland and raising their two grandsons while Beth was serving out her sentence in nearby Coffee Creek. It had been difficult, but they had managed. The wedge that had grown between him and Jan had begun when Monty had been accidentally shot in the hand and hip by his older brother Ryan. The two had been foolishly in a race to see who could break down and reassemble Jan's pistol which had been carelessly left on her nightstand. Ryan had just finished ramming the clip home to stop the clock when the rest had become history. In the aftermath, Jan had sought refuge in her position as a religious counselor which had become more important to her than her roles as mother and grandmother—at least that's how Galen saw it. And suddenly their world views had changed from those of a couple looking out over the same landscape to those of two individuals subsisting on separate continents.

And this separation had meant that the boys no longer lived under the same roof, either—Monty had followed Galen to the apartment and Ryan had remained in the house with Jan. To Galen, the resulting informal custodies of their grandsons had been the opposite of what was healthy. Ryan was just beginning high school and was the more volatile of the pair—yet in need of his own space, patience, and understanding—neither of the last two of which Jan seemed to possess lately. In Galen's view, Jan's heavy-handed attempts at Christian spiritual counseling were uncompromising and were smothering the boy. Beth was like-minded in this and had rebelled against her mother's solution that only a strong Christian devotion could ease her son's trauma from the accident. Instead, Beth had insisted that Ryan take advantage of the professional counselling available to him through the correctional facility. Ryan had at first revolted against any kind of help at all, and early in the summer had scared them by going missing for a few days and then getting involved in a smattering of fights. The COVID restrictions had left him to simmer at home and he had cooled down considerably by the beginning of the school year.

Monty, on the other hand, was well on his way to recovering from his wounds and had been the more buoyant, jovial, and outgoing younger brother. He was the one who needed the extra time that his grandmother could provide for physical therapy appointments and exercise opportunities that Galen's busy schedule couldn't easily accommodate. This was, of course, before the need for mental health counselling of some sort became increasingly evident in Monty—mostly through his surliness and anger issues—and Galen's latest outburst hadn't helped on that front in the slightest.

Galen slowly walked around the side of the house until the motion-sensor lights came on and then he made his way down the uneven steps to unlock the lower-level door. As it swung open, Monty came limping around the corner from the living area with a hungry look on his face. "Hey, Gramp. About time!"

Galen reached out to tousle the boy's hair, as was his normal greeting, but Monty pulled back. Galen stood and gave the boy a serious appraisal. He didn't seem mad, but he didn't seem particularly happy either. He could see as he set the pizza on the sideboard that the exchange over the phone had caused no real harm. And as a confirmation of this, Monty reached over to the counter opposite and held up the ruined Timbers shirt, launching into a description of the tragic event and of the rest of his virtual school day. They set pepperoni pizza slices on their plates, and Galen turned on the news as they sat in front of the television for dinner.

"Hey, Buddy," said Galen. "Just so you know, a lot of my yelling is because of these damn shingles, but that's no excuse. I'm sorry for being impatient with you." Monty was about to say something when Galen held up a finger and added, "But just don't, with a capital 'D', ever call me at work—I could be in the middle of a big bust or something."

"Honestly? How often are you in on a big bust?" chided Monty.

"But I could be," admonished Galen, and he caught up on the national news while Monty was busy on his phone and the remainder of the pizza.

With the usual complaints and excuses on Monty's part, Galen insisted they go for a walk after dinner. Monty's isolation and injured hip meant that it was important for him to get out and about, even if it had become mainly an evening and weekend event. Jan had been able to help Monty with exercise during the weekdays when they were all living under the same roof, but since he was now with Galen, and the detective was away during most daylight hours, necessity dictated that it become an evening routine for the two of them. Galen himself had actually begun to enjoy taking in the night air.

The pair headed toward the Willamette River, which coursed through the city many blocks away, and so far they'd never made it the entire distance before turning back. Walks in a hilly spot like Mt. Tabor Park would be perfect for Monty's stamina and his hip, but as with most other parks or trails, it was unlit and closed every evening. As he strolled past a glistening slime trail with a large banana slug at the end, Galen pictured a younger Monty who, on similar evening walks when they'd first moved to Portland, had loved running ahead to find and fling slugs with a stick. The silent Monty trudging with a walking stick beside him now ignored both them and him.

Chapter 7.

GALEN HAD just emerged from his morning shower when he heard Monty rapping on the bathroom door. "Hey Gramp," called the boy. "Your phone has rung like five times since you've been in the shower, and it's always the same number. I think it might be important."

"Thanks," said Galen, who quickly toweled off, threw on his robe, and was soon on his phone—tapping on the top name in his call log, 'Jenkins', to reply.

"Hey, Stan, I see you were trying to reach me. What's up?"

"I know it's on the early side, Galen, but I thought this was something you'd like to know ASAP. The guys downstairs have processed a cell phone found on the body of a street person—and they think it might be Armlin's."

"Robert Armlin's phone?" Galen was dumbstruck. "Are you kidding me, Stan? Do they know where Armlin is?" *Armlin? His phone? Is he alive?* he wondered at the same time, aware that this last thought came, oddly, without much sense of hope. "We haven't had any alerts that Armlin's number has been active recently, have we?"

"No, unfortunately there's only a thin connection between the phone and Armlin, and nothing to show that he's used it for a long time. It's pretty battered and has a cracked screen. It had a prepaid SIM card in it, so it obviously wasn't Armlin's number that registered when it was used. Luckily though, there were some pictures and notes on the SD card that was left in the slot, and they pointed to Armlin. Here, let me shoot you one of the images."

A few moments later, Galen's message alert vibrated, and he brought up the picture. There, with a loving grin on her face, was Armlin's wife Emma. Galen's throat suddenly tightened. "Yeah, Stan, that's Emma," he managed.

"Same as I gathered from the file photos," said Stan. "The phone company is getting back to us on the numbers that were called from that SIM card, and we might have a list of those by the 8:00 a.m. meeting."

"Where was it found?"

"Apparently there was an OD up near the St. Johns area where the homeless are now camping along the Peninsula Crossing Trail," said Jenkins. "There was no ID on the body, but after a picture of him was sent from the hospital morgue, the boys in Records quickly identified him as Sheldon Anderson, originally from Silverton, just outside of Salem. Fingerprints have now been confirmed. Anderson's been in and out of rehab and the psych clinic, and we've had him in the tank numerous times for D and D. It looks like smack finally took him down. They found his arm riddled with puncture marks."

"First another ransom note, and now this. When did they find the... Anderson?"

"Let's see." Jenkins searched his notes. "Yesterday morning around ten."

"And Ms. Armlin had another sketchy ransom note left on her porch yesterday morning. It mentioned a money drop in St. Johns."

"Ah," said Jenkins.

"I know, it seems odd. Thanks, Stan, see you at eight." said Galen as he swiped off the conversation.

He sank down on an as yet unfamiliar stuffed chair in the pre-furnished basement apartment and tried to incorporate this new development into the remainder of the Armlin case. *Two months since the other ransom note, and now we get a dup plus his phone shows up?* as he sought an explanation for the appearance of Armlin's cell. *Maybe the tide is finally turning on this case?* he wondered, finally with a slight tinge of optimism.

Chapter 8.

ALL THE earlier Zoom problems—someone cooking breakfast somewhere in the background, another spouse asking what else was needed from the grocery, Nelson's partner wandering in and out of the background, Cushing's blurry camera, and Pembrook's image jiggling about as he balanced his laptop on his knees—were now solved, and the meetings ran smoothly.

Tom had seemed diminished to Galen during his captain's first Zoom conference upon returning from New York. He had been, naturally, compressed into a small frame on Galen's laptop, but he had also seemed less himself. Galen had soon realized that Tom was the type of person who was a presence when in physical proximity, and he somehow managed the same command over the phone, but Zoom was definitely not his element. He'd been brought down to the same level as the rest of them. Tom had mastered the medium over time, but Galen was glad to be part of an in-person conference with him once again. A large screen showed frames of more than half of the attendees, but Tom, Galen, Jenkins, and Pembrook sat spaced around the large conference table, masks in place.

Tom brought the meeting to order and first addressed the discovery of Sheldon Anderson and of Armlin's cell phone. After covering the basics, he continued, "We've heard from the phone company, and there were several calls made from that SIM card over the past month, including four in the late afternoon the day before yesterday, probably just prior to Anderson's death. I'm forwarding the list to you all, but let's see…" and he seemed to be looking at his Zoom audience, but was actually consulting something on his laptop screen. "He made earlier calls to a Silverton number listed with the same last name of Anderson, so Sheldon was probably contacting some relative living in the area. Those last four calls were to a number that's currently inactive and we're still waiting on details, but it looks like another prepaid SIM."

Galen asked, "Any calls before that, Captain? Any to known contacts of Armlin? Any attempts to phone Emma?"

Tom Weston shook his head. "I know what you're wishing for, Galen, but we checked that out first thing. Nothing suggests that Armlin made any of the calls."

Galen sank back in the swivel chair. He then suddenly sat back up and was speaking just as Tom resumed. "Why the hell did Anderson have Armlin's phone, and who did he call on his last day? There just has be some connection with Armlin if Anderson had his phone. How did he get it in the first place?"

"All great questions, Galen," said Tom, "and you're just the person to look into them."

"Then I think we need to get Brenda in Forensics to take a DNA sample from Anderson, and the results need to be checked against any found on the two untraced ransom notes. It's just too much of a coincidence for both the second note and Armlin's phone to show up on the same day. Could be a connection."

"But Anderson was likely dead when the note showed up on Emma Armlin's doorstep," countered Pembrook.

"I realize that Michael, but it's the only lead we have," said Galen.

The remainder of the meeting dragged on for Galen, even during his own report on the reemergence of Erin Carlson. It must have been a slog for his captain as well because Tom ended the meeting saying, "And I can't wait to get everyone back in the office and get out of these fucking Zoom meetings! Pardon my..." he was then muted on screen but those around the table heard, "fucking French!" at which point the projected login screen was suddenly the only thing on display.

Chapter 9.

GALEN HAD contacted Brenda Rigby in Forensics for her to begin her work on acquiring and analyzing Anderson's DNA, and he had also requested further details on the call records from the phone company which were still forthcoming. So, with some time available in the early afternoon, Galen felt compelled to check in on Erin Carlson and see how she had settled back in with her husband. This was partly routine and partly to make up for the lack of full attention he'd given the case even though the outcome had been positive and very pedestrian. He knew that her husband, Mike, would still be at work at the Butler Tire Center, and thought it would be a good opportunity to gauge the situation when Erin was away from her sister and her spouse.

He turned onto SE 112th Ave, a treelined street that climbed a hill from the wetlands after crossing Johnson Creek. He knew the address from previous visits with Mike Carlson, and so didn't need to slow much before making the left turn into the driveway on the steep slope. His feet crunched on the gravel as he approached the house, and this roused the barking of a dog inside. This name he remembered—Scruffy.

Galen rapped on the door and as soon as it opened a gray mass of fur seemed to be surrounding his legs from all sides at once with a wagging tail following it about. "Hi, Scruffy," said

Galen as he reached down to pet the squirming mass. Scruffy was aptly named since each hair in his fur seemed to point away from its neighbors. He wasn't sure if he'd ever seen the dog's eyes, but Scruffy's tongue—definitely.

"Hello, Detective," said Erin Carlson as Galen rose from greeting her pet. "Thanks for calling ahead."

"Hello, Ms. Carlson," said Galen. "I just wanted to check in and see that you were settled back here at home. I've had cases where a sudden change of heart could turn into another missing person report."

"Erin, you can call me Erin. Oh no, I'm here for good. Won't you come in?"

"Thanks, Erin. Shoes?"

"That's fine—you can leave them on," as she showed him to a sofa situated under the large front picture window. "Some tea or coffee?"

"Sure, a cup of tea would be great," he replied. As she disappeared into the adjoining kitchen, he took in the room—older furniture, but well-kept, prominent large-screen TV on the opposite wall, some dog toys on the shag carpet. Where he would have expected to see curios or knickknacks given the decor, there were arranged crystals, various candles, and a Himalayan salt lamp.

Erin was soon back with two mugs of herbal tea, set them on the low coffee table, and took an easy chair beside the couch.

"So, how are you, Erin? Are you happy to be back home?"

Erin took a moment to answer. "I'm OK," she said nodding slowly. "And fairly happy to be back."

"We can recommend counselors if you think someone like that would help. Believe it or not, what you've just been through can be a huge stressor," Galen mentioned, without making any judgements in how he said it.

Erin scooped up her mug and sat forward with her elbows on her knees. "No. Mike's happy to have me back, and that's at least something." She took a sip of tea and was suddenly surprisingly candid. "When I said before that I needed some affection when I sought out the affair, I was wrong—that wasn't quite it. What I really need is to get comfortable with myself."

Galen gave her a questioning look, and she continued.

"I'm no glamour queen, but I was a cheerleader in high school, and just like every other girl and young woman, I wanted to be noticed, and got used to it when I was. Women know when men's eyes are following them and not all of us hate it. Mike used to look at me that way, too."

Erin set her tea mug down. "Then, I became invisible. I can walk down the street, and no one even notices anymore. I had a job at Joann's and quit—not because I didn't like the work—I got tired of just being an extension of the cash register. Sure, I had friends there, but most people looked right through me when they checked out."

Galen didn't say so, but he knew the feeling—at least at some level. Whenever he would walk through a student district, he was suddenly part of the landscape. All eyes were keyed in on others of the same age group, and he was definitely nowhere close to that generation.

"I thought an online dating service would bring back that same… spark," said Erin. "Have someone out there interested in me again. You know how that turned out."

"Yes, I do. And I hate to tell you this, but this aging thing isn't going to get any better. Believe me, I know."

"Oh, I sure know that, too. That's why I've decided I have to get happy with who I am. I've been to some shops and am going to focus on wellness. I think some of these crystals might already be helping," as she pointed to the collection near the TV. "This boutique I like has a new-age book club I just joined, and Jodi is being very supportive. You don't need to worry about me, Detective. I'm just one among legions of women dealing with not being the center of attention anymore. I'll be OK."

Driving back to headquarters, Galen realized that Erin had a different look in her eyes than during his previous interview with her. Rather than being sad and defeated, they'd radiated a calm acceptance, and he'd been glad to see it.

Galen tracked down the location of Anderson's belongings to the Bureau's North Precinct on Martin Luther King Jr. Blvd. Several officers in riot gear were stationed outside the entrance, and the street was still littered with debris and tattered signs from a protest that had flared into a small riot the night before. He brought out his badge and displayed it while he was still well away from the men so that they wouldn't be on edge as he approached, and they nodded as he passed by them and entered the building.

The soiled clothing had been disposed of, and Armlin's phone was with the IT staff, but what remained in the small evidence bag was more than Galen would have expected from a homeless man: an unused syringe, a needle with the cap on, a small bag with a dusting of what must have killed the man, a bus pass, a Fred Meyer gift card, a phone charge cable, and a set of two keys—one for a house and another possibly for a padlock. There was an art deco 'M' on the keychain and the design looked vaguely familiar to Galen, but he couldn't immediately place where he'd seen it before. The detective immediately discounted the idea that the keys belonged to Armlin since there was no Prius key fob, the car which Armlin drove, and they both looked shiny new—like duplicates. *Now, why would a homeless person have a phone, a Fred Meyer card, and a set of keys on him?* wondered Galen. *Stuff he found on the street or on someone?*

He decided to log the keys and the gift card out of custody, since they seemed like they would be able to provide him with the most information. Out of curiosity, Galen headed back to headquarters by driving south on Albina to where a short curve turned it into N. Mississippi. Sure enough, just past the curve, 'The Red House', as it was now known, stood out from its neighbors by the signs and banners that had sprung up on the porch and on the steep empty lot next to the house. A few tents and a small crowd were on the lot as he drove past. The Kinney's, who'd owned the land for decades, had defaulted on a recent mortgage but were claiming the right to remain on their property. When the court ordered their eviction, a resistance had sprung up that soon became a major movement and another reason for protest in the north side of the city—adding to the ongoing demonstrations over the killing of George Floyd. Thus, the riot gear on display near the North Precinct. Portland was in upheaval and with all of the opinions flying about in the newspapers, Galen found himself wondering what Robert Armlin's take on matters would have been.

Chapter 10.

WRAPPED IN multiple layers and donning a wool cap to ward off the early evening chill sat John Doherty at one picnic table among several arranged along the side of Kells Brewery on NW 21ˢᵗ. He'd been a longtime regular at Kells Irish Pub located near the Willamette River just off Burnside, but COVID and the riots had lately closed this old haunt, and he'd adapted.

A light mist had begun to fall, giving a soft edge to the streetside lamps, and Galen greeted John with a smile as he walked up and maneuvered himself into the bench opposite. "Hi, John," he said, and again felt awkward not removing his own jacket and hat at a pub. Such was the new normal with outside dining regardless of the weather. "How's it going?"

"Hey, Galen!" said John, lifting his glass of stout and a smile of his own in greeting. "Still living the dream."

"Sorry it's been a while since I've been able to join you. Ever since Jan and my separation, I've been needing to spend more time with Monty."

"And how is the little rascal doing?" asked John, as a server set a Harp Lager down in front of Galen. The detective was learning to not be surprised when this happened, except that this was a new server, and he raised his eyebrows in response. She smiled and tipped her head at the man behind the bar who waved back through the paned glass.

Galen lifted his pint to their favorite bartender, took a sip, and then answered John. "Truthfully?"

John nodded while his expression showed the coming reply might not be what he'd originally expected. They both turned for a moment to a sudden far-off roar from the protests taking place many blocks away.

"You know Monty," Galen then continued. "He was something. He'd taken the shooting in stride. He'd easily adapted to living away from his grandmother, was loving taking Zoom classes for school, was, and still is healing like something from a sci-fi movie—and he'd kept a pretty positive attitude throughout it all."

He shook his head and continued. "But... Monty's not in the cast of 'The Little Rascals' anymore. He's just graduated to 'The Breakfast Club.'"

John then also shook his head. "Hormones?"

"And how," replied Galen with a smile, and then more seriously, "but it's really more than that. It's like getting shot, being separated from his mom and gram, and being isolated from his friends by COVID have all finally eaten away enough layers to where they've exposed a nerve. And it's hurting him."

The two old men looked at each other. Galen could read that they'd both been there on so many of the same levels.

"And," Galen drew out dramatically. "There's another problem. One big problem."

"What's that?" asked John, responding with a conspiratorial grin on his face. "Drugs, suicidal thoughts, gang membership?"

"No—worse," and Galen lengthened an already drawn-out pause. "The saxophone."

"Ah! God have mercy!" exclaimed John.

"You've got that right," laughed Galen. "Maybe if he could just learn to tune it or something…"

"It's the embouchure," John drew out the last word while pursing his lips. "Expect the loud goose-mating kind of honking until he develops his embouchure."

"How long does that take?" groaned Galen.

"Oh, years in some cases…" as he laughed, and Galen nearly choked on his beer.

Galen remained perpetually hopeful that beer was the cure for shingles, knowing that, in the end, it always seemed to make the symptoms worse—but at the same time making him care less that it did. At least the beer made it easier to ignore the stinging on his left lip, although since much of it was now also numb, he constantly felt like he was drooling and so wiped occasionally at the corner of his mouth to stem the phantom drips.

The pair continued to catch up with each other, as it had been a few weeks since Galen had joined John at the Kells Brewery. John Doherty was a writer and editor for *The Messenger*, a free-press, leftist publication that thrived in Portland. He had been best friends and gone to school with Robert Armlin, which was how Galen had come to meet him while working the case. John was on the opposite end of the political spectrum from Galen, but somehow the two had struck up a friendship regardless.

Galen was struggling about whether to mention that there was a potential lead concerning John's old friend. The beer didn't loosen his lips, but it did persuade him to not want any news—good or bad—to come as a later surprise. "John, I can't give you any specifics, but I wanted you to know that, after all this time, a hint of something possibly connected with Robert has come up."

John's eyes jumped to meet Galen's, and as quickly dropped. He studied the foam on his stout and asked without looking up. "Is this going to be good news, Galen, or bad?"

"I honestly don't know, but I didn't want it to be a complete surprise if something develops. Of course, there's always a chance, too, that this is just a coincidence and that nothing will come of it."

John took this in and then glanced again at Galen. "I've finally accepted that he's dead," he said, suddenly grinning, "but I hope he's recovered."

The skies let loose when Galen was halfway back to his car, and he pivoted to see John turning up his collar and hunching over his beer.

CHAPTER 11

"I FEEL like a spy," said Emma as she gracefully took a seat in the black Escalade Galen had checked out of the Bureau's small fleet of vehicles. He hadn't dared give her a ride to the ransom drop-off point in his musty sedan, and rather enjoyed holding an umbrella and playing chauffeur this morning. Emma was dressed in what were, for her, very plain clothes, as if she were ready for a simple day working in the garden, were it not for the rain.

Galen closed the passenger door beside her, rounded the front of the car to the driver's side, and settled in behind the wheel. "I think we're ready," he said, and as he did so, he could see that her calm exterior belied a very nervous woman. He hoped what he had to say wouldn't add to her anxiety. "But before we go, I need to tell you something, Emma. It's purely coincidental, but yesterday we found your husband's phone…" as she swiveled around to face him, "in a very battered condition on the body of a homeless man."

"Could this mean…?" she began hopefully.

Galen was already shaking his head. "The phone hadn't been used by Robert for probably months and it had a different SIM card in it. The only reason we know it was his is that it still contained an SD card with some of his pictures. We'll make sure we get copies of those to you, but it looks like the man somehow obtained the phone and was using it as his own. We hope to know more about him soon, but our best guess so far is that he simply found it."

Emma sank back into her seat. "Thanks for telling me, Galen. So, this has nothing to do with the ransom demand?"

"I'm sorry, but I'm afraid not."

They were leaving her neighborhood when Emma said flatly, "That's probably for the best. I didn't want to get my hopes up."

He chose Highway 30 heading north out of the city on the west side of the Willamette River, and they soon crossed the river on the incredibly high St. Johns suspension bridge into St. Johns. Galen wound through tree-lined neighborhoods and ended up at the south end of George Park. He cracked open the windows and turned to Emma. "OK, Emma. We're ten minutes early, and here's what I'd suggest. You wander across the street and into the park. Walk around for a while in the most exposed areas and then find a bench fairly near that garbage can on the Northeast corner. It looks like your raincoat is long enough to protect you, and you'll have the umbrella. At noon, get up and walk slowly but purposefully up to the garbage can. Take your time opening it up, and then drop the money into it. Don't look around to make sure anyone saw you, just close the lid and walk back the way you came. I'll be here with binoculars, and I can see the bin from here. We have people placed around the area—see?" He pointed to a woman with a wet corgi on a leash. "That's detective Cushing walking a dog near the swing sets. We also have a video camera running in the fitness center across the street and another in a van parked in the opposite direction. You'll be totally safe. We'll monitor the vicinity and the drop point and see who shows up."

Emma's nervousness seemed to have evaporated as she opened the side door. She took off her mask and with a determined look said, "Well, wish me luck." Which Galen did before she closed the door and checked traffic prior to crossing the street.

Emma was back in the car twenty minutes later and they, along with all the other officers stationed in the area, watched nothing much happen. Twice there was some excitement as the bin was approached and Emma had grasped Galen's forearm in anticipation each time, but it was used both times merely as a trash receptacle. The team waited an hour with no results after which an officer retrieved the money bag and returned it to Emma.

She clasped the wet plastic bag to her chest, and the detective expected tears when Emma suddenly spat out, "What is wrong with people? Who would do such a thing? Claim they held someone's life in their hands and then just treat it as a joke!? I can't stand it!" Then the tears came. They sat in the car until Emma had cried it out, and she then took several deep breaths as she wiped her face dry. "I'm sorry, Galen," she said in a defeated tone. "I told you I didn't want to get my hopes up, but my heart must have said otherwise. Things really are back to where they were before I got that damned note, and now I am too."

"I'm sorry about that, Emma," said Galen, "but we can't just ignore these things in the remote chance that something might come of them."

"I know, Galen. Thank you and the others for trying."

Galen shrugged and said, "It's our job. But one of the worst parts of it is when leads like this end with nothing to show for the effort."

"Well, at least it was a beautiful day even given this rain," said Emma as they were again on the St. Johns bridge. She admired the view of the water and remarked on the gorgeous colors showing on the hills before them. "And, I enjoyed chatting with you, Galen." They had talked about a range of topics during the long wait, but the conversation had centered on Emma's plans as she was looking more and more certainly at a life without Robert.

"Me too, Emma. Me too."

CHAPTER 12.

THE NEXT morning, he made the phone call that every law enforcement officer finds difficult. He wanted to express his sympathy, but at the same time he was desperate for any information he could gain from a conversation with the next of kin.

"Hello?" came a raspy, but obviously elderly female voice from the other end of the line.

"Hello, Mrs. Anderson?" he greeted her in a neutral tone. "This is Galen Young from the Portland Police Bureau. I'm sorry to hear about your son, Sheldon, but I wanted to check in with you." He had verified beforehand that the hospital had notified Ms. Anderson of Sheldon's death and had confirmed through Records that the phone number was that of Sheldon's mother.

"Do they know what happened to my boy yet? They wouldn't tell me a dang thing when they called yesterday, and the cops who came by didn't know nothin'."

"No, ma'am," said Galen, "we're not sure of the cause yet, but your son was found in a camping shelter in the Saint John's section of the city—a place where people are taking refuge until the pandemic cools down," echoing what had been conveyed to Sheldon's mother in the previous call and taking care not to reveal too much of the man's rough life in the event that she wasn't already aware.

"Oh. Well, it's still good to hear from somebody who knew about Sheldon. Say, he wasn't in any kinda trouble, was he? You're the cops, after all."

"No, ma'am," said the detective. "None that I'm aware of. I was wondering if I could ask you a couple of questions about your son though."

"I guess so, but I might not know the answers. Sheldon's been outta touch for a long, long time."

"Fair enough, Mrs. Anderson. The reason I called is that we found a phone on Sheldon and the records show that he rang your number a couple of times over the last month. We need to know more about why he had the phone and why he called. It seems it was a new phone to him. Do you mind talking about that?"

"Well," she was silent while she thought this over. "Them were private conversations... but, no, I guess it won't do no harm."

There was an unexpectedly long break with some liquid sounds in the background, causing Galen to eventually prompt, "And, so?"

"Oh, yeah. Sorry, I got to thinking about Sheldon finally having a phone—he never seemed to bother with one before. Anyway, I hadn't heard from that boy in a month of Sundays when he suddenly calls me out of the blue. I didn't even recognize his voice it had been so long..." There was another lengthy pause, and Galen heard a glass being set down. "He sounded real happy on the first call. We caught up some and I learned that he'd been mostly in Portland all this time. Can you imagine? Here I thought he was in California. He was real excited that he had a job. He didn't say that he wasn't working before he got it, but the way he talked, I could tell that it musta been a while."

"What was his job?" asked Galen.

"He said that he was hired to look after some old coot and that it was a pretty cushy job. He got this phone, some money, and all he had to do for it was make sure the old guy was comfortable, stayed put, and was fed."

"Stayed put?" Galen jumped in. "Why 'stayed put'? What did he mean by that?"

"I kinda wondered about that too, but Sheldon was so excited, I didn't ask at first. Later I did, and he said the old man was a little nutty and they didn't want him to wander off."

"They?" asked Galen. "Did he say who he was working for, or with?"

"You sure ask a lotta questions, Mr. Young. I don't know. He never said." She paused again. "Is that it?"

"If you don't mind, what were the other calls about?"

"Well, there were only a coupla others. We just yapped and caught up. He talked a lot about TV since he hadn't watched any shows in a real long time, but got to watch a lot in the house he was in. He liked that Duck Dynasty all right."

"He was in a house? Did he mention where?" Galen couldn't help but ask.

"Yeah, of course he was in a house! What kinda stupid question is that? Never said where," replied Mrs. Anderson in a curt manner.

"Oh, sorry, yeah, that was obvious… Do you mind telling me about the last phone call?"

"Well, you know Sheldon, he could never hang on to one job for very long."

"Yes, so I understand."

"He was sorta bummed that he had to leave it, but he said that the old guy got too much for him to handle. He was having trouble feeding him and Sheldon said he couldn't deal, so he had to quit."

"And the old man? Did he say who was looking after him now?"

"Nope."

"Did he ever mention where he got the phone?"

"Nope, just that it was part of the job. Look, is that it, Mr. Young? It's well into teatime."

"Just one more thing," said Galen, suddenly realizing that his breathing had slowed. "Did he tell you the name of the old man?"

"Nope. But I never asked," she replied. "Is that it?"

"Yes, and thank you for your time, Mrs. Anderson. I'm sorry again about your son."

"That's OK. It was good to at least talk to him over the phone. Portland all this time, and he never thought to visit. Just like that Sheldon. Thank you for calling, Mr. Young."

Galen rang off with a tight feeling in his stomach that he hadn't had for several months. Not since Robert Armlin had disappeared.

Chapter 13.

A DETAIL emerged from a review of the video tapes taken during the attempted ransom exchange which no one had noticed at the time. The camera in the fitness center showed a man in a hoodie wander up the sidewalk from the east to the convenience store across the street, take a moment to survey the park, and then enter the shopfront. The windows in the store were filthy and rain-streaked, but the camera could pick him out loitering behind them. When he exited the store, he took a moment and glanced down the street to Galen's black Escalade, turned and stared for a moment directly at the camera in the fitness center, pivoted and walked away. On closer inspection, they could see that the man behind the window looked jittery or agitated, shifting from foot to foot. The officer stationed inside the convenience store hadn't pegged him as suspicious, but the cashier who had sold the man a can of Red Bull, described him as "hopped up, probably on meth or something." Facial recognition identified the man as Hal Langford, a suspect brought in twice in the last three years in connection with a methamphetamine drug ring, but no charges filed against him would stick.

Detective Deb Cushing tracked Langford down to a used car lot that employed him near the airport, and she reported on the results of her subsequent interview with him during the morning conference the next day. "I honestly don't know," said Cushing. "He said that he stopped by the Shopper's Friend convenience store to get a Red Bull when he was out for a walk. He works at the Like New Cars near the airport, but says that he often takes a drive or walks during his lunch hour to take in the air and relax." She took a moment and shuffled the papers in front of her. "But, 'relaxed' is the last word I would use to describe him. Despite his jitters, his mannerisms while he was telling me this made me suspicious. I can't put my finger on it, but he was acting like a kid caught with his hand in the cookie jar."

"Did you ask him if the name Armlin meant anything to him?" asked Galen.

"Yep, and the odd thing was, he didn't act any differently with any of the other questions I posed to him. I even brought up Anderson's name on the off chance, just to gauge his reactions. It could be that he's just nervous around the police, no matter what. I don't know what he's done wrong, but I don't think he knew anything about the ransom drop."

"Well, why don't you follow up anyway, Deb," said Tom. "I know you're busy with other cases, but see if you can find any kind of connection between Langford and either Robert or Emma Armlin or Sheldon Anderson. Otherwise, it looks like our ransomer is just yanking our chain."

The meeting ended with Galen describing his interview with Ms. Anderson and informing the others that Brenda in Forensics had found no match between Anderson's DNA and the DNA found on the ransom notes. He then stayed behind with Cushing and Pembrook to talk about a missing person case the two were working on that was connected with the protests.

After fifteen minutes, the three were heading for the conference room door when Jenkins momentarily blocked the entrance as he stepped in. "Hey, guys," he said by way of greeting. Deb Cushing, with no mask to hide it, gave a slight smirk as if she were used to the male-oriented phrasing. "Galen, I have something you might be interested in," continued Jenkins, revealing a sheet of paper and pointing toward the table for the two of them to take a seat.

Cushing and Pembrook hovered as Young and Jenkins sat. "Records called and wanted me to pass this on to you. They were taking care of the final paperwork for the Erin Carlson mis-pers case when a notification came up for that very name. Apparently, Carlson was killed in a hit-and-run accident last night."

"Ah, shit!" said Galen, suddenly taken aback. "I spoke to the poor woman just the other day. So, what happened?"

"According to the report, she was out walking her dog—it was dark and raining at the time—and a vehicle apparently slammed into her and flung her down a bank into some bushes in a deserted lot. It was so bad that the dog was hit too. The Labrador of another dog-walker found her a few hours later. There was no evidence of tire or skid marks, no witnesses were found, none of the neighbors noticed anything, so there is not much to go on. The officers on the scene talked with the husband, who was of course shocked by her death. He'd been at work and got home after the ambulance had arrived. He said she usually took the dog to a nearby dog park—especially in lousy weather like last night. He couldn't understand why she'd decided to walk from home, because they both knew how dangerous the stretch of road in front of their house was."

"Who's investigating?"

"The Central District has it—the Carlsons live just off of Foster on 112th."

"Yeah, I know. I've been there a few times—even the day before yesterday. Thanks, Stan. What a horrible thing to have happen," said a downcast Galen.

Jenkins gave him an empathetic pat on the shoulder. "I hope they catch the bastard."

"I'm sorry, Galen," said Cushing. "I know how hard it is to work on a case and then have it end like this."

Galen remained fixed in his chair as the others expressed their sympathies and drifted away. *Poor Erin. She seemed like she had a plan for getting her life back on track, and now this.* He clenched his fists even more tightly while he thought, *Maybe I'm getting old, but this didn't have to happen. Everyone just seems to be driving faster and faster to the point that cars are now lethal weapons in their own right.*

Chapter 14.

THE RAIN forced Galen and Monty to stay in that evening. Monty was particularly disagreeable and antsy which Galen took as a good sign—it meant that the boy's body was accustomed to the daily exercise they'd been getting. Over a dinner of pork chops and mashed potatoes, he suggested that they go and visit Jan—a comment which received yet another half-hearted response from Monty.

Pulling into the familiar driveway felt so natural, and the house so welcoming, that Galen found himself wondering why he was living somewhere else. The reasons came flooding back, but didn't completely swamp his nostalgia for the way things had been. For someone with a healing hip, Monty proved to be very spry and ran in a hopping fashion to beat the rain before Galen had unbuckled his seat belt. The door went unopened on the first knock, and Monty pounded again, shouting "Gram! It's me!"

Jan opened the door with a warm smile. "Hi, Monty!" she said as the boy wrapped one arm around her and leaned into a hug. She pulled the tween into the house, but so far, hadn't established eye contact with Galen. She'd left the door open, and he found the pair sitting on the couch with Monty catching her up on all that had happened since their last visit, Jan stroking her grandson's injured hand the entire time. Not wanting to interrupt their moment, Galen mimed a cup of tea over Monty's head. She nodded with the slightest of smiles, and he disappeared into the kitchen to make some cups from an herbal assortment tucked into a jar on the counter. After setting her mug down on the coffee table in front of the pair, he took his own and knocked on and then opened Ryan's bedroom door. Jan had mentioned that Ryan was at his girlfriend's this evening to Monty, but Galen thought he might learn a little about his older grandson through the state of his room. It was neater than on his last visit, and the work setup for school looked well organized. He closed the door, unsure whether this improved state showed the influence of his grandmother or his new girlfriend, and he suspected the latter.

They'd finished their teas, and Monty and Jan had eventually wound down their conversation. Galen had turned on the television to a soccer game in the other room with the sound muted, and the onscreen action began to hold more and more of the boy's attention as he would turn around to peer at the display, until he finally drifted over to one of the seats in front of it and switched on the sound.

"More tea?" asked Galen as he sat at the other end of the couch from Jan.

Jan glanced into her empty cup still cradled in her hands, and then over to her estranged husband. Taking longer than he expected, she finally said, "Sure, another cup would be great." Whereupon Galen rose and took her cup along with his own back into the kitchen.

"How are you doing, Jan?" he asked as he retook his spot at the opposite end of the couch. He vaguely noticed that, ever since their separation, he'd switched to calling his wife by her first name rather than the familiar 'hon'.

"Fine. I've been so busy lately, it's like a miracle. You know, it really was a good thing that we moved to Portland when we did. So many people are looking for counseling, what with the pandemic, the election, and all the crazy stuff happening out in the streets. You should see it on the news, cities are burning everywhere. I get referrals and have to refer them to other counselors. People are searching for some stability right now, and I'm glad I'm here."

"That's good news," said Galen. "I mean for you—not for the people looking for help."

"Of course," said Jan and took a sip of her tea.

"How's Ryan doing? I never seem to catch him at home anymore. How's his girlfriend?"

"Oh, Amelia's a sweet girl, and she's perfect for Ryan. He's really come around since this summer. She's keeping him grounded and interested in school. They're Presbyterians, so I was a little worried at first, but you can tell she has good values."

Galen was trying to recall what being Presbyterian meant, when Jan continued in a lowered voice. "By the way, I don't see what you were saying about Monty. He doesn't seem any different to me at all on any visit. He's still his sweet self and isn't moody in the slightest. Are you sure he's not just secretly resentful about your total focus on work, and not on him?"

Somehow, this comment brought a moment of revelation to Galen. It was as if he could suddenly see the world through Jan's eyes. In here, Beth and her incarceration were nonexistent. Her negligence with her handgun had been a mere hiccup. Her grandsons were perfect, and it was only her tight rein that kept them that way. And the reason for their separation had been him. He'd questioned the viability of her counselling her own grandson, while sticking up for Beth throughout it all. He'd been consumed by work and had neglected the best interests of the family in the process. In here, where she was following a divine calling, he was the one consorting with all sorts of disreputable souls and was responsible for everything that had happened in their relationship.

"No, I spend as much time with him as I can, but this past year has been hard on him. He's so used to being around me that he lets his guard down. He really is going through something right now."

"Well, if that actually is the case, he should be spending some sessions with me."

Beth had expressly given Galen directions that Jan was to have as little therapeutic role as possible regarding her two sons.

"Maybe you're right, Jan. Maybe it's nothing. If Monty really was going through something, I know you'd notice." He was about to add more, but wanted to nip this direction of the conversation in the bud. Instead, he rose and stretched. "Well, I guess I'd better get Monty back to the apartment and get him to finish his homework before bed. Thanks for the tea."

Jan was all hugs as she woke a now-napping Monty in front of the TV screen. They bid each other a good night as he and Monty headed for the car and the place they now lived.

On the short drive back, Galen had a second revelation. He and Jan had built a life together in Pendleton where they had the space and time to deal with each problem as it developed. Every approaching storm had been easily seen from a long way off, and it was a lengthy walk to the neighbor's if there was something that needed discussing. Even issues with their daughter had been as if they had occurred in slow motion, and they'd had the chance to be candid, thoughtful, and measured in their responses. Everything about Portland and their family was now more crowded, busy, and complicated than it had been before. And now, after seeing inside Jan for a few moments, Galen had to sadly admit to himself that they were never getting back together.

CHAPTER 15.

THE TYLENOL had worn off so that, once awakened by a bad dream, Galen found it impossible to drift back into sleep. His left cheek was on fire, and after stewing over Erin Carlson's death, he soon found his thoughts again lost in the Armlin case.

In the dark and still-unfamiliar bedroom, Galen reexamined all of the interviews he'd conducted during the course of the investigation: there was, or course, Armlin's wife Emma; his boss and his coeditor at the Oregon Sentinel; John Doherty, one of Armlin's dearest friends and now a friend of Galen's as well; and members of Armlin's social circle—all of their conversations still fresh in his mind. He had read through most of Robert Armlin's editorials during the search for the missing editor to get a picture of the man he'd never met. The resulting image was of a humane, thoughtful, and exceedingly open and frank individual. He then recalled his interviews with the kidnapper, Gary Rockney, who, except for a slip or two, had stonewalled him at every turn. Then he remembered his questioning of Rockney's associates—his girlfriend, his boss, and his workmates at Miracle Furnishings.

Miracle Furnishings! thought Galen suddenly. He didn't sit bolt upright in bed like in the movies, but his eyes widened at the realization. *That's where I've seen the 'M' on that keychain before – the Miracle Furnishings logo!*

He was in the furniture store's parking lot and watched as Mr. Nerland arrived and opened for business. Fifteen minutes more passed as he listened to the radio, allowing time for all of Miracle Furnishing's employees to clock in for the workday. He said hello as the soft-spoken salesman he'd met on his last visit opened the door for him, noting that the thin, immaculately dressed man seemed even more ghostly than ever behind his white mask. Galen made his way windingly through the maze of elegant furniture to Oliver Nerland's office at the back of the showroom.

Nerland nearly tipped over his coffee mug as Galen rapped gently on the doorframe, not expecting anyone to be in the store so soon after opening. "Hello again, Mr. Nerland," Galen began, "I appreciate this is unexpected, but I have a few questions that I hope you can answer," assuming that Nerland would remember him from his previous visit. Instant recognition would obviously have required more coffee on Nerland's part, especially since Galen's face was mostly obscured by his black mask. The store owner stared intently at the detective, but appeared to be drawing a mental blank. "Galen Young, detective with the Portland Police Bureau?" he prompted, drawing out his identification as he said it.

The lights came on. "Oh, yes, Detective Young. Forgive me," offered Nerland. "I'm sorry it took me a moment to place you. How have you been?" Galen didn't bother with "Fine," but instead gave a nod of his head. "Ah, good. You said you had questions? Is this still to do with Mr. Molitor?" Rockney had been working as a delivery person for several years under the pseudonym Molitor while at the store.

"Yes, Gary Rockney, as we now know him," replied Galen.

"Ah, yes, yes," remembered Mr. Nerland. "That is still difficult for me to get used to after all the time he worked here." He gestured to a plush leather seat suspended in a curved wooden frame. "Please, help yourself," as Nerland walked around his teak desk and sat stiffly in his own leather chair.

"Before I take a seat, could you please have a look at this keychain?" asked Galen, drawing the keyset out of his pocket and laying it splayed out on the desk in front of Nerland. "Does this logo look familiar?"

"Why, of course," said Nerland, pulling open a side drawer and extracting a small crystal bowl containing a dozen of the same keychains. "That's one of our gifts to our customers when they make a purchase. Why do you ask?"

Galen gave an inner sigh. "So, you give them out to everyone?"

"Yes, unless they choose our monogrammed pen or a napkin holder."

"Any chance you keep a record of who chooses what?" asked Galen.

"No, it's totally up to them," said Mr. Nerland somewhat quizzically. "Why? Are you looking for someone who chose a keychain?"

"Yeah, this key ring might be connected to a missing person case, and we're trying to locate the owner."

"May I?" asked Nerland gesturing toward the keys. Galen nodded and the store owner picked the set up and examined the two keys. "Sorry, this is our keychain, but I have no idea who these belong to."

"Thank you, Mr. Nerland," said Galen, reclaiming the keys and folding himself into the luxurious chair for a moment, while dreading the thought of going through all the sales records to try and discover some connection between the customers and Sheldon Anderson, but... *the only possible real connection would be through Rockney who worked here, otherwise this is hopeless...* "You don't by any chance give them out to your employees, as well?"

"Why yes, we encourage them to leave something after a delivery. I'd imagine nearly every employee has taken one for himself. It's good for advertising."

"Are any staff around today who worked with Rockney, ehr, Molitor?"

"Well, we're pretty short-staffed at the moment. There was a kerfuffle about COVID-19 protocols, and I recently had to let several workers go and make some new hires, but I believe two of them are loading a delivery van as we speak. Here, let me take you there," Nerland said, beginning to rise.

"No, that's OK," said Galen through his mask. "I remember the way. Thank you for your time, Mr. Nerland."

"Certainly," replied the owner as he sank back in his chair, subtly conveying his happiness that there was now an excuse to not shake hands.

"Oh," said Galen as an afterthought, "could I have a list of those employees who worked with Rockney around the time of the kidnapping—even if they aren't employed here now?"

"Why yes," and he ticked the names off on his fingers. "In deliveries we had Soto, DeAngelo, Perkowski, and Rawlins, but Perkowski and Rawlins were both let go, so let me give you their addresses," and he jotted down some information from an iPad he'd brought to life. "Soto and DeAngelo should be in back, if they haven't already left for a delivery," handing the detective a slip of paper.

Galen thanked him again and headed for the delivery dock farther to the rear of the cavernous store. He approached what he initially counted to be three men loading the van, but as he made his way around an island of stacked mattresses, he found two employees reflected occasionally in a mirror while lifting a plastic-wrapped sofa and maneuvering it into the cargo space. A pleasing salsa tune wafted from the small adjacent delivery office.

He was surprised at the music, given that Emmanuel Soto was one of the two men wrestling the sofa into the van. He had interviewed Emmanuel about the Davidson kidnapping to the beat of heavy rap. "Hello, Emmanuel," Galen said as the two emerged from the back of the van and approached a waiting loveseat. "I'm surprised that you don't have your usual music on. This is listenable."

Emmanuel studied Galen up and down, peered momentarily into his eyes, and then said in recognition. "Detective…"

"Young," Galen grinned back behind his mask.

"Jung," Emmanuel echoed back. "Nah, that stuff before wasn't my music. That Rawlins liked it on alla time, and he liked it loud. Mine's the chiller stuff."

"And who's this with you?" asked the detective.

"This here is one of the new guys, Derek… somethin'."

Derek, standing a head taller than Emmanuel, instinctively reached out his hand to introduce himself. When Galen subtly shook his head, Derek said, "Oh, right. Sorry, I forgot," dropping his arm. "I'm Derek Springer."

"And when did you start work here, Derek?"

"About ten days ago," he replied. "Me and three other guys all started at the same time."

"So, where's DeAngelo?" asked Galen, peering into the empty delivery office.

"He just left in the smaller truck for a delivery."

Emmanuel was shaking his head at a memory. "Man was that weird that Gary was like a kidnapper, or what? Who wouldda thought?"

"Yeah, and that's why I'm here again," said Galen more seriously. "Do either of you gentlemen recognize this ring or the keys on it? Are they either of yours, or do you know who they may belong to?"

Both Emmanuel and Derek examined the keychain quickly and both shook their heads. "Nah," and "No," they both muttered simultaneously. Galen had expected as much and repocketed the keys.

"Mr. Nerland mentioned that he had to let some people go," said Galen. He turned to the shorter of the two. "Why was that?"

Emmanuel looked at the ground and thought for a moment. "Well, since they got their asses fired anyway, I guess I'm not tellin' stories. There were a coupla guys who wouldn't follow the rules. They like wouldn't keep their masks on and hated wearin' gloves. Somma the customers started complainin' that they didn't feel so safe no more."

This tallied with what Nerland had mentioned. He then asked, "Emmanuel, just to check again, who besides you was working here during the time that Rockney... Molitor disappeared with the girl?"

"Lessee," thought Emmanuel. "There was me, DeAngelo, and Rawlins."

"Only the three of you?" asked Galen. "What about," and he consulted the slip Nerland had given him, "Perkowski?"

"Nope, I'm sure Jason weren't here when Gary trucked. The reason I remember is that I had to start goin' out on deliveries, too, because that Jason like split at the same time as Gary. We really hadda push to get the stuff outta here."

"He split?" asked Galen. "I thought he was let go just two weeks ago?"

"Yeah, he was just canned, but when Gary flaked out, so did Jason—he suddenly hadda take care of his sick mother and took like three weeks off. I know you gotta take care of your momma, but it was bad timing. With them gone, the rest of us had like serious overtime. Just bad timing."

"I'll say," muttered Galen, and like a UFO, Jason Perkowski suddenly became a noticeable blip on his radar screen.

CHAPTER 16.

HE RECEIVED a text message as he was heading north, back toward Portland's city center, and Galen was surprised to see it was from Carol, his superior's wife. Galen, Tom said you were out this morning. If you're driving near our house, could you stop by on your way back? There's something I need to give you. Their home wasn't far off his route, and now curious, he texted back that he would be there in about half an hour.

Carol Weston was seated on her front porch swing and began donning her mask as Galen pulled up and parked out front. She gave a little wave as he closed the car door and made his way up the walkway which was whimsically decorated with embedded glass and ceramic tiles. Tibetan prayer flags were draped across the porch, and a myriad of wildflowers were blooming across the yard.

Carol's eyes twinkled over her aqua-colored mask as she greeted him and gestured to a wicker chair for him to take a seat. "Hi, Galen," she said. "Thanks so much for dropping by—I know you're busy, but this should just take a second."

"Sure, Carol. How have you been during all of this?" he asked, not bringing up that he was curious about what had brought him here in the first place.

"It's been a strange time, hasn't it? I haven't seen you since the whole pandemic started." She knit her eyebrows in sudden concern. "And Tom said that you were hit with the shingles, and that they weren't going away. My mother had the same thing, and she was in agony for years."

Galen sat still, unsure how to respond. He didn't want to come across as a macho stoic, but he didn't want to whine either. Then he remembered that this was Carol, who always appreciated the truth. "Yeah, they're terrible, but... I'm starting to adjust to them. It's like if you never had TV, and then moved in with someone who had it blasting all the time. It's always there, but after a while you begin to tune it out."

Carol suddenly burst out laughing. "I'm sorry, but that hit so close to home. We don't watch TV. At least I don't anyway, but whenever I'd visit my mom, she'd always have the talking heads going at full volume. I don't know if she even paid attention to what they were saying. After Dad died, they were his substitute so she wouldn't feel so lonely. And it might have taken her mind off the pain." She stared seriously at him for a moment. "I'm sorry you're hurting and the real reason I asked you here was to give you these," and she handed him a paper bag that had been sitting next to her chair. "I don't know if you're interested, but I think that either of these might help."

Galen reached gingerly into the bag and took hold of a large round object which he slowly withdrew. "That's a CBD bath bomb," she said as he pulled it out of the bag and twisted it in his hand. At Galen's blank expression, she continued. "I've read that CBD products are some of the best for managing the nerve pain from shingles. You plunk this bath bomb into the water, and as you soak, your body absorbs the healing and analgesic properties of the CBD."

"Um, thanks Carol, but I never take baths—just showers. And CBD? Isn't that from marijuana?"

Carol pointed at the bag. "Yep, the next is too—hemp or marijuana. Just take a look."

He reached in for the next—a small box. "That's a vial of CBD drops. I chose one that has more CBD than THC, but still has some THC to take the edge off. You put a dropper or two under your tongue or in your tea. I can guarantee that it's very therapeutic. I use a 1:1 mixture for my joint pains, and it works wonders."

Galen juggled the box between his hands, and then juggled it a little more.

Carol grinned, or he imagined she did, and said, "These are totally legal in our state now, as you should already be aware. They can both help you so much that I thought you'd better get them from me, because you probably weren't very likely to go and buy them for yourself."

Or ever buy them, mused Galen, but he said, "Well, I appreciate the thought, but, honestly, I can't see myself ever using either of them." He dropped the two gifts in the bag and offered it back to Carol.

"No, no. You keep them. You never know when they might come in handy. Just maintain an open mind and the right time for them will present itself. My treat."

"Well, thanks for thinking of me," he said as he set the bag on his lap and wondered whatever he would do with them. *Maybe the dumpster?* he wondered.

"And how are your boys?" asked Carol. "It must be hard for them with you and Jan separated now."

It was no mystery how Carol had come to know this—Tom must have mentioned it at some point. "Oh, so you heard?" he asked to show that it was no surprise that she knew.

"No, but I do know now," responded Carol. "I just had a feeling."

Once again, Galen found himself surprised by Carol and her intuition, but still suspected that she must have heard the news from Tom. "The boys are fine. I only see Ryan once a week or so since he's staying with Jan and we're all so busy, but he has a new girlfriend who seems to be helping him after the accident. He got into some scrapes this spring, but so far the transition into high school seems to be going OK. Monty's another matter. If you ask me, he's finally showing the signs of trauma that he should have displayed right after the shooting. Physically, I get him out as much as I can, but with work, COVID, and school, we can only take walks in the evenings."

Carol leaned toward him and then said, "I'm trying to be more active too—besides joining in the BLM demonstrations. I could really use a hiking partner to get me motivated. Do you think Monty would be interested? There are a lot of local trails, and my hours are flexible."

Galen tried to picture the two of them together on a walk— one an older female Tarot reader, and the other a moody teenage boy—and wondered what they would even find in common to talk about. He personally doubted that Monty would be interested, but said, "I'll sure ask Monty and see what he thinks. Thanks, Carol, I'll let you know."

"That would be great. Thanks again for stopping by, Galen."

"Sure thing," he said, standing and picking up the bag she'd given him. "And I appreciate the gifts, although, like I said, I probably won't use them."

"You never know," as she saw him down the porch steps. "Don't forget to ask Monty."

Galen assured her he would as he headed for the car with doubts about what was in the bag, and about the future of the hikes. As soon as he closed the car door, Galen stashed the bag Carol had given him under his front seat, and not since attending underage drinking parties in college, he felt like a criminal.

CHAPTER 17.

No crowds were evident on the river side of the Portland Police Bureau headquarters as Galen turned into the building's parking garage entrance. A glance up the side street, however, had shown a now familiar scene as he caught a glimpse of what looked like an encampment of protesters in the park on the opposing end. It was easy finding a space in the nearly empty subterranean lot, and he only encountered a few masked officers on the way to his floor. He threw his coat into an empty chair and got right to the reason he'd come in. A search of records for Jason Perkowski revealed several interesting items, but provided no indication of his current address. Perkowski had faced two charges for drug possession which had both been thrown out on technicalities, and had received one misdemeanor for theft that had resulted in a suspended sentence. He had worked at Miracle Furnishings for the past four years without incident until his recent firing. But Galen was interested in something else, and he soon found it. The statistics about Perkowski's parents—his father had died in 2002, and his mother in 2013.

Interesting, thought Galen. *He wasn't taking care of his sick mother after all. So, who was he taking care of then?*

He called downstairs to IT/Research and was mildly surprised to have someone answer. "Hi Andy," he said. "I expected that maybe all of you guys in The Tombs were now working from home."

"Hi, Detective Young," Andy replied. "Nope. We keep our social distance, but a few of us need to be here to hunt up the physical records. What can I help you with?"

"Well, I've done a preliminary search on the whereabouts of a Jason Perkowski," and he spelled out the name. "Born February 22, 1983, in Rosedale, and for some reason I can't find a valid physical address for him. I checked with his employer, and the last entry was a trailer park out near Troutdale, but he's no longer there. Maybe you'll have better luck?"

"I'll see what I can do. Are you going to be in the office for a while?"

"Yeah, at least a few hours. If it takes longer, you can call me on my cell."

"Will do."

"Thanks, Andy."

Galen had just started in on some filing and about ten minutes had passed when his phone rang.

"Hi, Andy, that was fast," Galen answered in surprise.

"Some are just so easy," chided Andy, dragging out the last word. "Nothing came up on bank records, and I called around the Troutdale RV or trailer parks, and the one he'd been at said he'd moved out about two and a half months ago. OK, then I looked for one closer to his place of work, Miracle Furnishings, right? Sure enough, a J. Perkowski is renting a space just south of Portland at Vista Trailer and RV Park right below Milwaukie off 99E. Based on Google Maps, it's not much of a vista though. The owner says Perkowski's been there for two months and pays in cash only."

Galen sat back. *He's right, that was easy,* he thought. "Thanks, Andy. That's exactly the information I needed. Have I mentioned that you're underpaid?"

There was a chuckle from the other end of the line as Andy hung up.

It took Galen a moment to remember the geography of the area and he consulted a jurisdictional map just to be certain. The Vista Trailer and RV Park on 99E lay to the south of Milwaukie City which was Portland's southern neighbor. This meant it fell under the Clackamas County's Enhanced Law Enforcement District. He dialed the sheriff's office in Clackamas and, after making his request, found himself temporarily listening to light jazz—apparently a police department favorite.

"Hi, Galen," said Sheriff Dan Monroe after the receptionist had put him through. "What can I do you for?"

Galen was acquainted with Sheriff Monroe through some of the multiple cases which had transgressed the boundary between Portland and its neighboring jurisdictions. Most of these rural neighbors had, over time, swelled to fill in the empty spaces that had once defined the boundaries between them. The gap between Milwaukie and Oregon City which comprised the Clackamas County district was now so densely packed that it could easily be ranked as its own municipality.

"Hi, Dan," said Galen. "I'm calling to request a check on a person of interest—it seems that one of our fine citizens has taken up residence in your neck of the woods, and I'd like to locate him as soon as possible regarding a missing person—or a possible murder." Galen hated uttering these last words, but they were probably the ones which most closely resembled the truth.

After Galen had given him the details about Perkowski, Monroe said, "Sure thing. I'll have a couple of our deputies check him out and let you know what they find." It was all said at an official level, mainly because Monroe was friendly but held onto a certain wariness due to Portland's tendency to insinuate itself into his business.

"Thanks a lot, Dan, I appreciate it."

Chapter 18.

He awoke with a dry mouth, a headache, and a niggling feeling that something was amiss. A long hot shower, a hearty breakfast of eggs with hash browns and toast accompanied by two mugs of strong coffee finally alleviated the headache, but did nothing to stop the feeling that something was off. He went to his bedroom and checked his pants pockets to make sure that he still had his keys, phone, and wallet. Everything was accounted for, so that wasn't the cause. He finally put it down to the change in routine last night.

His car was still in the Bureau parking lot since he'd walked to the nearby tavern which had hosted the retirement party in a large open courtyard, and had taken a cab home. A desk sergeant who'd become a department fixture had required a rousing sendoff, and Galen had planned ahead for a long night out—having Monty stay over with his grandmother that evening, and arranging transportation after the celebration. But, now he needed a ride to work. He was about to call a cab, or maybe try that Uber thing, when he realized that the Bureau was on Jan's way to her office, too, if this was a scheduled workday for her. *Should I ask her?* he wondered while dialing her at the same moment. *What could it hurt?*

"Galen, I was just about to call you," said Jan, a little agitatedly. "I wanted to bring Monty back to your apartment and I need to talk to you about something."

Wondering what she had in mind, Galen said, "Any chance you can drive me to work while we discuss it?" thinking that no matter how bad it was, it would be worth the lift.

"Sure," his estranged wife said, and then, "that would be great. See you in a few minutes."

Galen felt an annoying schoolboy trepidation at what she might have to say—probably something to do with the sins of his overindulgences last night. To distract himself, he put the dishes in the sink and tidied up. Grabbing yesterday's newspaper, he glanced at the cover and then sifted through pages as he waited for Jan. He'd just scanned Metro news and was flipping past the Obituaries Page to get to the Sports section, when there she was—a picture of a younger Erin Carlson was staring back at him. He read the obituary with mild curiosity.

Erin Carlson has passed away unexpectedly to join her mother Margaret (Faulk) Shute, her father Phillip Schute, and a younger sister, Mary Schute, in our Heavenly Kingdom. Erin was born in Racine, Wisconsin on January 14th, 1982. She grew up on the family farm where she always enjoyed the newborn calves, chicks, and lambs. She was head cheerleader for the Racine Case Eagles where she met and fell in love with her husband Mike Carlson who was a guard on the basketball team. The couple was married in 2002.

Mike was in sales, and when a job came open with a tire company in Portland, Oregon, the couple jumped at the chance to be nearer to the ocean, which had always been Erin's dream. Her surviving sister, Jodi, and her husband soon followed them to the coast, and Mike and Glenn Knowles worked together at Butler Tire Center since 2004, becoming co-owners of the business in 2018. Erin loved her job at Joann's Fabrics, where she worked from 2006 – 2018, and many in the neighborhood will remember her help and friendly smile.

Erin loved quilting, reading, bowling, and canning. She always entered in local craft shows and fairs where she won multiple blue ribbons.

She had many friends in the area and will be especially missed by her bowling team and her quilting guild. She had a new loving friend who was especially dear to her, and who will now miss her for eternity.

Erin is survived by her husband, Mike Carlson, her sister and her sister's husband, Jodi and Glenn Knowles, and her nephew Bobby Knowles. May she rest in God's loving arms.

Plopping himself on the kitchen chair, he wondered about a sentence that had jumped out at him: *She had a new loving friend who was especially dear to her, and who will now miss her for eternity.* As he recalled his meeting with Erin and her sister, he'd been left with the strong impression that she wanted the affair to remain secret and kept hidden from all but the three of them. And yet, here it was in black and white—it appeared now that Erin had told her husband about her affair after all. Who else could the 'new loving friend' be but the lover? And she'd been run down on a rainy night, probably soon after telling her husband about her liaison. Had anyone investigated Mike Carlson after the accident? Adultery seemed like the perfect motive for him to do his wife in.

Galen was lost in thought when Monty threw the door open. "Hey, Gramp! I had the best time with Ryan—and on a school night, no less! It was so rad for us hang out—why the heck are we living here, away from home? Ryan and me think that you and Gram should like totally stop your stupid fighting and get back together," flinging his backpack on the floor and limping over to the sofa. "Oh, and Gram's waiting for you."

"Hi, Monty," said his grandfather as he headed toward the door. "Sorry about last night, but I had some things to take care of. Remember you have to log-on for your classes in half an hour, and no phone time while school is in session."

"K, Gramp," said Monty in a distracted tone, already making the most of his phone time during the remaining window. "See you this afternoon."

"You, too." Galen grabbed his things, shut the door, and climbed the steps to see what was on Jan's mind.

They exchanged the normal pleasantries on the drive toward the Burnside Bridge, the nearest of several crossings which led over the Willamette River and into the heart of downtown. A heavy mist kept the wipers on a quick intermittent setting—if it was any denser, it would become rain with full-on wipers required. Jan mentioned how good it was to have Monty in the house again, and actually described the time spent with her two raucous grandsons in just-short-of glowing terms.

"That's great, Jan. Maybe the two of them should be together under one roof. We could trade off."

"Now, you know that just won't work, Galen. When the two of them are together, they distract each other, get into those video games, or fight like dogs. Neither one of us can handle the pair of them by ourselves." She concentrated on a left-hand turn. "When Monty was saying how great it was to be with his brother, he also hinted that he was lonely. You should spend more time with him."

"I'm giving him all the time I can afford right now, Jan. The boy needs some pals and someone who's around more than I am. I still think that we should swap, and Ryan should be staying with me."

"Are you joking? Let all those hormones loose, alone with a girlfriend all day in your apartment in a basement? You obviously have no idea how much I have to orchestrate things to make sure that the two of them are chaperoned as it is. Nope. He's not staying with you. No way."

Jan was navigating the complex and nearly invisible driving lane changes as they approached the bridge when she became more serious. *Uh oh,* was Galen's first reaction and he braced himself for a dressing-down for a night out—when here he was, a man in his sixties. "Galen, I just received some news this morning before you called."

He looked at her and saw that she was now gripping the wheel tightly with both hands and had her head leaning forward, trying to concentrate on the constantly evaporating image of the car ahead of them. "It was from the Coffee Creek Correctional Facility." Now the words came more slowly and thickly. "They told me that the COVID-19 virus has been detected in multiple inmates—and Beth is one of them." Galen was momentarily shocked—both at the content of the message and that Jan stated this last bit with a catch in her throat. She'd always had issues with their daughter, and with her increasingly strict religious outlook, she'd often expressed her opinion that Beth wholly deserved the time she was serving in prison.

And then the immediacy of her news hit him. "Is she all right? Is Beth showing symptoms? Is she in quarantine?"

Jan's eyes swelled with tears, and, as they had already crossed the bridge and were now heading toward the Portland Police Bureau headquarters upriver, she sought and quickly found a loading zone to pull into. Then she lost it, sobbing uncontrollably while still gripping the wheel. Galen leaned over, hesitated, and then put an arm on her shoulder, gently rubbing her back. "Damn it! It's her fault for being put there in the first place!" she groaned. She then took a deep breath and said, "They told me that she has a fever, a cough, and is beginning to have trouble breathing. How could that be? She's so young and fit."

He knew that the virus hit indiscriminately, but said, "Hey, you're right, Jan, she's strong and in good health. She'll pull through just fine."

"But what if she doesn't? What about Monty and Ryan? Just when she was getting interested in them again, this happens. I haven't breathed a word to them yet." She dug into her purse for a Kleenex and used it to dab at her eyes and blow her nose.

"No, and that was good thinking. Where is she being treated?"

"They have limited facilities at Coffee Creek, but she's one of the first stricken and has already secured a spot in their care ward. I asked what would happen if it got worse, and they said that if it got to the point that they couldn't handle it, they'd transfer her to a real hospital, maybe OHSU." This, at least, came as good news. The Oregon Health and Science University was one of the largest hospitals in the city.

Galen and Beth had always been close, and it tore him up to hear this news, but as usual, he found himself immediately adopting the strong, supportive role. At some point in her troubled past, Beth had broken a connection with her mother that Jan would never allow to be repaired. He suspected that it was probably the time that Beth had tried to sell her mother's engagement ring to support her meth habit, but so much had happened during the relatively brief period of Beth's collapse that he couldn't be 100% sure. Regardless, Galen was touched by Jan's concern, but knew to wait awhile for its true depth to be revealed.

Jan finally looked over at him while searching for another Kleenex with her hands. "Our Beth," she breathed. "She deserves some time in prison, but not this. What should we do?"

"We'll just have to take it a step at a time, Jan, and keep ourselves informed. Like you said, she's been in good physical shape, and you know she's a fighter."

This brought the glimmer of a smile to Jan's lips, and she reached over to lightly touch her husband's arm. "She is that," she said. "When should we tell the boys?"

"Let's just wait and see how things develop over the next day or so. Then we can tell them if she doesn't improve. No need to worry them just yet."

She nodded, wiped her eyes again, put the windshield wipers on full, and pulled back into traffic.

Galen found himself worried about his daughter, but was also just as amazed at the concern Jan had expressed about her health. He held a momentary image of a reconciled mother and daughter in his vision, but after forty-two years of marriage, he also knew that a sea change of that magnitude in his wife was highly unlikely.

CHAPTER 19.

THE BUREAU was becoming aware that working remotely was a hinderance to good police work. There was obviously no getting around the need for personal connections and spontaneous confabs. It was time for the morning briefing, and far more than half of the detectives were gathered in the conference room.

For once, it was a slow news day with only two new cases, but since few of the outstanding ones had yet been resolved, it meant that the department was managing to motor along with gunwales just above the waterline. Cushing reported a successful conclusion to one of five cases under her purview, and both Jenkins and Pembrook remained swamped, especially by earlier and continuing out-of-town requests for information regarding possible missing persons who might be present at the Portland protests. There were several local homicides, and most of them appeared to be of the domestic variety—all related to the strains of economics, quarantine, or politics.

When it came time for Galen's report, he provided an update on the Robert Armlin case, and briefed them on his discussion with Sheriff Monroe who was going to have his men speak with Perkowski. He was about to turn his slot over to the next detective when he asked, "You know when you get one of those feelings?" They all did, and so the faces of those around him and all the little faces on the large display screen were now engaged. He saw Tom nod, and he continued, "Well, I'm sure no one noticed, but let me read the obituary of Erin Carlson, that recent missing person of mine who had a brief affair down in Salem. She was the recent victim of a hit-and-run near her home." He read through the obit, emphasizing the line that mentioned a new 'loving friend.' "The thing is, the last time I talked to her, she was adamant that she wouldn't tell her husband about the affair. So, if she did admit to it to him, wouldn't this be a motive for his doing away with her on a dark rainy night?"

"I hadn't read the obit, Galen, but that does sound odd," said Tom. "Any interviews of the husband after the hit and run—anyone?"

There was a pause while computers were consulted, and then Pembrook said, "No detectives, but uniformed questioned him, and Carlson said that he was still at work when Erin called him and said she was taking her dog for a walk. He thought she'd drive somewhere to do this, but apparently that wasn't the case. Uniform checked the car he had just parked out in front of the house and found no signs of a collision. He seemed to be genuinely shocked and confused, and wasn't a suspect at the time."

"What I don't get, though," said Galen, "is why he would even mention the man she had an affair with in the obituary? Who in their right mind would do that? Either he's one of the most forgiving husbands I've ever met, or he had a reason for stating that in the obit."

"What if it was some other friend?" asked Jenkins. "What if this new 'loving friend' was some... say, some woman she met over coffee somewhere, and she meant a lot to her?"

Cushing immediately broke in. "Who wrote the obituary though, Galen? Did he write it, or someone else?" The meeting was silent for a moment, and Galen was just about to ask, "What do you mean?" when Cushing continued. "I'm just hearing it for the first time, but to me, the obit you just read seemed to be from a woman's perspective. What if her sister wrote it and wanted to spite Mike Carlson somehow, and so she included that bit about someone else who made Erin happy for a while?"

"But, were they at odds—Jodi and Mike?" asked Galen. "I didn't get that impression."

This brought a shrug from Cushing.

"Given what we don't know, I'd like you to look into all this a little further, Galen," stepped in Tom. "Next up?"

Sheriff Monroe reached him later that afternoon.

"Galen, it's a good thing you called when you did. When my deputies arrived, Perkowski had hitched up his truck to his trailer and was just getting ready to pull out."

"That's great," said Galen, wondering at the timing of Perkowski's decision to leave. "Were they able to detain him for a few questions?"

"I don't think that's going to be a problem," replied Monroe. "He took some swings at my guys, and once they corralled him, they found both drugs and an unlicensed firearm in his possession. He'll be available to you for questioning anytime you like—he's ours for the foreseeable future."

"Wow, smart move on his part," joked Galen. "Do you mind if I stop by there tomorrow morning?"

"Sure, Galen, but remember, he's already been transferred to our jail down in Oregon City," said Monroe.

"Oh, right. And just so you know, Dan, I'm investigating a link between Perkowski and Robert Armlin, and I sure as hell hope it pans out."

"Armlin? That editor who went missing a while back?"

"Yeah, it's still a work in progress, but I believe there's a connection between Perkowski and Armlin. Or at least I hope there is."

Why didn't I notice? Galen wondered, feeling immediately inadequate as he set the phone down. He'd questioned some of the Miracle Furnishings staff after Rockney's arrest, but hadn't thought about any employees who may have been away on leave. *If Gary Rockney didn't get rid of Armlin by himself, he would have passed him off to someone he knew—a friend or coworker—to take care of the problem while he scooted out of town. That person would have been busy with Armlin and not at work.* Tired and frustrated, he rubbed at his face which awoke the prickling sensation on the left side. *But if it turns out that this Perkowski had Armlin, what's the connection with Anderson, the homeless guy, and those keys?*

CHAPTER 20.

GALEN PULLED into the Vista Trailer and RV Park just at dawn the next morning. Andy had been right—there was no vista except for the surrounding parking lots, and several of the RVs looked like they would never see another new sight again. The lot wasn't that large to begin with, but he immediately knew which space was Perkowski's—the only one with a truck still attached to the trailer hitch and occupying the fourth spot in from the front entrance. After the night's rain, the morning was foggy, and a heavy dew lay everywhere—especially visible across any green spaces and the windscreens of the vehicles parked next to their trailers. His own footprints followed him as he made his way across a strip of grass to the trailer door. He had no search warrant and no authority here, so entering the trailer would be impossible, but for some reason he just had to see the trailer. He stood on the narrow stoop, wiped the dew away, and was up on tiptoes to peer inside. From what he could see, everything appeared to be the habitat of a slovenly, drug-using bachelor—just as he suspected it would. He was itching to search the interior and couldn't help but try the locked door-knob to no avail.

He sat in his idling sedan before heading to the Clackamas County Jail in Oregon City located further to the south and dialed one of his Portland Bureau coworkers, Detective Deb Cushing, since she always provided a good sounding board.

"Hi, Galen, how are you this fine, early, morning?" Deb asked with a slight emphasis on the word 'early'. Galen checked his watch. *Uh, oh, 6:15 a.m.,* he finally realized.

"Oh, sorry Deb, I can call back later if you're busy."

"Busy would be if I'd already started my day," she joked. "What's up?"

Galen repeated what she already knew about the discovered phone and keys in Anderson's possession, and then followed that with his interview at Miracle Furnishings, what he'd learned about Perkowski, and the fact that the man owned a trailer which he was in the process of moving when he was detained.

The line was silent as Cushing mentally sifted through the information Galen had given her. He heard the rustling of bed sheets and a door close in the background. "So, he lived in one trailer park until about the time of the kidnapping, and two months ago moved into another one? And he was on leave from the furniture store for three weeks when Rockney bolted?"

Galen nodded into the phone, remembering to say, "Yeah," as he was reshuffling the same information.

"So, where were he and his trailer during that three-week gap between when he checked out of one mobile home park and into another?"

"Now, that is an excellent question, Deb," said Galen, feeling a little embarrassed that he hadn't yet realized the obvious. "I'm heading over to Sheriff Dan Monroe's in Oregon City right now to ask Perkowski that very thing. We both know I'll be lucky to get an immediate answer, so is there any chance you could start the search on our end to find out where the hell he was during that time?"

"Galen, there is a huge chance I can do that," said Deb, and he could feel her grin through the connection.

"Thanks a million, Deb. I'll let you know how the interview goes."

"OK, Galen, I'll keep you apprised of what I find, too—good luck."

"You, too, and thanks, Deb," as the pair rang off.

Chapter 21.

"CONTINUE TO Southeast McLoughlin Boulevard," said 'Bitchin' Betty' from the GPS unit as Galen glanced over his shoulder at that very same road.

"Thanks, Betty" he said sarcastically as he backed out of the space near Perkowski's trailer, "I would never have thought of that." He punched in the address to the Clackamas County Jail and chose a route that would take him on backroads to avoid the nearby snarl with Hwy 205, especially given the morning rush hour traffic that was just getting underway. He was nearing the county's law enforcement complex when he remembered that it wasn't even seven a.m. yet and pulled over to search for a nearby place to have breakfast while he waited for office hours to begin. The GPS soon had him parking next to a neighborhood Shari's which he was happy to find open and sparsely populated, even given the restrictions which further limited seating. He ordered and took his time over a meal of which his wife, Jan, would never have approved. Galen surreptitiously ran his hand along his belt line. *Of course, she's right*, he sighed.

And Jan was right about so many things. It was just unfortunate that those things were always about other people's issues. He'd really thought at first that they'd be able to keep their marriage together despite all that had happened, but since the separation, he no longer saw their living apart as a mere trial. He'd come to see his wife as a lighthouse—shining her beam outwards and illuminating all of the rough seas ahead for others, but unable to see anything going on close to shore—inside herself. She was a spiritual Christian therapist, and by all accounts had worked wonders with her clients, but she was, in fact, a bit of a shipwreck at home. In his own mind, he could easily see what her problem was, and that was in dealing with her own guilt. However, since he was no psychologist himself, he wasn't certain that he was right about this. To him, her perceived failure in raising their daughter, Beth, so that she would eventually turn to drugs, and her horrible mistake in leaving her handgun in plain sight for their grandsons to discover, combined to create the shoals she stood over, but which lay in constant darkness to her.

And lately, Galen felt adrift. *For Monty's sake though, I still need to keep up a relationship with her, and we need to fix Monty's continuing separation from his brother Ryan,* he thought as his leisurely breakfast had stagnated into pushing his hash browns around on his plate—and he loved hash browns. This isolation was becoming too much. He and his grandsons couldn't visit their mother at the Coffee Creek Correctional Facility, especially now that Beth was infected, Jan, with some exceptions, had shut down all but rudimentary communication after they had agreed to the trial separation, Ryan had his new girlfriend who consumed all his attention, and Galen felt like he himself was in a padded room, only connecting with everyone remotely. Visions of the open spaces surrounding Pendleton with its proximity to his brother in Joseph and the Wallowa Mountains suddenly overwhelmed him, and he found himself once again regretting the move they'd made to Portland. He had been retired, they had owned a house in the middle of plenty of acreage, and Jan had been reasonably content. The pandemic would have been a breeze there. Instead, they'd moved to the city with its ensuing congestion and trials for the struggling family.

The clink of glasses from the nearby counter brought him back from thoughts of eastern Oregon and he motioned to the server that he was ready for his bill. He gave the masked server a huge tip, just for being there, and would have tipped his hat if he was wearing one and still in Pendleton, but instead gave her a friendly wave on his way out.

"Oh, damn it to Hell, Galen, I'm sorry I didn't have time to call," said Sheriff Dan Monroe when Galen showed up at his office thirty minutes later. Galen gave him a questioning look as the sheriff continued. "I'm afraid our Mr. Perkowski is currently unavailable."

"What happened?" asked Galen.

"Well, it's possible the boy was a little more heavily into the drugs than we expected. During this morning's rounds he started going... well, going psychotic—'flailin' and wailin'' as one of the deputies put it. He's in the hospital for the moment, but the doctors say they'll quickly have it under control once toxicology lets them know what the boy's been taking. Or, of course," Monroe paused with a smile, "knowing Mr. Perkowski as I do after only a few short hours, it could all be just an act."

Galen shook his head. "One of those, huh?"

Monroe affirmed it. "One of those. How about if I give you a call once he's back in our custody and under control?"

"That would be great, Dan. I need our only lead to be coherent. Let me know as soon as he's available."

Monroe assured him he would and apologized again for not apprising Galen of Perkowski's unexpected absence.

If not Armlin, then Carlson, thought Galen once back in his car. He pulled out of the parking lot and headed north toward south Portland.

CHAPTER 22.

MUCH TO the chagrin of the car behind him, Galen slowed after he crossed Brookside Drive in Southeast Portland and tried to picture the scene of the accident. It wasn't difficult to see how there could have been one—no sidewalks, a narrow two-lane stretch of road on a steepening hill, blackberry brambles tangled intermittently on either side, and one or two steep ditches flanked by tall trees. *This is hardly pedestrian friendly,* he thought. The Ford F-150 behind him was now apparently trying to push him uphill, it was so close, and Galen put on his blinker to turn left at the steepest pitch of the road. He'd just begun to make his turn when a car dipped down from the crest and was heading for him. He decided to gun the motor and turned into the driveway just as the oncoming car sped past behind him. He could hear the truck that had been on his tail gunning its engine as it made its way more expediently up the hill.

Mike Carlson had agreed to meet him at around noon and his Jeep Liberty was parked in its normal spot in front of the house. Galen pulled into the graveled space next to him, noticing that Erin's Honda Civic was parked in the small carport along the lower level of the house which was situated on the steep slope of the 6900 block on SE 112th. Signaling the end of a solid stretch of rain, the midday sun cut through the clouds and glistened off of every surface, and its appearance indicated that clearer skies were thankfully in the offing.

Carlson opened the front door just as Galen knocked and stepped back to welcome him inside. "Hi again, Detective Young," he said. And then before Galen could reply, Carlson was asking, "Have you found the driver? The fucking bastard who killed Erin?"

"No, unfortunately not," replied Galen, finally pulling up his mask. "And again, I'm sorry for your loss, Mr. Carlson."

"Who would do such a thing? Just drive away?" Carlson still gripped the door and stared for a long moment down the hill and through some trees toward the scene of the accident. Eventually he closed the door and motioned for Galen to have a seat in the living room. "Want a beer?" he asked as he lifted one he'd already opened. Galen was surprised that Carlson had started so early in the day and shook his head, to which Carlson shrugged as if this was to be expected. Then he asked in a more subdued tone, "Then what brings you by, Detective? I don't have anything that can help beyond what I've already told your guys."

"But just to get me up to speed, can you tell me again what happened to Erin? All I have right now is a sketchy report to go on."

Carlson sighed. "Yeah, sure. I was at work, and Erin called around dinner time to see how I was doing. She said that she had lasagna ready that just needed to be reheated, but that Scruffy was itching to go out, and it was pouring at the time. I told her to just let him go in the yard, but Erin must have decided to take him out. She walks him down the street to the Brookside Wetlands in the summer, but in weather like that evening, she'll drive him over to Lents Park to play with other dogs. I got home to flashing lights all up and down the fucking street." He sank back in his chair, "You know the rest."

He tilted the beer can up in a long drink, and then slammed the now-lighter aluminum down on the side table, adding some buckles to the smooth sides in the process. "We should've never moved to this fucking place! Coming from Wisconsin, Erin hated it here after the first winter. Fucking rain, crowded big city. Here I am owning a tire center and I hate these fucking cars! Driving too fast, distracted, living in the fucking things. You should hear them race down our hill!"

Yep, the same guy I interviewed when Erin was missing, thought Galen. *Erin described him as a milquetoast - I wonder what the other guy in the affair was like?* He could see that Carlson was saddened but not absolutely crushed by his wife's passing. "Did you help walk Scruffy?" he asked, remembering the raggedy dog that seemed to spend most of its time looking for pets during his previous visits. "I noticed the steep hill and no sidewalks," Galen remarked. "How were you able to navigate it even on a good day?"

"We had a pattern of when to switch from one side of the road to the other. It's not bad if there's no traffic. But nowadays there's always fucking traffic—isn't there?"

"Yeah," Galen agreed. Portland was no longer the sleepy big-little city that had apparently existed before he'd moved here. "I don't want to take too much of your time, Mr. Carlson, but there is one thing I wanted to ask." Carlson met his eyes. "When did Erin tell you about her affair, and how did you take it?"

"What?" erupted Carlson. "What the fuck are you talking about? Erin would never have an affair!"

Oooh, thought Galen. *Maybe Cushing was right – maybe he didn't write the obituary.* "Well, I just assumed that she had one based on her obituary. It mentioned a special friend."

"Oh, that," said Carlson, immediately calming down. "You know Erin took that break from me over at a girlfriend's when we were having our problems? That friend, I think her name is Sarah, must be the one—she's also some friend of Jodi's."

"Did she talk about this friend?" asked Galen.

"No, not much," said Carlson, suddenly seeing where Galen was headed with his questions. "But there wasn't a fucking affair. Like I told you, I suspected she was having one a couple of times this past year. She started always saying she was going to the library for the afternoon. Who wouldn't be suspicious, since she never went there much before? So, I followed her—twice, and sure enough both times she went to the fucking library. I asked why, and she said it was a nice quiet spot to read."

Galen gave no outward response. He remembered that this was where Erin had conducted her online dating, with her husband none the wiser. Carlson seemed genuinely convinced that his wife had been faithful. "So, you didn't write the obituary then?" he asked.

"Nope. I just couldn't do it or get the words right. Jodi wrote it for me. For us."

Then why did she add the bit about the new friend? wondered Galen. "Thank you, Mr. Carlson. I think you've answered all my questions. We'll let you know as soon as we have any more information about Erin's death."

As the front door closed behind him, an orange cat that was sitting on the warm hood of Galen's sedan jumped down and skirted past him, heading for a safer spot under the Honda Civic. Galen sat in his car and rather than make the long run down to Tualatin, he decided to give Jodi Knowles a call.

"Hello?" answered Jodi, "Detective Young?"

"Hi, Ms. Knowles. Yes, it's me again."

"Hi, Detective," she responded, and then just as Carlson had, "Did you catch the bastard that ran over my sister?" Bobby—Galen had finally remembered his name—was howling in the background.

"Um, no. We're still chasing down leads. I'm sorry that I don't have any news on that front, and I'm very sorry about your sister's death." Galen had sent a sympathy card, but this was the first time they'd spoken since the accident.

She heaved a heavy sigh. "Yeah, we all are. Who would expect such a thing? Makes me afraid to go out on a walk even in our neighborhood. Bobby, pipe down! Just a second." Jodi was off the phone, and Galen could hear the refrigerator open and close in the background. "Sorry about that," when she came back on.

"That's quite all right, I know what toddlers can be like. Is this a good time for a few questions, or should I call back?"

"No, no, now is fine. What do you need to know?"

"I wanted to ask about the obituary you wrote for your sister. I'm a little surprised and curious why you added the sentence about Erin having a 'new loving friend who was very dear to her?' I thought that Erin wanted to keep the affair secret."

"She did want to keep it secret! I never wrote that line and it shocked me, too, when it showed up in the paper! I thought Mike would be royally pissed if he found out and wouldn't want anyone else to know about it... but he still added those words for the world to see. Maybe he just wanted to let the other guy know that he knew for some weird reason. He hasn't mentioned that he knew about the affair to me, and I don't dare bring it up because I don't want him to know that Erin came running to me first after the affair if she didn't tell him... but she must have said something."

"Are you certain, Ms. Knowles? I just spoke with Mr. Carlson, and he said he assumed you wrote that sentence and that it referred to your mutual friend—the woman Erin stayed with."

"What? I for sure never wrote it, and if Mike didn't add it in then who the hell did?"

That's an excellent question, thought Galen as they wrapped up the conversation, and he crawled back out of the car to go and have another chat with Mr. Carlson.

He'd been as tactful as he could be, but Galen was glad to be out of the house as Mike Carlson hadn't taken kindly at all to further suggestions that his wife had been cheating on him. The sun was now shining in its full splendor through the tree-tops as Galen made a multi-point turn in the driveway to avoid backing out onto the deadly road. As it was, a car was braking at his tail the moment he turned right and down the steep slope to head back to the Bureau.

Chapter 23.

Tom had decided to cancel the increasingly packed morning conferences, saying that he preferred to meet with each small team in person around a large table, and that he wanted to keep those sessions as brief as possible. He still wanted collective brainstorming, 'but only in microbursts' as Cushing had phrased it.

The missing persons team gathered that afternoon, and Galen updated them on the delay with Perkowski, described Cushing's continuing search for Perkowski's whereabouts during those three weeks, and he detailed his meeting with Carlson. "Mike Carlson is in total denial about his wife having had an affair, and it doesn't look to me like this could just be a front. He also has an alibi for the time of the hit and run. He said that two employees were with him in the tire center till 6:45 p.m. and that he worked till 7:30 p.m. It's a twenty-minute drive from his workplace at the tire center to his home. The coroner estimates that his wife was struck by a car or truck just after 6:30 p.m., and the ambulance was on the scene at 7:45 p.m., about five minutes after she was found. Given the timing, I don't see now how Carlson could have anything to do with his wife's death, but I'm going to check in with the two employees to verify that they were at work when he says they were.

"The real mystery to me right now is who wrote that bit about a special friend in the obituary. If Erin's death wasn't a total accident, that one line points to a motive. Both Carlson and his sister-in-law, Jodi Knowles, swear that Jodi wrote the version of the obit just as it appeared, except for that single sentence. So, who put it in? And why?"

"Well, who knew about the affair?" asked Pembrook. "From what I've heard, Jodi is the only person who knew about it besides Erin Carlson and her lover, so either she's lying, or she told someone else about it."

"Yeah," said Jenkins, "but either way, we need to know how and when the obituary was altered. I think you need to get the original, Galen, and talk to the newspaper to see which version they received."

"OK," said Tom. "Galen, check with the Tualatin Police Department before you question Jodi Knowles more formally—I don't want us stepping on their turf without further permission—and then crosscheck with the Oregon Sentinel. Do you need any help with this? We don't even know if there was intent yet, so I don't want a lot of our time wasted on it right now. You can join Cushing and Jenkins on one of their cases if nothing develops soon."

Galen had always thought of their captain as a meetings person, but COVID-19 had obviously changed all that. It felt like he was giving them the bum's rush to wrap the meeting up. They'd concluded all the issues on the table and were filing out when Tom said, "Hold on a second." Only Jenkins had left the room, but the others turned in mid-stride, retook their seats, and sat forward. "I know you had a feeling about this Carlson case, Galen, but the old-school part of me says look at the motive. Maybe it doesn't matter what someone wrote in an obit. Nine times out of ten, it's going to be someone close to the victim, and in my mind that means it's either the husband or the guy she broke off the affair with. If the husband isn't showing any promise, then it's probably the jilted lover."

"We don't know much about that jilted lover at this point, Captain," said Galen.

"Well, I'd put some energy into that, if it was me," said Tom, subtly giving Galen an order. Galen remained seated while he thought about how he would accomplish this as the meeting concluded and the others headed back to their offices, leaving him in the empty room.

The Tualatin Police Department had said they had no problem with Galen questioning Jodi Knowles in person given that she was connected with the recent missing persons case of her sister, so he was once again unaccompanied on this visit to the Knowles' home. The outdoor toys had been piled into a soggy corner of the lawn to await either a long break in the rains or the next summer.

"Hello, Detective," whispered a weary-eyed Jodi as she opened the door before he knocked. "Bobby's sleeping," she whispered again while holding a finger to her lips. She motioned for him to enter the hallway, and then quietly closed the door behind him. The pair walked shoeless and on tiptoe as they crept their way to a small room that must have served as a craft room/office by the looks of it. "The little devil," she said in a slightly louder voice as she pulled the door shut. "The only time I get any rest is when he does."

"Thanks for agreeing to speak with me, Ms. Knowles," said Galen. "I just have a couple more questions that might shed some light on whether someone was purposefully intending to run your sister down that night or not. If these don't lead anywhere, I'd say it was a random event and whoever did it simply fled the scene."

Wincing at the thought, Jodi said, "You think someone might have done it on purpose? Who would do such a thing?"

"It's unlikely, but we do have to look at all possibilities, just to be certain."

She then visibly tensed and picked up a picture that she'd set on a nearby sewing table for just this purpose. She thrust the framed image of much younger sisters on a lakeside picnic toward the detective. "She didn't deserve this!" she hissed with her hands shaking. "This was murder! Whether someone meant to do it or not!"

Galen understood this normal reaction to a loved one's unexpected and violent death. "She didn't deserve it, Jodi," he agreed. "But if it was a premeditated murder, we'll find who did it when we have enough information."

"What else do you need then?" she pleaded.

"My primary interest right now is the wording of the obituary, and when exactly that extra sentence was inserted.

Both you and Erin's husband swear that you didn't include it, but I need to see the original—the file that was sent to the newspaper."

"Well, I can show you the file, and the email it was sent in, if that helps," as she swiveled her chair to the computer situated next to the sewing table and re-woke the screen.

Galen read both the Word version, and the email with attachment, and noted the names, date-stamps, and sizes of the files. Their numbers all agreed, and neither version contained that additional sentence.

"Thanks, Jodi," said Galen. "Hey, one more thing. The man Erin was seeing in Salem? She said that he was a liquor distributor, and that's about all I know. She wouldn't identify him when I was here, but did she mention his name to you? What can you tell me about him?"

Jodi was quick to answer. "Not a damn thing, and that kind of pissed me off if you want to know the truth. Here this asshole practically abuses her, and she won't tell me anything about him?"

"Nothing?"

"No! All I got from her was that he was a big-time supplier of all of the bars and stores around, he had a so-so house in an iffy neighborhood, that he had two big honking trucks, he loved his guns, sports, and... well, that's about it."

"No description of him, nickname, anything that slipped out?"

"She said he was big, heavy, liked camo gear, and he stepped outside to smoke a lot. That's about it—sorry, Detective."

"That's OK, Jodi. It's more than I knew before," said Galen.

He then thanked her without feeling the need to probe more deeply to see if she was concealing anything from him. He'd been in the room with her when her sister had told him about the affair, and all seemed to be consistent with Erin's brief account of events. And now he had a vague description of her lover.

He wanted to check in with the Oregon Sentinel about the obituary wording when he returned to the office, but following his captain's suggestion about the two most likely suspects, he rang the Salem Police Department where he was put in touch with the Investigations Unit. "Detective Blowers here, and you're Detective Young from the PPB?"

"Yes, Detective Blowers, Galen Young, and I'm looking for some information about one of your citizens."

"Todd, Galen," replied an amiable Blowers, "who is this person you're interested in?"

"Well, that's just the problem, Todd," said Galen. "I know virtually nothing about him. He's apparently a liquor distributor, owns two trucks, likes camo gear, guns, smokes, and is large."

"You're kidding me," laughed Blowers, "that's not much to go on."

"I know, Detective, but this guy might be connected with a murder, so I'd really like to find out anything I can about him."

"OK..." said Blowers as he took a moment to consider this. "There can't be more than half a dozen liquor distributors in our little town, so I'll have our people look into it. I don't suppose you have a name, or you'd have said."

"Nope, that's all I got."

"Jeez, you're not giving us much, but I'll see what we can do. I'll call in the next day or two and let you know if anybody shakes loose."

"Thanks, Todd," and the two ended it there.

Chapter 24.

SHERIFF MONROE called the next morning and announced that Jason Perkowski was back in the Clackamas County Jail in Oregon City. The medical center's toxicology report had indicated the residuals of a mix of several drugs in his system. "I thought it was either an act, or Perkowski was having a panic attack," Monroe had explained. "I guess the guy was going through something like the DT's or something. Or else he was just waking up to the reality of his current situation."

Eager for any information he could obtain about Robert Armlin, Galen hit the freeway south to Oregon City as soon as he reported to his captain. He met with Sheriff Monroe and briefed him about the pertinent details concerning the Armlin case along with his suspicions of Jason Perkowski's possible involvement.

"So, Armlin just disappears from the face of the earth, you have circumstantial evidence that Rockney and him had an altercation, and the thing that ties Perkowski in with this is that he worked with Rockney? And Perkowski happened to be gone when all of this occurred? You also have a key ring with the Miracle Furnishings logo that was found on some bum? I can see where you might hope for possible connections here, but isn't this all a little thin, Detective?" asked Monroe after the briefing.

"Don't forget about Armlin's phone that was found on Sheldon Anderson along with those keys. The evidence may look thin in its pieces, but put together, these are the strongest links I've seen yet in this damn case," said Galen. "Especially since Perkowski conveniently left work just as Rockney did God knows what with Armlin and fled with the girl. I think we should have a look in his trailer. I think we're finally getting somewhere."

"Now, Galen," said Monroe, trying, but at the same time failing to sound more convivial, "if I walked into your patch with a similar case, what would you think? You know that I can't act on the flimsy information you've given me and that no judge in the state would ever issue a warrant based on what you've laid out here. But..." and he paused a moment, "we're way ahead of you." His eyes showed that he may have been grinning behind his mask—and that he perhaps had been this entire time. "Luckily for you, we'd already requested a search warrant based on the drugs we found on him."

Galen was momentarily taken aback. "Well, that's great! Do you need any forensics help? We'd love to find evidence that Armlin was in that trailer."

"Nah, that's OK, we got it. I understand my team is searching his trailer as we speak."

Galen nodded appreciatively and then asked, "Say, you don't mind if I have a little chat with Perkowski while you're holding him?"

"Not at all, in fact I think I'll join you. I'm not saying that I don't think he may be involved in your Armlin case, it's just that we can't do more than talk to him at this point anyway, and I'll be interested in what he has to say."

The interview hadn't gone well, and to Galen the results were like the one-sided grillings he'd given Gary Rockney. Perkowski had admitted that he and Rockney had worked together and that he'd been shocked that his coworker had ended up being a kidnapper. He'd sworn, on the other hand, that he had absolutely no idea who Armlin even was. When Galen had pressed about his lying about caring for his sick mother, Perkowski had answered, "Hey, I needed some time off, and wanted to use sick leave—what do they care whether I have a mother or not—it's not like it's a crime or something. What are they going to do—fire me?"

Galen had then shown him the key ring with the Miracle Furnishings logo and the two attached keys. "Do you recognize these keys?" he'd asked. To which Perkowski had erupted in laughter. "Yeah, a house key, and a key to something else," he finally managed. "How did I do? Two for two? Why, are they yours?"

"Nope," Galen had replied, realizing how ill-timed his question had been. "And you don't know to whom they might belong?"

"Honestly? Do you know how many of those chains we've given away? Hell, I even leave them as a tip for a meal sometimes," had been the answer.

Galen had paid particularly close attention to Perkowski's eyes as he'd asked his last question. "Do you know a Sheldon Anderson?" There hadn't been a flicker of recognition, and no tell-tale sign that Perkowski had ever heard the name.

"No. Why?" Perkowski had asked, totally deadpan, and in keeping with his taking the entire interview as a joke—"Oh, wait. Isn't he that flute player with Jethro Tull?"

The downcast detective was just walking into the parking lot when Cushing rang his cell phone. "Hey, Galen. Good news. We traced where Perkowski was holed up during those missing three weeks. He had checked into a small RV park of about twenty spaces in the woods outside of Astoria, near the coast. I talked to the park owner, and he remembers Perkowski, but not by name. Perkowski had checked in under an alias, but couldn't hide his plate numbers. The owner always goes by license plate numbers since so many people give false names. Ever since the Twin Towers, he says he's especially careful about this. Anyway, that plate number he remembers, because Perkowski asked to be parked at the edge of this small field away from everyone else and in a spot next to the trees without any RV hookups. The owner remembers telling him that the price would be the same as a fully serviced stall and the guy didn't even put up a fight. By way of requesting the secluded spot, Perkowski had claimed that he had a couple of dogs that were very sensitive to noise, but the owner said he never saw a single dog the whole time he was there."

"This is perfect timing, Deb—thanks," said the detective with relief. "I just had a frustrating interview with Perkowski, and I'll need more ammunition the next time I talk to him. The sheriff here told me that they'd applied for a search warrant of his trailer for drugs, and he's agreed to direct forensics to conduct a thorough going-over of the trailer for any other evidence as well. I want proof that Armlin was there, and Monroe seems to agree that it's a priority."

"I was hoping for something like that," said Deb. "That camping trip of Perkowski's sure sounds suspicious to me."

"I agree, Deb. Can't wait to see if anything turns up," as they rang off.

Chapter 25.

He was sure it was her. "Hey, Carol, wait up," shouted Galen as he approached the recognizable figure. Turning to the sound of her name, Carol Weston was draped in a long coat with a pair of ski goggles strapped to one arm, carrying a cardboard sign, and was obviously enjoying the brief appearance of early afternoon sun before joining the crowds. Galen had been contemplating his two main cases while strolling along the Willamette River walkway after lunch when he'd spied her.

"Hi, Galen," said Carol with an open smile on his approach. "What a gorgeous day, isn't it?"

"It sure is that," responded Galen as he caught up and matched her stride while they walked along the wide, promenade that paralleled the river. The sun danced on the wake a boat was throwing out as it passed.

They kept a few feet apart in deference to the virus, but neither felt the need for masks in the breezy, open space. She gave him a quick appraisal and then asked, "Did the CBD products help? How are your shingles?"

"Oh, I..." began Galen, "the shingles are the shingles, but I haven't had a real chance to try out what you gave me yet."

Carol smiled knowingly. "You're not going to get stoned by trying them, you know."

"No, of course not," responded Galen vaguely, as he had absolutely no idea what kind of effect CBD oils or tinctures would cause. "I've just been waiting for the right time."

"The right time is when you're in pain and need some relief—that's all they do, and you should give them a chance," said Carol.

"I will... and soon. It was thoughtful of you to give them to me."

"Just remember, they won't do any good if you don't try them," she prodded. "Any word as to whether Monty's up for some walks or hikes?"

"I told him you were interested, and he said that he'd think about it. I'll ask him again tonight and let you know."

"OK, anytime, that would be great," said Carol. "I could really use a hiking buddy." She then changed course. "You know, Tom and I never had kids, but we often joke that we should try and rent one sometime. It wouldn't work for us to have a young person around all day, every day, but they sure give a fresh perspective to things, don't they?"

After a nod from Galen, she added, "Something about seeing the world through the eyes of someone who is new to it all..."

They walked in silence for a few minutes with Carol occasionally closing her eyes and turning her face directly into the sun, and then Galen asked, "So, the demonstrations have brought you downtown?" glancing at the cardboard sign.

"Yeah," said Carol, "As I mentioned, I just feel like while all this is going on, I need to show my support."

Galen looked over and then asked, "So sort of a civic duty?" He knew the answer given Carol's leanings, but the question seemed to be the one expected, though he wanted to skirt getting into politics.

Carol shook her head. "Surprisingly, for me it's more personal."

He was accustomed to not fully understanding where Carol was going at any particular moment, and so asked, "What do you mean? You're…" He felt like he saved himself by not continuing with *you're not Black,* but wasn't sure if he'd caught himself in time.

Carol gave an enigmatic twist to her lips and then continued on a few paces.

"I know. I'm not. Your deceased editor, Robert Armlin, wrote an opinion piece on Martin Luther King, Jr. Day several years back, and I still remember it. He asked how we living in Portland, where there are relatively few people of color, could know if we were racist or not. We wouldn't have the types of encounters necessary to make it immediately obvious. We needed to be very vigilant and examine ourselves more deeply to watch for it. I did watch for it. And I found it somewhere I didn't expect. I had to cut ties with a good friend recently over this, and so these demonstrations are a way to reaffirm that I made the right choice."

"What did your friend do?"

Carol sighed as if with the regret of having committed a major crime. "Last summer I helped an old college roommate move from Montana to Arizona, of all places. She rented a

U-Haul, and I flew over to Billings to drive with her down to Phoenix, and then I flew back from there after we had moved her into her new digs. We decided to see some sights along the way and took a few days. We stopped at several places to eat—remember the pre-COVID days when we didn't give something like that a second thought?" Galen nodded. "And we didn't camp, but stayed at hotels, so we ran into all kinds of people, but never really engaged with too many of them. Just a normal trip. Right?"

Galen glanced at her to show that he was listening, but felt unsure where this was heading.

"But, here we passed or interacted with dozens of people, and the only ones she made any mention of at all were the few Black ones, and every comment ended up being negative in some way. To her they were all either murderers or drug dealers when they were really just regular folks."

Carol stopped, set the sign down, and leaned up against the cement wall with the river running below them and watched a pair of ducks swimming in the sunshine. "And that's why I'm joining the protests," she said. "I can do something in a group that makes a difference without the immediate hard consequences it has on the individual level." She looked sadly over at Galen, but he could already tell what she was going to say. "Jeanne was one of my closest friends, but I couldn't keep quiet. Just before I left, I confronted her about her attitude, hoping that it wouldn't ruin our friendship. She thinks she's enlightened, but she is really a subtle racist and couldn't see that in herself. She blew up at me and asked how I could possibly think that of her. She doesn't even know that the way she sees Blacks isn't or shouldn't be normal, and it cost us our friendship."

She was shaking her head. "I've wondered if I did the right thing. I could have kept my mouth shut and still have a friend—after all, isn't that one of the most important things in life?" Carol suddenly broke out laughing and the ducks jumped. "Here I took what I thought was the high ground but I'm still beating myself up about it. Isn't that ridiculous?"

Galen's reaction was immediate. "No, not at all, Carol. The way I see it, friends are rarer than we ever know because they don't stay with us forever. Jan and I moved here, and apart from the people I work with, I don't have any friends left—I may even be losing Jan. And most of my current workmates won't even last as acquaintances after we don't have work in common—just like what happened to me out of college, and again after leaving Pendleton. I know why you would feel bad about losing her—friends are precious."

Carol gave him a soul-searching look and then a sad smile. She wrapped her fingers tenderly around his arm and said, "Thanks for that," as she pulled away, picked up the sign, and headed back to the scene of all the action.

CHAPTER 26.

THE BACKGROUND music hadn't changed since he'd last contacted the Oregon Sentinel, and a calliope version of *Don't Worry, Be Happy* looped while he waited to be connected with someone in the Obituary Section of the newspaper. The tune finally paused, and he had human contact. "Oregon Sentinel obituaries, Bob Krauss speaking. How can I help you?"

"Good afternoon, Mr. Krauss. I'm Galen Young with the Portland Police Bureau. I was wondering if I could ask you some questions about a particular obituary."

"Yes, Mr. Young, I should be able to help you, as I could with anyone in the public. What did you need?" asked Krauss, sounding, ironically to Galen, exactly like a mortician—solemnity shadowing each word.

"There was an obituary for Erin Carlson published on September 22nd. My questions are about how you received the original, and any changes that might have been made before it was printed."

"Sure, just a second. Let me pull up that file," said Krauss. And a few moments later, "Ah, here it is. I received it on September 19th from Jodi Knowles, the deceased's sister."

The date matched the last version on Jodi's computer. "Do you have the time for when the file was last saved?"

"Well, that would be the day of the printing," replied Krauss.

"How about the original that was attached to Ms. Knowles' email?"

"Just a second…" there were clicks and soft classical music in the background. "Yes—Detective?" Galen responded that he was on the line. "3:03 p.m. on the 19th." Which corresponded exactly with what Galen had written down at Jodi's house.

"OK, now my next question is about the inclusion of the sentence beginning 'She had a new loving friend,' near the very bottom of the printed document. As you can see, it's not in the original, so, I was wondering if you received another version? Or if not, can you tell when that sentence was added?"

"Ah yes, I see the sentence. Just a moment while I check."

Galen held for two minutes, thankfully with no calliope music to accompany his wait, and then Krauss was back on the line. "This might take a little longer, Detective. May I call you back?" Galen agreed and gave him his contact information.

Fifteen minutes later his phone rang. Galen briefly considered putting Krauss on hold for a moment so that he could enjoy the light jazz that the Bureau provided, but answered on the fourth ring instead.

"Detective Young?" asked Krauss, and assuming that it was, continued immediately, "I found my notes on the document. Mr. Knowles, the deceased's brother-in-law, called the next morning on September 20th asking about Ms. Carlson's obituary, just to make sure that it made it to my office, and he said he needed to update what was sent in. He then read out that new sentence very slowly, so that I would get it right."

"OK, thanks, Mr. Krauss," said Galen while he was wondering how Glenn Knowles had come to hear of his sister-in-law's affair.

Phone calls to Jodi at home and to Glenn at the Butler Tire Center resulted in emphatic denials from each of them that Jodi had told her husband about the affair. After his initial shock at this news of infidelity, Glenn swore that he never suspected such a thing and hadn't made any contact with the Oregon Sentinel. He then spent several minutes giving Galen a piece of his mind about the detective's implications that the family would have had even the slightest ill thoughts toward Erin, whom they loved very much.

Tapping a pencil in time with the song that was now firmly planted in his head, Galen first brushed aside his initial reaction to Glenn's browbeating, and then took careful notes about his conversations thus far, including Glenn's adamant denial that he had phoned in the change. If he and Jodi were to be believed, Galen was ultimately left wondering how he could possibly track down someone who had impersonated Glenn Knowles over the phone—quickly realizing the futility of that path. *But as far as I know, only Jodi, Erin, and I had knowledge of the affair,* he thought. *Obviously, someone else was aware of it... of course, the liquor distributor in Salem was, too. But he would be an idiot to draw attention to himself. So, assuming that Erin hadn't revealed it to anyone, Jodi must have been the source.*

He decided on yet another telephone interview given the late hour and the time necessary to make another trip to Tualatin, at the same time regretting that he would be unable to read Jodi's face as they spoke.

"Hi, Jodi, this is Galen again," he greeted her more familiarly now.

When he posed his question, Jodi was adamant that she hadn't breathed a word to a 'single solitary soul.'

"How about the friend that Erin stayed with?" asked the detective.

"Oh, no. Erin made it clear that Sarah didn't know a thing about it."

"Is there any chance that someone else overheard you discussing the affair? Possibly when you were on the phone somewhere away from home? Maybe at the grocery store with someone? At a friend's house? "

"No, we never talked about it on the phone, except when Glenn was gone and Bobby was napping. And we were never together..." There was a long pause. "You know, the only time we both meet... met outside our homes was to have our hair done. The salon was remodeled into separate rooms, and we shared one so that we could have some sister-time together. We did whisper about the affair while our hair dried and stuff, but I'm sure no one heard us."

Ah ha, thought Galen, *maybe.*

"Oh, and you probably already know that she was seeing a therapist for the last few months about her problems with Mike? Maybe she consulted with him about it when they resumed?" There was a pause, and he heard some banging and a high-pitched voice in the background. "Isn't it sad. You think you have all the time in the world. I was going to ask her if that therapist could convince her that what she went through with that man in Salem was a true trauma, like a PTSD, but I never had the chance. Now I..." and she trailed off.

Galen sympathized, but pressed on to ask her for the details about both the hair salon and the counselor, and then thanked her as Bobby began making an even bigger fuss, presumably for his afternoon snack.

Galen Googled the addresses of the therapist and the hair salon to get his bearings and then put his computer to sleep, grabbed his keys, lifted his coat off the hook beside the door, and was reaching for the knob when he stopped, staring through the frosted glass at the envisioned interviews to come. He followed them through their natural course—the first with the hair stylist, and the second with the therapist—and both had ended providing him with no more information than he had now. He would chat with each one, ask about their relationships with Erin, and their last sessions with her. And then he would ask two questions. The first would be, "Did you know about Erin Carlson's recent affair?" to which the stylist would likely reply, "No, what affair?" to help protect his client's integrity, and the therapist would reply, "I'm sorry that would breach the confidentiality of my meetings with my patient." Then he would ask, "Did you phone in a change to the obituary of Erin Carlson?" and given the answers to the first question, he knew this was fruitless. He simply had nothing substantial to help press them for the information.

He rehung his coat, put his keys back on the desk, and started to think this through. He was glad that he had so much more time by himself to do just this very thing during the pandemic. He was becoming gradually adjusted to the pace and demands of his relatively new job in the big city, but to him nothing would ever compare to the small office, open spaces, and laid-back atmosphere of Pendleton where a case as big as a double-murder or as small as a missing pet squirrel could each unfold in their own timeframe.

I have nothing, and I'll get nothing if I start asking questions now, he thought, picking up the pencil again.

Before he could begin tapping, he was back on the phone to Bob Krauss. Luckily there was no being put on hold this time since he had Krauss's direct number.

"Oregon Sentinel obituaries, Bob Krauss speaking. How can I help you?" like a recorded message.

"Hello Mr. Krauss, Galen Young here, we spoke earlier?"

"Ah, yes, hello Detective, was there something else you needed?"

"Yeah, I was wondering how common it is for someone to call in a change to an obituary prior to publication."

"Oh, it happens all the time. You see, people are under a great deal of stress when they write them up and so the obits require a high degree of editing. I often call people back for clarifications or to fix obvious mistakes, and they call me with additions or deletions. This happens especially as more time passes, and more and more relatives become involved. Most are really straightforward, but for some I go around and around with the writer, which can cause days of delay before publication."

"And do you verify the caller? You know, to make sure the person is who they say he or she is?"

There was a pause. "Um, no, I don't even know how I'd do that. I can't just ask... You have no idea how extremely fragile many of these people are, Detective. I don't want to say anything that might set them off, because the grieving process is hard enough on them as it is."

"I see," said Galen. "My problem is that it appears that none of the relatives involved phoned in a change to the Erin Carlson submission, and yet someone did. And frankly, two of them are very upset about the addition, now that they each realize that the other hadn't been the one to add the sentence we discussed." Galen sighed theatrically into the phone for emphasis. "This single addition could reveal a motive for the possible murder of Ms. Carlson in the first place, and yet I'm completely at a loss to find out who the hell called it in."

This had the desired effect as the import of that small but substantive change sank in. "Oh, I see," replied Krauss. "I had no idea that a murder was involved."

"Yes, I believe that the submitter was serving notice that he knew about an affair with the 'special friend' and wanted the rest of the world to know about it, too. And if he knew about the affair, he might have had a motive that could turn a hit and run incident into a homicide."

There was silence on the line, and then Krauss said, "I'd like to be of help, but I frankly don't see how I can. We get so many notices, and I'm in so many back-and-forths with the writers. It's a zoo, if you want to know the truth, Detective."

"I'm sure it is. It is here, too," replied Galen sympathetically. And then something came to him. "By the way, just out of curiosity, have you ever had anyone call back after the obituary was printed saying, 'Hey, how could you print such-and-such a lie? I never said that?'"

The response was immediate. "Oh, yes!" said Krauss. "What a headache that caused. It was the Olsens... I think it was the Olsens, but give me a minute to look up the file." Galen was on hold to blissful silence, but also with some anticipation as he awaited Krauss.

"Detective?" asked Krauss, and then, as before, he plunged ahead without a response. "Yes, it was the Olsens about three months ago. They had submitted an obituary, but then they were furious after it was printed. I don't know why I didn't make the connection with your situation—they nearly took us to court over it, but we printed a retraction, and they were mollified by that."

"What was the change?" asked Galen. "What did you retract?"

"Well, it was one sentence—actually a sentence pretty similar to the one you were talking about. A brother phoned it in, but they later said that Kim Olsen didn't even have a brother. Should I read it?" Krauss asked, but then after a pause he suggested, "How about I email you the obit we printed and highlight the sentence we retracted?"

"That would be great, Mr. Krauss. Thanks so much, and I'll get back if I need more information."

"Quite all right, Detective, and don't forget that all of our obituaries are archived online if you want to do some digging yourself."

Galen wasn't sure if Krauss was aware of the ironic pun he'd uttered in his usual solemn manner as he disconnected.

Chapter 27.

THINGS WERE winding down for the day, and Galen was too. He needed caffeine, and met with Pembrook and Cushing over cups of hot beverages in one of the small meeting rooms off of the cafeteria. "They both turned up," said Pembrook, as he sipped at his coffee through the small hole provided in the plastic top. At raised eyebrows from Galen, he elaborated. "The two missing protesters—we found them both. One claimed to have been abducted by the Feds, but the government still denies any activity at all in our area. His story has some holes in it, and since he's now been located, we're not going to do any follow-ups. The other case was based on a frantic and, it turns out, premature call by a spirited teenager's parents. She was at the protests, but went to a friend's house as it got late, and forgot to check in—for two days."

"Is there really anything to these reports of Federal agents yanking people off the streets, Michael?" asked Galen.

"The press says yes, and the Feds say no," answered Pembrook. "So, who knows? I actually think that they are grabbing people to try and tamp down the demonstrations and put the fear of God into the lot of them. Doesn't this sound just like the Feds anyway? No coordination with other agencies?"

"I've heard that some of our uniforms are helping them out," said Cushing.

"Who can blame them?" asked Pembrook. "Night after night of being yelled at and assaulted? I'd like to help them out myself."

Cushing drilled her eyes into him. "But you wouldn't—would you Michael." It wasn't a question. Pembrook was about to respond, but Cushing cut him off. "Our job is to preserve and protect. That doesn't mean us. It means them. The public. No matter how much they sometimes piss us off."

Pembrook tried to seek the safer route, but couldn't help saying, "We all do what we have to... So, we were talking about the cases in front of us?" Their eyes locked, and Cushing finally eased her rigid stance and nodded.

Galen broke the awkward moment and told them about his recent conversation with Krauss, but they were both more interested in the Armlin case. Cushing filled Pembrook in on what she had learned about Perkowski's trailer being near Astoria during that critical period. "We should hear by tomorrow about the search of Perkowski's trailer—and I sure as hell hope they find something," Galen added.

"What if there is, in fact, evidence that Armlin was in the trailer?" asked Cushing.

"Yeah, Deb, I've been thinking about that a lot," admitted Galen. "It would mean that Armlin was alive for at least a week or two after his altercation with Rockney, and that Perkowski was definitely involved in whatever became of him. Whether or not this was all choreographed by Rockney from the start, or whether Armlin was unexpectedly dumped on his co-worker, I have no idea. And after Perkowski got him, what then?"

"He was in charge of disposing of Armlin?" asked Pembrook.

"God, I hope they don't find any blood in that trailer," said Galen, "and that we don't have to start searching those woods near Astoria."

"But if not, he must have taken Armlin somewhere else," stated Cushing.

"Yeah, that's likely." Galen replied. "And if it was back to Portland, I think we'll find that it ties in with how Armlin's phone came to end up in the hands of a homeless man. Anderson had a set of house keys on him, so he did have a home to stay in for a spell. Did I mention that his mother said Sheldon was proud of finally having a job—one of looking after an old man?"

"Yeah, you did. This is no mystery then, Galen," Cushing said matter-of-factly. "Rockney passes Armlin off to Perkowski who disappears with him for three weeks till things simmer down. Then he hides him in a house somewhere and hires Anderson to keep a watch over him. Case closed."

"My conclusion as well," said Galen, with Pembrook signaling his agreement across the table, "and I don't know if that's necessarily a good thing—for Armlin. We just don't have enough to go on yet." They were all silent for a moment. "The problem now becomes: if Armlin is in a house in this huge city, which house is it? Anderson's mother said that he left the job because the 'old man' was too hard to deal with and he was having trouble feeding him. What did he mean by that? Was it

Armlin's health? Did Perkowski take charge over Armlin after Anderson left?"

Cushing was shaking her head. "You're right. This doesn't sound good, especially if Perkowski, who's now in custody, is supposed to be watching Armlin and denies it."

"I can't wait to hear what forensics turns up in Perkowski's trailer—if there is anything there, we'll have enough to charge him for kidnapping at the least, and it'll also give us leverage in the interrogation room, because we'll need his cooperation to find Armlin."

Where the hell is Armlin? thought Galen as he sat at his desk, suddenly aware that a timer had been triggered when the two men they hypothesized to be responsible for Armlin were no longer up to the task. And he feared he had no clue when it would finish its countdown for the poor man—unless it already had. He was on edge as he sifted through what he knew and what had been found in Anderson's pockets. *And, where is that house where Anderson kept care of an old man?* He tapped on the Fred Meyer gift card lying on his desk and then logged onto the Kroger website, the parent company of Fred Meyer stores. He was suddenly curious to see if he could access the history of the purchases made on this card. He flipped it over and entered the required account number, but he had no PIN. After identifying himself as a police officer over the phone, he found a manager who could pinpoint the neighborhood store where

Anderson had last used the card. "Most of the purchases were made at our store on Interstate Avenue in the Arbor Lodge neighborhood," said the manager, "although the last one was made at our store in St. Johns on Lombard."

Near where Anderson was found. "When was the last purchase made?" asked Galen.

"Five days ago, at 3 p.m.," came the reply.

The day before we found Anderson, thought Galen. "And when was the next most recent transaction?"

"Two days before that at the Interstate store," said the manager. "It looks like the rest of the purchases on the card happened regularly every two or three days at that location for about..." as he was checking records, "two months or so. The card was recharged two times, and each was for $350."

"Can you tell how it was recharged and who purchased it to begin with?"

There was a long pause. "Yes, sir, it looks like cash was used each time. The name used was, um, John Smith."

"How about what was bought with each purchase? What was bought on the last visit to the store on Interstate?"

"Let's see," said the manager. "It might take me a minute to bring that up." He was soon back on the line. "I see 12-packs of beer were purchased nearly every time, and Ramen noodles, chicken soup, and Spaghetti-0's are big items. All of these were bought on that last trip, plus Gatorade, Boost protein drink, and straws."

"That's it?" asked Galen, with the manager confirming that this was the case before they ended the call.

Poor Armlin, thought Galen, realizing that Gatorade, Boost, and straws might point to someone in declining health. *Where is he? If Perkowski ties into this, he would know...*

CHAPTER 28.

THE EMAIL from Krauss was in his queue when he next opened his mailbox. He read through the obituary of Kim Olsen, the 34-year-old mother of a now-deceased daughter. A sentence in the last two paragraphs jumped out at him.

Kim will be missed by her loving husband Richard, her sisters Rose and Jemma, her sister-in-law Laura, and her many nieces and nephews. She will also be missed by a recent special and close friend with whom she spent many happy days, and who loved her dearly.

Kim will join in heaven her parents Ruth and Joel, and her daughter Lianne who left us too soon.

Galen stared at the screen. *Yep,* he thought, *that highlighted line is very similar to the one inserted into Erin's obit. Too similar.* Galen spent the remainder of the day researching the Olsen family and the circumstances surrounding Kim Olsen's death. The family was average in nearly every respect—income, employment, housing, and education. The police report stated that Kim had been out for a late afternoon jog on the Springwater-on-the-Willamette Trail, but had failed to return home that evening. She was discovered in the river waters the next morning with no indications whether the death had been due to accident, suicide, or foul play. The death had finally been ruled as accidental.

Following the recent evening they'd spent together at Jan's, both brothers had decided that just because their grandparents were separated, there was no reason that they should be, too. Both had lobbied Galen and Jan separately to say that they deserved more time together, perhaps even switching between households as 'a team,' as they put it. However, in light of his recent conversation with Jan, he realized that she would be against the idea as anything more than an occasional thing.

Given the age difference and the fact that Monty was still in middle school while Ryan was in his first year of high school, Galen was touched and appreciated that the two boys would want to stay together—whereas it hadn't been that way with his own brothers. The rough times for him had been more physical than mental as was typically the case these days, but he knew that being a brother was not always an easy road.

Galen had also observed that his grandsons' relationship with one another was becoming more dynamic. Ryan had shunned his younger brother after the accidental shooting that had injured Monty and had only recently come to terms with his own culpability and guilt. Galen saw this as a positive development, but one that could quickly change. Knowing that Monty was himself now finally dealing with the same traumatic issues, and that he was entering a phase of carving out his own independence, Galen found himself doubting the long-term existence of 'a team.'

The lobbying had one immediate effect, however: Jan's acceptance of Ryan joining him and Monty at their apartment for dinner that evening.

The only snag was Amelia. Ryan had insisted that his new girlfriend be included, and Monty had complained that he just wanted one-on-one time with his brother. Ryan had won in the end, and Galen was interested to meet Amelia and see how things went. He drove the short distance from his apartment to his old house, leaving Monty to heat up the spaghetti sauce and butter the garlic bread.

Jan opened the door on the second knock and quietly whispered, "There's no new word on Beth's condition. I don't know what that means, but I hope it's a positive sign," before stepping back into the living room, and then fading away into the kitchen.

I hope so, too, thought Galen, *although no news isn't always good news.* And this brought his worries to the surface again.

"You guys ready?" he asked in a purposefully upbeat tone, as Ryan grabbed a bag of chips he was bringing to the dinner and stood next to his grandfather. His girlfriend pushed herself out of the sofa, confidently walked across the room, and stopped before them, throwing her hands out to the side for a moment and letting them fall back against her thighs. There was no hand-holding nor outward signs of affection between the two, and Ryan was so flustered that he forgot to make the introductions. Galen was afraid that the situation was becoming too awkward as Ryan froze, when Amelia smiled and held out her hand in greeting.

"It's so nice to meet you, Mr. Young. Ryan keeps bragging about how great it is to have a real detective for a grandfather."

Ryan didn't blush, but almost. "So good to finally meet you, too, Amelia," said Galen. "Are you and Ryan in the same classes?" which was enough to break the ice and for both of them to begin talking normally—at least, normally for teenagers. On the drive to the apartment and over the course of the evening, Galen learned that Amelia's father was a judge with whom he had a vague acquaintance, that her parents had recently divorced, that she had an older sister who had just graduated from high school, that she played French horn in the concert band, and that she loved school. *That's all I need to hear,* thought Galen as they were sitting around the table slurping spaghetti and cracking jokes—not everyone of which Galen understood.

Monty was mopey and reticent at first, but finally accepted Amelia over a game of Snap. She had silky red hair, a laugh that drew everyone in, and an empathy that radiated out to whomever she met. By the time he'd driven Amelia to her front door and Ryan back to Jan's, Galen was hoping that Ryan would marry this wonderful specimen of a human being, knowing, of course, that time and circumstances weighed heavily against this ever happening.

During the trip back to the apartment and Monty, Galen remembered how traumatized Ryan had been by the accident and how devastated he'd been after his subsequent break-up with his previous girlfriend. *The boy seems to have bounced back all right,* thought Galen. *And thank heavens for that.* Of course, Jan had taken it upon herself to counsel Ryan, and he'd benefitted from a Coffee Creek Correctional Facility therapist arranged through Beth prior to COVID, but Galen was putting his money on Amelia as being the real reason for the changes in his grandson. While parking his car, he also wondered how much of the credit his increasingly vainglorious wife would claim.

CHAPTER 29.

GALEN ARRIVED at the Bureau office building the next morning after a pleasant evening but a nearly sleepless night and was just exiting the elevator on his floor when his cell phone buzzed. "Galen?" came the voice of Sheriff Dan Monroe when he answered.

"Good morning, Dan," replied Galen, immediately side-stepping any small talk, "any word from Forensics?"

"Exactly why I called," answered Monroe. "I just got word that Armlin's fingerprints are all over the rear bedroom and the bathroom of that trailer. We don't have the DNA results back yet, but Forensics said there were two different hair types collected, and that many of them were gray."

"Great!" said Galen, although this was the exact opposite of what he felt, given his concerns about Armlin. He was silent as he processed his next moves in another interview with the suspect, and Monroe was patient. After several long moments, he asked, "When can I see him?"

"Perkowski isn't going anywhere—ever, apparently," answered Monroe. "But I'll expect you sometime this morning."

"I'm on my way," said Galen. He was punching the elevator button and tapping his Captain's number as soon as the call ended.

"Tom," Galen rushed on as soon as he had him on the line, "I just received confirmation that Armlin was in Perkowski's trailer, and so I'm heading down to Oregon City to question him. I also learned yesterday afternoon that Anderson was in the Arbor Lodge neighborhood using a Fred Meyer gift card for the last two months. I think it's likely that if he was keeping Armlin in a house as we suspect, the location has to be in that northwest quarter of town, and it's probably within walking distance of that Fred Meyer store."

"It sounds like you're on the right track, Galen. There are plenty of answers we need from him besides the obvious, aren't there? If your theory's correct that Perkowski passed Armlin off to Anderson for safe keeping, why did he choose the north side of the city in the first place? Maybe because it was so far from where he's been living that he was trying to muddy the waters? A friend's house? And why trust somebody like Anderson with that kind of responsibility?" asked Tom. "We definitely need Perkowski to confirm the Anderson connection and tell us where the hell Armlin is."

"Yeah, and find out who's taking care of Armlin now," said Galen. "I hope to God someone is."

"Me, too. Let me know as soon as we have any solid info concerning his whereabouts," said Tom, immediately after which Galen was exiting the elevator and heading for his car.

He headed south on 99E toward a specific location, but his thoughts were all over the map. He imagined Emma's ecstatic face in Goose Hollow if they found her husband safe and in one piece after all this time. Galen also tried to shut out the unbidden images of her devastation should they be wrong and Armlin had met the end that they'd suspected all along. The familiar route south near the correctional facility also reminded him of his daughter Beth, and his continuing worries about her wellbeing. *When will they let us know more?* he wondered as he tried to catch sight of the facility that was now much too far away. He was so proud of how determined she'd become to make something of herself and take more direct control of her son's lives. This big change in her attitude had occurred just prior to the pandemic, and although difficult from her position in jail at the time, her wishes to be more involved were now rendered impossible. Then came his thoughts about her sons— Ryan with the promising new girlfriend who'd come into his life, and Monty who was entering a phase Galen was unsure he could keep up with.

The detective realized that he must have been subconsciously paying attention to the GPS instructions, because he found himself pulling into the Clackamas County Jail parking lot without having been consciously aware of the route he'd followed to get there. He sat in the car and dug at his jaw, finally downing two more Tylenol before donning his mask and wearily pushing himself up and out of his sedan. As he shut the car door, he wondered if he was up to the coming task. *Goddamn these viruses!* he thought, and again became aware of the beat of his heart as a dull rhythmic pain in the root of one of his teeth. He was finally growing to accept the reflection of the haggard, lined face he had just seen in the driver's side window as his own.

Sheriff Monroe met him in his office and introduced Galen to the Clackamas County detective who would join them in the interview room. Galen and Detective Ibanez had been in several workshops together, so they were already acquainted, and he gave her an elbow bump as Sheriff Monroe choreographed the proceedings. "Galen, we have a lot to discuss with this guy. We found meth and more than an ounce of coke in a ceiling panel. We found Armlin's fingerprints and probably his gray hairs all over the back of the trailer. And we discovered a small arsenal in the metal storage locker in the truck bed. Perkowski has danced in and out of custody several times, but I think his card is now full. We have a ton of questions that pertain to the County, but the most urgent thing right now is to find out what he knows about Armlin, so we'll let you lead off with your interrogation. How does that sound?"

"Sounds great, Dan, and I appreciate it," replied Galen as they rose and headed to the interview room. "Hey, you don't have any coffee available by any chance?"

"Latte or mud?" asked Monroe with a grin.

"Mud sounds perfect right about now."

Five minutes later, a thick coffee along with a squashed gooey pastry had Galen feeling like he was temporarily out of the ozone.

Perkowski was already seated alone in the bare room, and for the moment, Sheriff Monroe and Detective Ibanez decided to join a guard and observe from behind the one-way glass partition he was facing.

Galen placed a fresh cup of coffee in front of Perkowski and set his own next to his notepad. He knew the risk of having the suspect throw the hot coffee at him from across the table, but he was willing to take the chance in order to establish a hint of rapport with the man.

Perkowski had no qualms about the offering and began almost greedily sipping at the hot brew.

"How are they treating you, Jason?" asked Galen in a concerned manner.

"Hey, this is jail man," came the reply, "and it's rough like always."

"But you haven't served much time before, have you?"

"Just holding cells, but they're bad enough."

"I imagine so," said Galen. "Have they told you why they're holding you now?"

"Yeah, I know. I got a little hot and took a coupla swings at some of their patrolmen. It ain't a big deal, and they got no right to hold me for something as small as that. I never connected, but they punched me plenty. It should be those cops that are in jail."

Galen looked down, consulted his blank notebook, and then opened a folder with random sheets thrown in.

"You know, Jason, it might be a little more than that. They found some drugs?"

"I ain't saying nothing about them finding anything, but it was an illegal search, so whatever they found doesn't count for squat."

"OK, we'll put that to bed for the moment," replied Galen. "So, the reason I'm here is to ask you about Robert Armlin. He's an older man in his seventies and was a well-known and respected editor of a local newspaper—The Oregon Sentinel. Do you know him?"

"How would I know some newspaper editor? Especially some old guy? That ain't in my hood." Even to Galen, this didn't sound like gangsta. Not in the slightest.

"OK, well, the thing is, we found his fingerprints all over the interior of your trailer. Do you know how they got there?"

"No idea. Maybe he broke in? He's a thief? Is my stuff, OK?"

There was no visible change in Perkowski's expression or demeanor, no hint that the detective had hit a nerve. *Oh, great,* thought Galen. *Another Rockney,* who had given him nothing but grief in the several interviews he'd attended while the kidnapper was incarcerated in Wyoming. And another perp who still refused to offer any indication of what had become of Armlin.

"No, he's not a thief, and your stuff is OK." *Even though you'll probably never see it again,* he thought. "We have records that your trailer was parked in a camping spot outside of Astoria just after Robert Armlin went missing. Combined with the fingerprints we found, we think you took Mr. Armlin there as a hostage until the search for him cooled down." Galen went with a statement rather than a question.

"I never checked in anywhere." There was a long pause as he saw Perkowski think this through. "Oh, yeah!" he said suddenly. "You mean the camping trip I took with my dogs?"

"Yeah, that one. Only you don't have any dogs, do you?"

"I sure did and took them camping. But then they got to be too much for trailer living, and I had to give them away. They were both white-haired, by the way."

Quick thinking on his part, Galen thought cynically but nodding as though in agreement. "How about your friend Gary Rockney... oh, sorry, Gary Molitor? Are you two still in contact?"

Perkowski shook his head. "Nah, we never were friends. I worked with the guy, but he was kind of a loner. Stuck to himself—even when we were out on deliveries."

Galen leaned back and took a sip of his coffee. He stared at Perkowski, and took another drink from the now cool, and increasingly bitter cup.

"OK, Jason, next I want to ask you about Sheldon Anderson." Still no visible signs of recognition or any physical response from Perkowski. *Damn,* he thought, *I wish he was hooked up to a lie detector.*

"Who?" asked Perkowski.

"The derelict you left to watch over Robert Armlin?"

Wide-eyed, Perkowski shook his head and thrust his hands out palm up. Apparently, the international symbol of not knowing what the hell the questioner was talking about.

Galen rubbed fiercely at his left temple, and suddenly in his mind's eye, he had launched himself across the table and was strangling the man on his way to the floor. *I wish,* he thought.

He took a deep breath to continue, but was interrupted by the door opening and Ibanez gesturing for him to join her outside. "Just a moment, Jason."

As he shut the door behind him, Ibanez said, "Galen, we thought you should know. We processed a prepaid SIM card that was found in Perkowski's glove box, and it matches the number your people had distributed about Anderson's calls. Anderson had tried to contact Perkowski several times on the last day his cell phone was used, but Perkowski either never answered, or had taken the SIM out of his phone."

Galen pressed his back against the wall in an attempt to relax his tense muscles. "Thanks, Theresa. I'd say this is the final nail in Perkowski's coffin." But when he met her gaze there was no certainty at all. "Now I just hope we can keep Armlin out of the grave."

The detective was all business when he reentered the room and sat across from Perkowski. "Let me lay this out for you, Jason. I'm not interested in the drugs and firearms they found in your possession. They're enough to hold you for a while—maybe for a very long time. I'm only interested in Robert Armlin. We have records that you checked out of your trailer park near Troutdale at the same time Armlin disappeared. You showed up two days later in an Astoria RV park with no dogs and chose a site far away from all the other RVs. Mr. Armlin's fingerprints cover the inside of your trailer. We expect some DNA results soon, too, which will make a final verification of his presence. Sheldon Anderson had the keys to a house, dangling from a chain that carries the Miracle Furnishings logo, and we now know that he tried to call you multiple times... recently. So, where is the house you stashed Robert Armlin in?"

"Detective, this is all bullshit. I know you're lying and trying to get me to say something that will put me away. I'm not falling for it."

"I actually could care less about you," said Galen evenly. "I do care about Robert Armlin and his safety." He mimed drinking from his coffee cup, even though it was long since empty, and then tapped it on the table. "Oh, did I mention that Sheldon Anderson is dead?" *Was that a glimmer of a response?* "Yeah, he died of an overdose five days ago."

To his eyes, Perkowski's expression seemed more rigid, but he still held the semblance of a smile on his face.

"So, I sure hope you have someone else watching over Mr. Armlin, because Anderson isn't currently up to the job." He felt this was too smug and backed off. "Where is Armlin, so that we can save his life?" asked Galen. "What house is he in? We know it's on the North side."

Perkowski was shutting down, but there was something new in his eyes.

"Please, let us help Armlin, because if not, I'm sure that you'll be facing murder charges when we eventually find him."

The something Galen had perceived in Perkowski began to resemble the look of fear, and the detainee replied in an even voice. "I'd like to have a lawyer now."

CHAPTER 30.

THE COURT-appointed attorney arrived half an hour later and spent another thirty minutes consulting with his new client and catching up on the case. The DNA evidence reconfirming Armlin's presence in the trailer arrived at the end of the consultation, which resulted in an additional hour of client/attorney time before it was agreed that the interviews could resume. Galen hated being put on hold, especially since he was now convinced that every hour wasted could mean serious consequences for Robert Armlin. He spent his downtime on the phone with his captain, fellow detectives, and the IT staff. They were working on the theory that Armlin was being held in a house in the vicinity of the conjunction of I-5 and 308 in northern Portland near the Columbia Slough. It was too large an area for door-to-door canvassing, and they had nothing else substantial to lead them to the correct house. So, for now, the Bureau was poised for action, but that didn't seem to count for much given the level of urgency they all felt. Detective Jenkins was interviewing staff at the Fred Meyer frequented by Anderson, some extra patrol cars were cruising the likely neighborhoods, but that was about all they could do for the moment.

The interview recommenced at 3:00 in the afternoon—this time with both Monroe and Ibanez joining the Portland detective at the table.

As before, Galen came right to the point. "Look, Jason. You have all the information that we do now. We have fingerprints and DNA that prove Robert Armlin was in your trailer. Confirmation that your trailer was in Astoria just after he went missing. Confirmation that Sheldon Anderson called your cell phone several times on the day before he died. And that Anderson had a keyring with the Miracle Furnishings logo on it—your place of employment. So, there can be no denying that there has been contact between you and both Armlin and Anderson."

He took a moment and studied the man who, based on glances and nods, now seemed to be willing to take advice from his attorney. Jim Nickerson, the lawyer, was young, well-dressed, and confident, but not cocky. He watched Galen evaluating his client and awaited the next expected move.

"You are currently being held for drug and illegal firearm possession, and now a suspected kidnapping charge has been added to the list. Your lawyer looks competent, so I imagine your sentencing will be reasonable when all is said and done."

Both Perkowski and Nickerson nodded at this, but Perkowski exuded confidence, while Nickerson seemed to be holding reservations.

"But imagine a murder charge," continued Galen. "With all of these other offenses on top of that? They'll put you away for life—no question." Nickerson's expression hadn't changed, but Perkowski's had.

Perkowski glanced nervously at his attorney, and then blurted, "Murder? Are you nuts? I know you guys. This is some kinda pressure tactic, and you're stepping way over the line."

"Oh?" asked Galen. "Which line is that? The one you crossed when you handed a kidnapped man over to a drug addict who ended up overdosing? The one where you are probably directly responsible for the death of a frail old man?"

"Frail?" erupted Perkowski. "That old guy is…" and then he shut up. He turned for support to his attorney, but Nickerson was staring down at his notes shaking his head.

"I don't think we need to go any further, and I need some more time with my client," said the attorney.

"But we don't have time," countered Galen. "This man entrusted the care of an elderly man into the arms of a street person. That person has died of an overdose, and if he was the sole lifeline for Armlin, who's taking care of him now? We don't know that any fatal measures were purposely taken—that would be straight-out murder—but if Armlin dies of injuries or starvation, that will be on both of your heads for not acting in a timely manner. We need to find him. Now!"

This last exclamation brought both men on the other side of the table to attention. "We still need a minute, gentlemen," said Nickerson. Monroe stood and spoke into the tape recorder, giving a brief intermission to the interview.

"Good job, Galen," said Monroe when they were once again out of the room. "I think he's going to crack."

"A guy like Perkowski?" asked Galen. "I'm not so sure. He's been guarded up till now and he's used to falling back on the judicial system to save him."

"No," replied Monroe. "I mean the lawyer. I think he sees the harm that Perkowski's done, and the damage that not cooperating with us will do him in the long run. He'll show that he's a good attorney if he can act in the best interests of Armlin."

"I was reading the same thing," added Ibanez. "He seems to be sharp and have a good heart. He's new to me—anyone know where he's from?" The other two shook their heads in reply as Ibanez stared toward the door.

After twenty minutes, Nickerson signaled that they were ready to reconvene. When they had all taken their seats at the table, the attorney addressed them. "My client says that he wants to work in the best interests of the missing man and has some information he would like to convey." Nickerson took a breath, and Galen could tell that he was having difficulty with his own personal feelings about the matter. The detective glanced at Ibanez, and she was studying Nickerson with an unexpected intensity as well.

Perkowski remained silent as his attorney continued. "My client claims that Gary Molitor came to him in great distress and needed someone to help him care for an elderly gentleman. He was told that the situation was urgent and that some greedy relatives with no interest in the old man as a person were searching for him, and Mr. Molitor wanted to keep him safe. My client says that he was asked to secrete the man out of town for a few weeks, and then find a comfortable place for him until he, Mr. Molitor, or as you know him, Mr. Rockney, could resume care." The stares from the other side of the table were unanimously incredulous, but Nickerson soldiered on. "My client says that Mr. Molitor put him in contact with a friend who had a vacant house in North Portland, and that Mr. Perkowski should take the gentleman there for safe keeping."

"Where is it?" Galen burst out. "Where is the fucking house!?"

There was momentary silence, and then Nickerson unexpectedly turned toward Perkowski and asked, "Just where is this house, Jason?"

"Yeah," muttered Galen and "Please?" whispered Ibanez while Monroe stared at the detainee with an expectant look. Perkowski, in turn, was now eyeing his lawyer in a mild panic.

"Well," began Perkowski hesitantly, while clearing his throat, "It was dark when I followed Hal to the house..."

Galen's mind raced. The ransom drop-off site. *Hal...*

"Hal Langford?" he asked suddenly.

Perkowski looked back at him in amazement. "How did you...?"

"Never mind that now. Where is Armlin?" Galen asked again in a commanding tone.

"Well, I'm not exactly sure."

Galen rose part-way out of his chair, and Perkowski threw out his hands in self-defense.

"It... it was past midnight and we met at the Sheri's off I-5 up near the river, and then took 99 south. I was driving my rig with the trailer hitched behind, so I really had to pay attention to traffic and his taillights. I don't really remember exactly where that house is. I think the street name started with a 'W' or a 'K', but I wasn't paying attention to the signs—only to his taillights, so I wouldn't lose him."

Galen glared at him and then glanced at Monroe who was shaking his head and asking, "A 'W' or a 'K'? Come on, Perkowski, we need more than that."

"There was a maze of streets—I really can't remember the name."

"How about the house?" asked Ibanez. "The number? Can you describe it?"

"Yeah, the house I remember. It was a lightish blue and had crumbling steps up to the front door. It was raised up over a basement. It was on an empty lot on one side and a big yard on the other, so it was perfect for..." and he realized he shouldn't say any more.

"Perfect for stashing a kidnapped man?" asked Galen.

"Now, let's be careful here," said Nickerson, although he himself looked like he wanted Perkowski to continue.

"And that's all I can remember," said Perkowski. They grilled him, but few more useful details about the location came up. When questioned about Anderson, he claimed that he'd never actually met the man, and that Rockney's friend, Langford, had been the one to dig him up. Langford had given them each SIM cards to contact each other in case of emergency, but Perkowski said that he never answered the calls because he didn't want to be involved anymore.

"So, then how did Anderson end up with a Miracle Furnishings key chain?" Galen had asked, which had resulted in a huddle between client and attorney.

Galen's initial anger at Perkowski turned into absolute frustration, and he was the first out of the interview room after they'd finished. He immediately rang the Bureau to have someone, anyone, begin a search of houses in the area with large lots on either side using Google Maps, and with features matching the general description of the exterior. Patrol cars in the vicinity of Arbor Lodge were provided the description and instructed to start driving a grid pattern of the streets, as well.

The time dragged. Perkowski was led back to his cell, Ibanez and Nickerson had struck up a conversation in the hallway, and Galen was trying his best to hold up his end of a banter with Monroe.

Twenty minutes later Tom was on the phone. "Hi, Galen. Andy from IT has found a matching house on N. Kilpatric."

"Fantastic, Tom!" replied Galen. "Get someone there!"

"We have. I've contacted Jenkins and Cushing and told them to be there ASAP. Dispatch is having the closest units respond immediately."

"If none of the responders has the key or no one answers the door, tell them kick it in," said Galen. "I'm still down in Oregon City, but I'll get there as soon as I can."

"I think they know to enter regardless, but I'll pass that on."

Galen took a deep breath and then added, "Oh, and you might want to have an ambulance there, too, Tom."

Galen was still ten minutes away from the address on Kilpatric when his phone rang. He recognized the tone Deb Cushing had adopted as she began, and his heart sank with each of her words. "Galen, there's no reason to hurry. It looks like Robert Armlin didn't make it. The EMT's are guessing that he passed away a few days ago."

"Ah, no," said Galen quietly. He focused on the car in front of him. "OK, thanks Deb, I should be there in a few." Visions of a stricken Emma Armlin, a bereft John Doherty, and other sad friends of Armlin played out in the space between him and the Washington license plate stuck to the rear of the car ahead. The rest of the drive was on automatic—again, mindless responses to the GPS instructions.

The street was jammed with police cars and emergency vehicles and Galen had to park a block away. The house was just as Perkowski had described it, light blue with a large lot on either side, and Galen wove through several patrolmen along the walkway and up the broken steps. The living room he entered was a mess of beer cans and half-eaten tins of Chef Boyardee. A television in the corner was still murmuring away and tuned to the Nature channel. Foot traffic and expressions indicated that Armlin was in the basement.

There was no heat in the house, making the dingy dwelling feel even more empty and inhospitable than it already was. The air grew even chillier as Galen descended the steps into the concrete-walled, dank, unfinished basement. On a cot in a corner lay a figure wrapped up in a large comforter, and as Galen approached, it looked like Robert Armlin was only sleeping.

CHAPTER 31.

WHAT A *crappy end to a shitty day,* thought Galen. He'd been sitting in his car in front of the Goose Hollow house for five minutes, exhausted and dreading this coming conversation with Emma. Lights were on inside and he'd called ahead saying that he was bringing her some news, unable to keep the sadness out of his voice when he did so. He hadn't wanted to wake her up at this late hour and have her unprepared, but he wanted to be the one to deliver what details they had in person.

Solar lights illuminated the walkway, but they seemed weak and anemic rather than tasteful to the detective. Emma's friend, Frank Grant, opened the door on his first knock.

"Hello, Detective Young," said Frank as he ushered Galen inside. "Emma called and said that you had some news about Robert? She asked for our support, so we know it can't be good. She's in the living room."

Both Emma and Marilyn Grant had been crying, however, he was met by brave faces. "Hello, Galen," said Emma. "Thanks for coming by so late, but you could have just said over the phone. I would have understood."

Galen shook his head, "No, I wanted to tell you in person, Emma."

She reached out and gripped his hand for a moment, and all three were silent waiting for Galen to continue. "We found

Robert late this afternoon in a house on the north side of town. There's still a lot we don't know, but the medical examiner estimated that he'd been dead for several days. I'm so sorry, Emma."

"Who would do such a thing?" asked Frank with a bitter edge to his question.

"We're still teasing that out, but it was almost certainly related to Robert's disappearance just after the Davidson kidnapping. Apparently, Robert was secreted out of the city for several weeks while we were searching for him, and then he was moved into the Portland house where he was kept for the past two months."

"But why hold him like that?"

"It appears none of those involved wanted to face kidnapping or murder charges. I think it's as simple as that. If they had let him go, he could have talked, and if they'd killed him, it would have been murder."

Emma was clearly holding back tears when she asked, "How did he die?" But Galen knew that she was really asking, *Did he suffer?*

"We'll have to await the coroner's findings, but I can tell you that he looked at peace, and there was no sign of physical trauma or ill-treatment."

"So, how then?" she asked.

Galen shrugged. "We don't know at this point, but it is possible that he was drugged while he was being held, and so perhaps an overdose is a very real possibility. Once again, I'm so sorry we didn't find him sooner." Emma's internal struggles with this information were subtly playing out on her face. "You'll be, OK, Emma?"

She struggled with a faint smile. "Maureen is flying out tonight to stay with me. And the Grants have been great." Then Emma couldn't hold back the tears any longer. He left the three in a knot after answering more of their questions as best he could. Galen's inclination afterwards was to drive straight to the nearest bar, but he knew that Monty was home alone at this late hour, and so he chose home.

CHAPTER 32.

HE CALLED in sick the next day. After the long and draining evening, he'd arrived at the apartment to find it empty. Oddly enough, he'd been expecting something like this from Monty, and so he hadn't panicked. He'd mentally nixed calling Jan at such a late hour, unless the situation became serious, so he'd reasoned out what he would have done at his grandson's age—starting to test his wings, but not yet daring to fly too far from the nest. Monty wasn't answering his cell phone, so Galen had headed out to search the nearby neighborhood, and sure enough, just as he'd stepped out onto the sidewalk, Monty had come—hood up, head down, hands-in-pockets-mode around the corner. He'd been tired and Monty had been oppositional, so after a few crossed lines of communication, the pair had headed for their separate bedrooms.

Galen made a huge breakfast, surprising a sheepish Monty as he emerged from his room, just before online class-time.

"Here you go, Monty. I've made some pancakes to get our engines started. Pull up a seat."

The boy was still groggy, but turned to log into his computer to be ready for the school day.

"Over here, Monty," said Galen.

"But I have classes, Gramps," eyeing the huge spread. "I can sneak some while Ms. Knudson calls roll."

"No, you won't," said his grandfather. "I called into your school, and you have a day off today."

"What?" asked a worried Monty. "Am I grounded because of last night?"

"No. I can see that we both need a personal health day. And that starts with these pancakes and bacon."

There was no 'Whoop!' he would have heard from his grandson a year earlier, but the boy did dig into breakfast with a relish.

Late that morning, Galen pulled his sedan into the small parking lot off of NW Cornell Rd. at one of the access points to the Wildwood Trail. Low clouds, light mist, and towering trees met them as they emerged from the car in the hills above Portland. A short drive up from the city, and they suddenly felt like they were in a much quieter, less tame environment.

Monty had been on the same long hiking trail nearer the Hoyt Arboretum, but never on this less-populated section. "Wow, this kinda reminds me of visiting Uncle Mack in the Wallowas. Cool!" Galen's brother lived in Joseph, a gateway to numerous hikes in the Wallowa Mountains, and the boys had explored much of the area over the years.

And... that's it for the conversation, thought Galen as Monty, walking stick in hand, struck out along the path that wound down to Balch Creek before rising again to climb the farther hillside, making sure to stay well ahead of his grandfather, except for some quiet time together staring down from the bridge at the rocky creek.

Galen knew that Monty wouldn't be too far ahead and found him staring out of one of the window spaces in a second level wall of the Witch's Castle. The old moss-covered stone house had lost everything but some of its sides and the floor which supported what remained of the second story. Galen climbed the short steps to join him and then they were both leaning on their elbows staring out of the same window.

"This is so rad," said Monty. "Who owns it?"

"I imagine that it belongs to the city now, or its parks department," said Galen. "It's something though, isn't it?"

"Yeah," Monty replied, and then thought for a while. "This is the kind of place I'd like to live. All by myself, and I'd shoot anybody who came near it."

Galen turned and stared at his grandson. "I'm sure you don't mean that, Bud. This is a cool spot, but you wouldn't need to defend it."

"Oh, yes, I would!" his grandson suddenly exclaimed. "I'd be a hermit and keep everybody out!"

"Monty?" began Galen. "You don't..."

"I mean it! They're all stupid!" and he sank down with his back against the cold stones, suddenly weeping.

Galen sat next to him and put his arm around the boy's shoulders, letting him cry it out. Eventually Monty recovered and wiped roughly at his wet face.

Galen removed his arm, and then asked, "So, what brought that on, son? What's the matter?"

"Everything!" shouted Monty, but the rest of the conversation was more subdued. Galen listened and it all came down to this: "Everyone's ghosting me, Gramps. I don't see anyone anymore, so it's all on Facebook, Instagram, or Tik Tok. But every time—every time—I add something to a thread, it just stops dead. Guys can talk about a... about anything, and I add a sentence, and it stops completely. I'm always the buzzkill on everything." He wiped at his nose with his sleeve and took a huge breath. "Ever since the accident, it's like I died instead of just getting hurt."

"I'm not going to say that it's all in your imagination, but here's two things. First—because of this COVID and everyone being hooked up remotely, there are lots of folks who feel exactly like you do. You don't know how many emails I've sent out and gotten no reply. Even Uncle Mack waits weeks before he answers if he does at all. And we're close. And second, believe it or not, you might be feeling the same way if you were in school every day. Now is the time that all the cliques happen and everyone's trying to be in the cool group and exclude everyone who isn't in it. But those groups are really just invented by the kids in them—they're not cool, they're excluders."

"But I'm on the outside of the outside," sighed Monty.

"The same thing that many in your school are feeling. We'll have to see that you get more real contact with friends—but it might be just a little longer until this whole pandemic cools down," said Galen, patting him on the shoulder. "You're going to make it through this rough patch, Monty. You're doing just fine."

Monty appeared to question this, but then nodded.

"Ready to keep going?" asked Galen.

The remainder of the hike they stuck together, pointing out to each other the late-blooming wildflowers, or the rare views of the city through gaps in the trees. Just before they reached the parking lot at the end, Galen said, "Say, Monty, I was just talking to someone who would really like a partner for hikes like this. Do you remember Tom's wife Carol?"

"Yeah, but I don't need a babysitter, and besides, she's kinda weird, isn't she?"

"She's different all right. But she really is just looking for someone who has some time to take some hikes with her. Give it a thought, OK?"

Monty tilted his head in a way that showed his doubts about the whole thing.

Chapter 33.

THE CORONER'S report arrived the next day. Despite the dismal conditions of his surroundings, Robert Armlin appeared to have been in reasonably good health externally. He'd been in fair physical shape, thin but well nourished, and had shown no visible trauma or needle puncture marks. Internally, it had been another matter, however. Based on the autopsy, the man had suffered a massive stroke, probably several days or a week before he'd died from a subsequent heart attack. The doctor had said that given the stroke, he would have been unaware of much in his final days.

Myrtle Street was much more congested than on his last visit, and just as was the case outside the cold house on N. Kilpatric, Galen had to park a block away from the Armlin home. The purpose of his visit was to tell Emma in person the cause of her husband's death, and relay that Robert had likely not suffered at the end.

Galen's thoughts had been focused on Robert Armlin all morning. He was surprised that he was still processing Armlin's death. He'd compartmentalized him as deceased months before, and had dealt with that, but then the editor had been resurrected, and he wasn't yet able to translate his recent passing into a new sense of closure. It was as if time was out of synch—Robert was still alive and yet not alive—for the time being.

A well-dressed and masked couple up ahead had just entered the main door of the heavily-beamed house as Galen mounted the few steps from the sidewalk to the immaculate walkway leading up to that door. He slowed his pace to gather himself as he approached, and then took a long moment on the front porch before donning his own mask and knocking. The door was immediately opened by a masked woman who closely resembled Emma, but because he could still see her eyes, he knew that this was Emma's sister. "Hello, Maureen, I'm…"

"Yes, hello, Galen. Good to see you again. Emma said you gave her the news earlier," replied Maureen. "We're having an impromptu memorial out back, but I don't expect you're here for that. Are you? You'd like to see Emma?"

"Yes, thanks," Galen offered, taking no offense that he wasn't expected at the gathering.

"I'll just be a minute," said Maureen as she went to fetch her sister.

Another couple strolled up the path and Galen stood aside as they knocked and were greeted by a young woman unfamiliar to him. Just as the door was closing, Emma emerged, wearing an orange outfit with a matching orange mask.

Galen was prepared for a wave, or perhaps an elbow tap, and so was surprised when Emma strode forward and gave him an immense hug. "Oh, Galen, thank you so much for coming by," she breathed. "And thank you for all that you've done to find Robert."

When they stood apart again, he said, "Emma, I'm so sorry that we didn't get to him in time. To think that he was still alive and practically under our noses all the while…"

"Isn't it just too much?" and tears began to form in her eyes. "But who could have known? You did your utmost, Galen. I know you did."

"Well, we tried, at least." And then he gave her the details of Robert's last few weeks.

"So, there's nothing anyone could have done, anyway," as her voice choked.

He shook his head and instead of apologizing yet again, he found himself grinning behind his mask for some reason and asking, "Orange?"

She laughed with tears now streaming down her face. "Hey, I wore black for so long thinking he was already dead that I can't stand that color anymore. This was Robert's favorite color on me."

"Good, it really suits you." Now, Galen was wiping a tear of his own and gave her one more hug before he turned and left her to her husband's memorial.

Deb Cushing had been busy. As they were wrapping things up at the derelict house the evening they found Armlin, Galen had mentioned to her that Perkowski had dropped Hal Langford's name during the interview. She'd taken the man who'd acted suspiciously at the failed ransom attempt into custody that very night. She'd finally been able to interview him late in the day that Galen had taken off, once Langford's self-induced drug-haze had cleared.

Apparently, Hal Langford possessed none of the caginess of Gary Rockney, nor the inflated self-assurance of Jason Perkowski. "He just started talking, and laid it all out," said Cushing at the wrap-up briefing that afternoon.

"Why do you get all the easy ones?" asked Galen with a grin.

"I think it has more to do with her bedside manner," joked Pembrook, which received a pained expression from Cushing, but she let it go.

"Anyway, it looks like Rockney was more involved than we knew…" she began.

"From prison?" asked Jenkins.

"Yep, in a way," continued Cushing. "Even from there, he had leverage over Perkowski, and to some extent, over Anderson and Langford, too."

"Through his girl-friend Ortiz, is that right?" asked Tom.

"Yes, Captain, and we have her in custody now as well."

Galen was surprised that Sara Ortiz was involved. She had seemed straight-forward and only connected as a love interest when he'd interviewed her in the early days of Robert Armlin's disappearance.

"All right, let's hear it," said her captain.

"Yes, Sir," said Cushing, taking a minute to refer to her notes. "The last thing that Rockney wanted was a murder charge added to what he would already face if he was captured.

When he met with Perkowski and transferred Armlin to his trailer, Rockney took several surreptitious photos of Perkowski with Armlin, who was already drugged by this point. He passed these photos off to Ortiz on his way out of town, which was his proof that Armlin was alive when he fled. These pictures gave Ortiz the leverage she needed to keep Perkowski in line—proof that he was with Armlin, so that if anything happened to Armlin, she'd give the pictures to the cops, us. She made sure that Perkowski knew about them, and he in turn let Langford know that if anything happened to Armlin, they were all screwed. Through Rockney, Ortiz was also the source of the money to Perkowski who then supplied cash and drugs to Anderson and Langford to keep them happy."

"What about the ransom notes?" asked Jenkins.

"That was Langford," said Cushing. "He said that he saw a chance to make even more money off Armlin, but both times he started celebrating before he had the ransom in hand and was too hopped up and addled to carry them through. Which was probably for the best, because we would have nabbed him in a second if he'd tried to take the money."

Galen cleared his throat, started, and then cleared his throat again. "And so, after Anderson OD'd, Armlin just…"

Cushing shook her head. "No, Galen. That's at least one good thing. Langford stayed with him until the end. He said that he knew that it was bad after the stroke, but that he also knew he couldn't call an ambulance. The stroke made him try for the second ransom, since he knew Armlin probably didn't have much longer. He stuck with him though, and fed him and kept him clean until the heart attack that killed him about four days later."

Galen shook his head. "They never thought to just let Armlin go?"

"I guess not. Each one up the chain had something on the one below, and no one dared try it—or even see that as a possibility."

"What a fucking circus," said Tom, which received unanimous agreement around the table.

As he had hoped, John Doherty was sipping a glass of stout and reading the Oregon Sentinel, the edition from the previous day with 'ARMLIN FOUND DEAD' dominating the front page. "Hey, John," Galen said as he slid into the bench across from him outside of the Kells Brewery. Neither of the two men were wearing masks given the distance and fresh air, and so Galen was momentarily taken aback when John awkwardly disentangled himself from the picnic bench and in two quick strides was smothering Galen in an embrace. "Oh, man, I'm so sorry about Robert," John nearly whispered as he released Galen and retreated to his side of the outdoor table. "But we've gotta toast him!" he choked out, and instead of sitting, he yanked open the pub door next to him and now in a clear voice shouted, "Seth! A Harp and a stout, quick as you like!"

Galen, and undoubtedly the rest of the pub, could see that John had already had a few, but he didn't mind, and expected to have some more with him. This, he knew, was going to be a wake.

"It's such sad news, but at the same time a huge relief," said John as he plunked himself down, "to finally know what happened to the poor guy." He then averted his gaze and brought a sleeve to his moist eyes as he began staring down into his glass. "I read the reports in the papers, but do you know the real circumstances of his... death?"

"John, I feel terrible about Robert," said Galen. "Here he was alive all this time, and yet we didn't have a clue about how to find him."

John looked up at Galen and said, "Yeah, when I think that here I was keeping on with my... He could have used so much solace. We could have talked about so much." His eyes dropped back down, and the sleeve came back up.

Galen gave him a minute and then said, "I know, I'm sorry. His circumstances were pretty much what was written. He was restrained by Rockney and passed off to Jason Perkowski who kept him in a trailer for a few weeks, and then he was hidden in a basement on the north side of town."

"But why?" asked John—a question Galen had been wrestling with since Sheldon Anderson had been found and his suspicions had begun to grow.

Galen started to recount the chronology of events as the Bureau knew them, along with the suspected motives driving those involved when he stopped partway through. John seemed unfazed by the pause. Galen had realized that his friend was really asking why a good human being could be treated so callously and how one person could act that way toward another. "I don't know the real answer, John. I've never been able to figure that out. How can the rules seem so clear to most of us, but be rewired in so many others? It could just be drugs and money—that's basically why the leverage that Rockney held over them stuck when it comes down to it. The fact that they could face murder or kidnapping charges were, in my opinion, really just an inconvenience to them that didn't matter as long as they had the drugs and money."

John shook his head and tipped back the last dribbles of his stout. "It really is a cold, cruel world then. Isn't it?" as the pint glass came down on the wooden table much harder than it normally would have. "So... was he at least treated decently? Is that too much to hope for? How did they keep him captive?" asked John.

The door behind him swung open and a server nimbly, given the cold, set down the two beers in front of them. "On the house, gentlemen—Seth insists."

"Thanks, Melissa, and cheers to Seth as well," said Galen with a sad smile as he clinked glasses with John. His expression turned more serious as Melissa hustled back inside. "This doesn't go beyond the two of us, right John? Not something for your newspaper?"

"Absolutely not," agreed John.

"And this might be difficult for you to hear—are you sure?"

John began to shake his head, but turned it into a hesitant nod.

"Promise to stop me if this is too much?" to which John nodded again.

"OK. There were healed wounds to both his wrists and ankles, so it looks like he was physically restrained at first. He had also suffered a serious head trauma, likely resulting in a severe concussion, probably received during his fateful encounter with Rockney down by Fanno Creek. After that it looks like he was heavily sedated—the coroner found no injection marks, but the basement had empty containers of oxycodone and tramadol, and it was likely that these were administered with alcohol. You know from the papers that he had suffered a stroke and then a heart attack, and the coroner is guessing that the drugs led to the stroke which was the underlying cause of his heart failure." Galen took a long drink of his lager and set the glass carefully back on the pine planking. "I'm sorry—that sounded like I was giving testimony in court. The best that I can say is that Robert was out of it so much that he probably didn't suffer, but the worst I can say is that they robbed a good man of his mind and his life."

As the evening spread across the city, they both spent rounds of beer toasting and talking about Robert Armlin's life, and Galen once again knew that he'd be taking a cab home. Suspecting beforehand that this meeting with John would likely turn into a wake, he'd asked Jan if Monty could stay with her and Ryan for the evening and overnight, and Jan had agreed that she'd pick him up before dinner. John and he both ordered the steaming Kells Shepard's Pie against the cold evening, during which Galen received two texts. Gramp! Great to spend time with Ryan! came Monty's, and Fortnite tonight! came Ryan's. Knowing Ryan as he did, he figured this must be the name of a video game.

As they sat, eventually under the pub lights on the dark street, both he and John were getting chilled and knew they'd had enough. They were finishing paying the tab when John tapped on the copy of the Oregon Sentinel he had folded next to him. "Did you read his obituary yet?" asked John.

"It's out already?" asked Galen. "That was quick."

"It'd been ready for some time, since we'd always feared the worst," answered John. "Here, you take this, but don't read it until later tonight."

"Why not?" Galen was curious.

"Because I wrote the damn thing, and I don't want any critiques till later," he said with a huge grin. "Here's to Robert!" Galen responded with a clink and a final swig.

They parted with slaps on the back and a quick hug, and Galen could tell that John was wishing it was his old pal Robert who was bidding him good night.

Galen was chilled to the bone and took a hot shower as soon as he was back at the apartment. For having drunk so much, he was surprised at how sober he felt, chocking it up to the dinner and the steaming flood he'd stood under for much longer than normal. He dressed in his sweats, reluctantly retrieved the newspaper from his overcoat pocket, and sank down on the small sofa to read Robert Armlin's obituary.

What to Robert Armlin were practical observations and well-considered opinions were to the rest of us Truths. His columns were filled with insights, revelations, and perceptions of the world that would make us subtly twist our own views of life, politics, and reality. The World of Journalism and the world at large are both greatly diminished by his passing.

Robert Armlin was born on May 28, 1947, in Ashland, Oregon and he spent most of his professional life in the state. He received both bachelor's and master's degrees in Journalism at the University of Oregon in Eugene where he met the love of his life, Emma Summers, and the two were married on July 3, 1970. As Robert often joked, he didn't want to get married on the day of independence.

Robert spent 40 years employed at the Oregon Sentinel in Portland where he and Emma settled down. He also always said that he would never call what he did for a living 'work' because he loved every minute of it. There is no need to go into a litany of the exceptional columns Robert wrote, because they will be forever archived in the annals of the Sentinel for anyone to read and enjoy.

Robert didn't take anything from the community, but only gave and served. He was on the board of directors of both the Portland Rose Festival and the Portland Symphony; and he was active in the Democratic Party, was a member of the Oregon Food Bank, and was a member of the Multnomah Athletic Club.

He loved travelling and visited, among other exotic spots, Egypt, Vietnam, India, Nepal, Thailand, China, Ethiopia, New Zealand, and Peru, bringing back tales of excitement and insight. He also loved fishing and had fond memories of trips to Canada, Alaska, and New Zealand in pursuit of the elusive trout.

He will be especially missed by dear friends connected with all the above clubs and societies, his various social groups, and those gracing the Goose Hollow Inn and Kells Irish Pub where he was not afraid to lift a pint against weather of all kinds – physical and metaphysical. He is survived by his loving wife, Emma, his brothers, Bruce, Kevin, Lance, and Walter, along with all of their wives, children, and grandchildren; bless them all.

May the words he wrote continue to inform and inspire.

Galen sighed. *What a great obituary,* he thought. *John outdid himself. I wonder why he wanted me to wait before I read it?* and chocked it up to John's modesty.

CHAPTER 34.

IT CAME as no surprise that Galen was in absolute misery the next morning. Sleep had come immediately, but abandoned him early. The left side of his face felt like his pillow must have been made of pins, he still had stabbing pains in his left ear, and now some of his lower teeth on that side were screaming at him. The headache from a hangover was only icing on the cake. He'd been eating Tylenol like it was candy, swallowing two more as he groaned out of bed, and found himself thinking wistfully about the CBD products that were still under the front seat of his car. He didn't know much about CBD, but he could just see himself hallucinating his way through the day. He opted for a heavy dose of caffeine instead, even though he'd read that both coffee and alcohol exacerbated the symptoms from the shingles. *Goddamn these viruses,* he thought again as he grabbed two masks he'd washed the night before and headed out the door to await the cab at curbside.

During the ride into downtown, Galen decided that he would try and reach Kim Olsen's widower by phone rather than conduct a face-to-face interview. The virus wasn't the reason for this tactic—he realized he had very few questions for the man: Did your wife have an affair? Did she see a therapist or hair stylist? If so, whom? It was most probable that there was absolutely no connection between Erin Carlson and Kim

Olsen, but if there was, the person who would know the most about either of their deep, dark secrets was a therapist.

He made it to the floor of his office just when the morning conference was scheduled to start, stopping first at the cafeteria for another large coffee to go. Galen shed his coat and dumped his briefcase and was heading to the meeting room down the hall when his cell phone rang. He'd received so many calls about renewing the warrantee on his 1995 beater sedan that he nearly ignored it, but the area code was local, so he took a chance as he strode down the corridor, ready to push cancel after the first few words out of the speaker's mouth.

"Mr. Young? Detective Galen Young?" came the voice of a middle-aged woman.

"Yes, speaking," said Galen. "Who is this—I'm in a bit of a rush."

"Mr. Young, this is Doris Karp, I'm the duty nurse at the Coffee Creek Correctional Facility care unit."

Galen halted in mid-stride and stepped back against the wall. "Oh, yes," was all he could manage at the moment.

"Your daughter, Beth, would like to speak with you in a minute," she began. "I tried your wife first, but there was no answer. Beth is now showing signs of a rapidly advancing viral infection and is beginning to have trouble breathing and keeping down any food or fluids. I just wanted you to be aware of this as you speak to her, because she may not be able to talk for long. To put you a little at ease, she is on oxygen and an IV drip, but she's not as yet on a ventilator. We're monitoring her closely, and we're prepared to move her to another facility if her health declines any further. Many patients stabilize at this phase, so we are waiting to see how far this progresses. Be assured that we will keep you apprised of any changes in her condition, and that we're sorry it is not going to be possible for you to see her until she improves. OK, here is your daughter," she ended abruptly.

There was some fumbling with the phone and then Galen heard a breathy voice that sounded like a small child's, "Dad?"

Galen tried to hide the catch in his throat as he answered, "Hi, Sweetie. It sounds like you might not be feeling so hot right now?"

"Oh, God," Beth whispered, "don't you ever get near this virus..." there came a mild fit of coughing, "it'll kick your ass!" A brief pause. "I'm not kidding..."

"Oh, Beth," said Galen. "I'm so sorry you caught this thing. But you're a fighter, right?" There was no answer. "Beth, you'll pull through this." He said as a statement of fact.

"Oooh. I sure hope so." Beth took some more labored breaths, sounding to him like they were through the oxygen mask which the nurse may have been holding over her mouth and nose for a moment. "My kids, Dad." Now, to Galen, this sounded like a plea. "Please tell them the truth—that mom's pretty sick right now—but maybe not how..." a few more coughs, "how bad it might be. I want them prepared, but not scared." Galen found himself gripping the phone and eased up. "OK?" she asked.

"Yeah, Beth," her father responded. "That's exactly what I'd suggest—you're such a good mom."

There was a long silence on both ends of the line.

"OK, Dad, I gotta go, but we'll talk soon, OK?"

"Beth, hang in there, Hon, I love you so much…"

"Mr. Young?" came the voice of the duty nurse. "I'm afraid that Beth has gone back to sleep for now. She's on several medications, so that's not at all surprising. Be assured that we're doing everything we can for her here."

"Yes, thank you so much for all you do," said Galen as they ended the call.

Pembrook was just emerging from the conference room, and Jenkins and Cushing were laughing at a joke Tom had told when Galen entered.

Tom looked over at him and began, "Hey, Detective, it's about time…" when he held his tongue. Even though they couldn't see the rest of Galen's face, all three present could tell from his eyes that something was amiss. They took seats around the table, and Galen related his phone call with his daughter.

The moment he was back in his office, he tried calling Jan to relate the news about Beth, but he was directed straight to voicemail. He needed to tell her more than a mere message could convey, so he hung up without leaving one. He'd heard that the virus was indiscriminate about whom it impacted, but he'd always thought that the young and healthy would come through unscathed. Beth had sounded like she'd been laid pretty low by this thing, and he found himself even more worried about her, which made him unproductive for the rest of the morning. Jan was refusing to pick up on each subsequent try, so he reasoned that she must be in sessions with her clients.

He did reach John, however, and walked through the driving rain to meet his friend at the nearby Bridge City Café for lunch.

"You obviously work closer to here than I do," said John, eyeing Galen's wet trousers and shoes as he displayed the soaked top half of his own shirt for a moment before rezipping his jacket. The outdoor seating meant that both would have to put up with the chill brought on by wet clothes and a light breeze.

Galen managed a smile, and John could see that the detective was not in a jovial mood. "It was great to celebrate Robert with you last night and to meet with you for lunch today, Galen, but I can see that something's up. What is it?"

"Thanks for joining me, John," said Galen, and he then described his phone call with Beth.

"Ah, man, that sucks," muttered John. "Here I am the semi-contented bachelor, and I can only begin to imagine what you're going through." Their order of turkey tikka club sandwiches arrived, and John eyed his suspiciously.

"And I can't imagine what my daughter is going through," said Galen.

"Then I'm twice removed from being able to appreciate her situation," said John taking an exploratory bite. He watched Galen take his first taste and then the men both nodded to each other, digging into the blend of interesting flavors. Halfway through, John set down his sandwich. "I honestly don't know how you do it, Galen. You're no spring chicken, if you don't mind my saying so; you're embroiled in important cases; you're raising two grandsons; you're having marital problems; and now your daughter could be beginning the battle of her life." He shook his head. "I know I should be offering words of encouragement, but I have to say that if Beth doesn't pull through, I don't see how you will. I really hope that she can beat this."

Galen stared at John, realizing that only a true friend would say something like that. It somehow made him feel much better than the usual sympathetic utterances ever would have. In spite of his continuing worries about his daughter, he found that the second half of his sandwich tasted even better than the first.

Feeling much more relieved and centered, Galen finally got down to work when he returned to the office. He took a deep breath as he dialed the phone number, hoping for a link between the two obituaries.

"Richard Olsen? This is Galen Young, a detective with the Portland Police Bureau. I was wondering if I could take some of your time to answer a few questions? This is regarding your wife, Kim?"

"Oh, sure, Detective," came the neutral voice of Olsen, and then on a more wishful note, "You've learned something new?"

"No, I'm sorry Mr. Olsen," replied Galen. "I just need to gather some information about your wife's contacts prior to her death—it might help with a case we're currently investigating."

"Oh, like her friends? I think your department already has a list of them from before."

"No, more like the appointments or regular meetings your wife might have kept as part of her normal routine?"

"Oh, like doctor's appointments? Book club? That kind of thing?"

"Yes, anything like that."

"Well, let's see. She only saw her regular doctor twice a year, but he was Dr. Rudd at the Portland Family Practice. Same with our family dentist, Wayne Wilson at Multnomah Dentistry. She was seeing a massage therapist for some lower back pain. Umm," he thought a little more. "She did have a book club that went virtual after the pandemic hit. Oh, and she was seeing a religious counselor to help her with the loss of our daughter."

"How about hair appointments, or visits to spas or salons?"

"Well, those were difficult because of COVID restrictions, and I cut her hair through the spring."

Not the hair salon, then, thought Galen. "So, it was a religious counselor, and not a psychologist or psychiatrist?"

"Yeah, Kim never sought help from them. Too hoity toity for her."

"OK. Can you give me the names of the massage therapist and the religious counselor?"

"Sure..." there was a long pause. "Here it is, Brandon Pierce with Eastside Chiropractic is... was the massage therapist. She absolutely adored that man, to the point that I was almost becoming jealous. And the religious counselor was... Janet Young with Christian Heart Counseling."

Galen was barely able to thank Mr. Olsen for his time before he hung up. *Jan was the counselor for Kim Olsen?* he was floored. His mind raced through the connotations—*conflict of interest, his own wife a murderess? No. Any real connection? A probable coincidence?*

He had to clear this up. Now. He tried Jan's phone again, and this time she answered on the second ring.

"Hi, Galen. I saw that you called a couple of times this morning, but I was in therapy sessions. What is it?"

He'd envisioned a delicate conversation about their infected daughter, but instead forged ahead on offense. "Jan, you were the therapist for Kim Olsen?"

"Um, yes, Galen, I saw a Kim Olsen. The woman who passed recently?"

"Yes, the Kim Olsen who ended up floating in the Willamette River. And you never said?"

"Well, now, why would I, Galen? She was my patient, and it was sad, but she died. You know I have to keep my involvement with my clients confidential, right? What is this about?"

"Was Erin Carlson also one of your patients?"

"Carlson? No, I've been seeing the Clarkston family, but not a Carlson. Why? Galen, this is starting to sound like an interrogation."

"No. Well, maybe it is, in a way. Look. There's a possible link between Kim Olsen and an Erin Carlson, and I just need to be sure that you're not that connection."

"A connection? No, I worked with Kim Olsen, but that's as much as I can tell you."

"And not Erin Carlson?"

"No."

Galen breathed easier and took a moment to switch gears. "Good. Thanks, Jan. The reason I called in the first place is that I spoke with Beth this morning, and she didn't sound good."

"They let you speak to her? How is she?"

"Like I said—not too good. The nurse said that she's already on oxygen, and that they're trying to keep her comfortable, but that if she goes downhill any further, she'll need to be transferred to a different facility. Like OHSU."

"Oh, my God!" exclaimed Jan. "That's so fast! I can't believe this is happening..." Galen was about to speak, but she continued, "What about the boys? Should we tell them?"

"Yeah, we should. Beth said that she wanted them to know about her condition, but not to scare them."

"Then you have to do it, Galen," was Jan's immediate response.

Me? Up till now, you're the one who seemed to care less about what happened to Beth... flitted through Galen's mind, but then he said, "Are you sure? You're the one who's been counseling Ryan all this time."

There was a long pause and then Galen could hear genuine emotion in his wife's voice, "Yes, but this is about their mother… their only mother." And then more softly, "I do my best, but I can't keep this up if something happens to her." The phone was muffled for a moment and then Jan said more evenly, "Hey, why don't you and Monty come over for dinner tonight, and then we can talk to them about it?"

"That sounds possible, Jan," a somewhat bewildered estranged husband replied. "Can we bring anything?"

Galen met with Jenkins and Cushing about a missing person case they were tasked with in the mid-afternoon. A professor with Portland State University, a sociologist and known philanderer, had failed to show up for classes during the second week of the semester. This had happened once before when the man was in his thirties and teaching in Flagstaff, Arizona, but to purportedly disappear with a graduate student when he was in his mid-fifties was raising some eyebrows. The most verifiable sighting of the pair had been at Cannon Beach a few days before, but the local authorities were having difficulty locating them after that. Galen left Jenkins and Cushing drawing straws to see who would make the trip to Cannon Beach.

Back in his office, his last call of the day was a reprise contact with Jodi Knowles. *She must be getting sick of hearing from me,* he thought as he dialed. He knew that with a toddler in the house there was never a good time, but he gave it a shot. "Hello?" came a haggard reply.

"Hi, Jodi, this is Galen, and I promise to make it quick."

Jodi laughed at this, and he heard a giggling Bobby in the background. "What does it really matter, Galen? He's either going to be laughing, screaming, or sleeping in the next second anyway. What do you need?"

"I just want to cross one more thing off my list, and then I swear I'll leave you alone."

She groaned in a good-natured manner. "OK, shoot."

"I'd asked before about Erin's recent contacts, and you said that she was seeing a therapist and your hair stylist. Neither of those two have helped with what I'm looking for and, to be frank, I'm running short of leads. Could you think back carefully about any other possible close contacts she made with anyone before she died? Even the most obscure person she might have shared things with?"

"No, there was no one else. I'm sure. We're living in the times of COVID, after all," she joked.

"Maybe over the phone or through Zoom?"

"I don't think so. But hang on," she said as a memory came back. "You know, Erin suffered from some terrible shoulder and neck pain after slipping on the ice last winter, and she was seeing a massage therapist for that."

Galen was suddenly paying very close attention on the other end of the line.

"Yeah, but she quit seeing him just before she left Mike for that nutcase in Salem. He started giving off some really weird vibes and she ended up saying that he was creeping her out, so she quit her visits with him. And just as well, if you ask me."

"And do you remember this man's name or where he worked?" Galen looked down and saw that he'd been tapping a pencil furiously on his desk, and dropped it, spreading his hand out to calm his nerves.

"Yes, it was Pierce, Brandon Pierce."

"Jodi, you're a wonder—thank you so much."

"What is it about Mr. Pierce that you…"

"I'm sorry, I can't really get into details right now, and it may really be nothing," he cut her off. "I hope you understand, but you've been most helpful," and he hung up after he assured her that he would let her know of any further developments.

Galen was immediately on the phone with his captain who agreed that Brandon Pierce should be brought into the station for questioning after background information was gathered. Galen arranged the interrogation for the next morning, and then spent an hour searching records for any information on the massage therapist. Pierce was roughly the same age as Erin Carlson, born in upstate New York, graduated from Ithaca with a bachelor's degree in English, moved to the West coast soon after, taught briefly at Rogue Community College in Grants Pass while also getting his massage therapy degree there, returned to Ithaca for five years where he worked as a massage therapist, and then finally moved back to Oregon four years ago to work for Eastside Chiropractic. He appeared to have no record other than some sexual harassment complaints while in Ithaca.

Chapter 35.

"*OKAY...*" Monty said slowly and in a highly modulated voice when Galen told him that they were going to have dinner with his grandmother and his older brother. He looked suspiciously at his grandfather. "Are you and Gram getting back together—is that what this is about?"

"Nope, we just thought it might be a nice idea," replied his grandfather. "If you finish your homework, we can leave by 6:00. I'm going to make a salad." *And lucky thing I stopped at the store on the way home for the ingredients; we're getting low on everything,* he thought while Monty limped over to his desk and Galen rubbed furiously at his jaw.

Aren't we the pairs? Galen thought as he cleaned and chopped a green pepper to add to the salad mix. Galen and Monty were both dealing with physical pain, and Ryan and Jan were dealing with emotional issues. Galen reflected that he and Monty were the lucky ones, as he pictured Jan and Ryan wrestling with their unseen demons. *Well, maybe Monty is joining them in that now, too,* he thought.

The joshing, laughter, and mild horseplay by the grandsons in the living room were in sharp contrast to the somber moods of their grandparents preparing dinner in the kitchen. And Galen ended up being more in charge of this part of the evening than he expected. Jan had wanted to prepare a hamburger casserole and had all the fixings laid out, but looking even more the old lady than her years, she was cautious in her movements and unable to stand fully erect without wincing. Her back was giving her fits, and her frustration was beginning to show.

"How did it happen?" asked Galen, genuinely concerned.

"Oh, it was just something stupid," she replied tersely.

"Did you try and move some furniture or lift something heavy?"

"No!" Jan gripped the counter and bit her lip. "No, when I pulled up in the car this afternoon, I just reached across to grab my purse in the passenger seat, and it's been hurting since."

"Why don't you go sit down, Jan?" asked Galen. "I've got this."

Jan let go of the counter gratefully and made her way slowly over to one of the kitchen chairs, wadded up a kitchen towel to put behind her lower back, and seemed to breathe easier. But this didn't lift the atmosphere in the room. Both of them were concerned about their daughter and about the reactions the boys would have to the news they had to deliver about Beth.

"Guys, don't you think this is how it should always be?" Monty asked as he and Ryan joined them at the table. A Seattle Mariners game was in the sixth inning on the TV in the living room, and three of the four of them kept their ears tuned in for any big plays.

"Seriously," Ryan joined in. "Aren't the two of you mature enough to work out your differences?"

At this, from a freshman in high school, Galen took a healthy drink from his glass of Merlot, and even Jan, who always limited herself to a single glass, was pouring another small amount for herself.

"Yeah, Gramp, just say you're sorry or whatever it takes. This is like our home—we should be living here too, instead of in some ol' basement," said Monty, piling it on and pointing at them randomly with his fork.

What a pair, thought Galen. "Well, Jan and I haven't been seeing eye-to-eye lately, and it's been better for us to stay apart for a while instead of continually arguing. That's not a healthy environment for any of us, so we separated to take the time necessary and see how it plays out." Jan made a sour expression across the table, and he wasn't quite sure what to make of it.

"Boys," Jan began in a lecturing tone, but then stopped. He knew that she was prepared to list all that had happened between her and Galen, and to the family as a whole. However, she showed remarkable restraint by asking for the salad dressing instead. He also knew she was aware that they had worse news to deliver and that there was no need to dig up the same old issues beforehand.

The conversation then became lighter, and the boys jumped up twice during the meal to see what the fracas was on the TV. The Mariner's slim lead had evaporated to such an extent that the next time there were sounds of celebration on the set, neither jumped up to see what had happened. Jan rose gingerly and, now walking nearly erect, went to the fridge to bring out a cheesecake for dessert. It was after the slices were served that

Galen decided to broach the subject of their mother's health. The bitter with the sweet.

"Hey, guys, I'm afraid I have some news that's a little on the sad side, but nothing to get too worried about yet."

The cheesecake on their plates was already half consumed, and both boys turned to their grandfather mid-bite.

"Probably not about the Mariners losing the game tonight?" asked Monty, maturely setting his fork down.

Galen grinned at this but then let his face grow more serious, so that they could begin to sense the gravity of the discussion.

"Okay... obviously not the Mariners," said Ryan.

"Nope, it's about your mom," said Galen. "We've learned that she's come down with the COVID-19 virus."

"Ah! I knew it!" exclaimed Ryan immediately. "Confined in a place like that—they say it can spread like wildfire in jails. Is she asymptomatic?"

Somehow Galen was surprised that his grandson was so well informed. "Unfortunately, not," he replied. "She started off with a fever, but now it's progressed so that she's having some breathing issues."

Monty was still registering this when Ryan asked, "She's not on a ventilator yet, is she?"

"No not yet, but they're..."

"A ventilator!" yelped Monty. "That's like totally serious! She's not gonna die, is she?" As soon as these words left his lips, tears began to swell in Monty's eyes. "Oh, My God! Mom!"

Jan was sitting next to Monty and reached over with a wince to bring him in close to her, gently saying, "Hey, Monty, she's OK, she's doing fine. It'll be all right."

Ryan searched his grandfather for more information as Galen explained. "I'm sorry, Ryan, it might be a bit of a struggle for Beth. You obviously know a lot about this virus and that it can hit people you might not expect it to—pretty hard. Your mom seems to be one of them. She was fine at first, but now she's having trouble getting enough oxygen. They have the capabilities to deal with that at Coffee Creek, but not ventilators. If she gets worse and it's evident that she needs help breathing, it looks like they might have to transfer her to OHSU or some other hospital. She's on the edge, and she'll either be staying where she is or moving to better care within the next day or so. We don't know any more than that yet."

"Yeah," said Ryan, now beginning to tear up as well. "And the worst part is, none of us can even visit her. It's been like five months since we've even seen her."

Monty was inconsolable after this, and the remainder of the cheesecake and the fate of the Mariners faded into the background for the rest of the evening. They all talked about what they knew of the disease, and in the end, Ryan did the best job of reassuring his brother and explaining how, with modern technology, Beth had very good chances, and that being relatively young and healthy, she should come through unscathed.

As Monty and Galen said their goodbyes and were driving home, Galen wondered at the changes that Ryan had undergone in the last few months, transforming from a troubled teen into someone already pushing the upper boundaries of adolescence. And he even perceived a gentler side to his wife that he hadn't expected to emerge, given her recent puritanical stances. *Maybe it was just because of her back pain meds,* he mused.

Chapter 36.

BRANDON PIERCE had been brought in for questioning, and Galen was sifting through the information he had on him prior to the interview when his phone rang.

"Detective Young? Todd here, Todd Blowers with the Salem Police Department?"

"Yes," Galen responded. "How are you, Todd?"

"I'm fine, but your request isn't in very good shape I'm afraid, Galen. Not a single one of our liquor distributors comes close to matching the description you gave, and we even visited each of their homes personally to check for car types and physical characteristics. Not one of them could possibly be who you described."

"Ah, damn, that's too bad, Todd," said Galen. "Sorry to put you through that. I know there wasn't much to go on in the first place, but I thought a good chunk of the male population in Oregon might match that description—two trucks, camo gear for clothing, and a big guy."

Blowers laughed out loud at this. "Well, you're right there—but not among liquor distributors in Salem, apparently. And you know what?"

"What?" asked Galen, somewhat needlessly.

"We even went the extra mile and checked out distributors county wide, and still no match. I'm guessing that you were misinformed about either the guy's job or his description."

"Yeah, and I'm guessing we were probably misled about even more than that," replied Galen. "Apologies for sending you on a wild goose chase, Todd. As it would happen, we're investigating a possible new direction in the case right now, but if this one doesn't work out either, I may be back."

"Sure enough, Galen, just let us know," replied Blowers. "Keep her steady," and they ended the call.

Galen had been so focused on the odd insertion into Erin's obituary and the connection with Pierce that he'd nearly forgotten about his request to Blowers concerning the man Erin had an affair with. *Alleged affair—with a phantom,* he now corrected himself.

Brandon Pierce was nothing like Galen had expected, although admittedly he hadn't given the man's physical appearance much thought. As the detective entered the interrogation room, he felt like he was stepping into the set of a movie production. Pierce looked like a star. Strong features with no single one of them dominating, striking gray-blue eyes, straight light-brown hair pulled back into a neat ponytail, strong jaw slightly muffled by a carefully trimmed short beard and moustache, thin but powerful physique. Galen could easily picture the man in any number of action movies, or steamy romances.

After logging onto the Bureau's interview recording system, Galen addressed Pierce directly. "Good morning, Mr. Pierce, I'm Detective Galen Young with the Portland Police Bureau, and I'm here to interview you concerning your acquaintance with two women—Erin Carlson and Kim Olsen. Do either of these names ring a bell?"

"Yes, of course, Detective," replied Pierce. "Both of them were my clients. And it's tragic that they both passed away so unexpectedly." Pierce's voice continued the movie star-like image—deep, melodic, and clear though not overly loud.

"The two not only passed away unexpectedly, but they also died in questionable circumstances," replied Galen. Then to gauge Pierce, he added, "And we're here to see if you might have had something to do with that."

Pierce's head shifted back while his eyebrows raised. "Me? What could I possibly have to do with their deaths?"

"Let's talk about that," said Galen, and he laid out the basics of the case. "Both of these women were clients of yours, and both met with, as I said before, highly suspicious deaths. You've come up as a link between the two where any connection at all between them would be extremely unlikely. Can you describe your clients? These two women?"

"What do you mean?"

"You know, how you saw them as people, what your relationships with them were like."

"Well, there's not really much to say. They were the same as every one of my patients—special and in need of healing. That's what I do—I heal, and I try and get them back to the kind of life they want, and deserve, to live. We all have our blockages, and my job is to open them up. To set them free."

Oh, boy, thought Galen, *would Carol ever love to meet this guy.*

"All right, let's talk about how special they were to you."

"Everyone is special to me, Detective," Pierce smiled. "Even you." He could see Galen balk at this and continued. "But my clients are even more special than the people I meet out in the public. You see, I'm a massage therapist, which is one of the best jobs in the world. I'm in physical and psychic contact with each and every one of them, and we develop a bond that can't be equaled... Well, except with a spouse or lover, perhaps."

Maybe too much, even for Carol, thought Galen. "So, similarly to a lover or a spouse, how would you react if you were spurned or if your feelings weren't reciprocated?"

Another, it now seemed to Galen, smarmy smile. "Detective, I'm talking about something bigger than egos and attractions. I'm talking about true connections on many levels."

Seeing this was going nowhere, Galen switched the direction of the questioning. "Did you cause either of these women harm?"

Nothing but the raised eyebrows. "You must be joking. I've just explained that I enhance life, not take it away. Don't be ridiculous."

"Then why did you call into the newspapers and make additions to those two women's obituary pages?"

Galen couldn't tell—there could have been the slightest flicker somewhere, the eyes, the cheek muscles? But then, he couldn't be sure it wasn't the lighting or if he himself had blink-ed at the wrong moment.

"Whatever are you talking about, Detective? Obituaries are written by their loved ones. Why would anyone outside of that close circle even contemplate doing something like that?"

And, of course, that was the end of anything productive in the interview. Galen thanked the lanky massage therapist while holding the door to the interview room open as he left, advising him to stay in town in case there were further questions.

Damn! thought Galen. This reaction was both because he had no solid evidence to help pin Pierce down, but also because he had absolutely no sense of whether this person was being straight with him or lying through his perfect teeth.

Galen pulled up his mask, but then quickly lowered it and rubbed at his left temple. Replacing the mask, he knocked on his captain's door.

"Hey, Tom," said Galen as he entered after the appropriate cue.

Tom was pulling up his own mask as Galen took a seat opposite him. "These frigging things," said Tom. "When will we ever be rid of them? Carol thinks they're here to stay—just like in Asia."

"She's usually right about that kind of thing," smiled Galen, probably undetectably to Tom.

"You can say that again," sighed Tom. "Say, speaking of Carol, I hear that she's going to be taking a hike with Monty. How do you think that will go?"

"No clue. I was surprised that Monty said yes, but he did like a hike we recently took on the Wildwood Trail. Kudos to Carol for offering to get him out."

"She says she needs any excuse she can get. But, what the hell will they talk about?"

"I've been wondering the same thing."

"Well, if they make it through an entire hike and are still on speaking terms, I'll be impressed."

Galen agreed and then came to the point of his visit. "So, I just wanted to get your opinion, Captain," a little more formally. "Personally, it looks to me like we're close to having something on those two initially unrelated cases. Erin Carlson has changed from being a located missing person into a likely vehicular homicide with intent—which we wouldn't have noticed without that strange addition to her obituary. And we found a similar insertion in the obit of Kim Olsen who, as you know, died under equally questionable circumstances. I've just spoken with Brandon Pierce, an unexpected connection between the two—their massage therapist."

"How did that interview go?" Tom asked curiously.

"Frankly, it was more of a fishing expedition, and I didn't get a nibble."

"And you needed my opinion on…?"

"Well, a couple of things. First, I'm now kind of stepping into Homicide's arena and want to make sure you're on board with that."

"Galen, you know how fluid this is—especially when a misper becomes a corpse. You have all the background on Carlson, and Homicide is over-tasked what with recent murders due to the riots and people going stir crazy. I've already checked with Majeweski in Homicide about this case and one that Jenkins is working on, too, and he said that he can use all the help he can get."

"Great," said Galen. "So, there's no problem in my digging into Pierce's past and seeing if anything pops up?" Tom shook his head. "And I also wanted to let you know that I learned this morning that Erin Carlson's new boyfriend was not a liquor distributor—at least as far as Blowers in Salem could determine. He had in-person interviews with all known local distributors, plus an expansion outward to the entire county which yielded similar—negative—results."

Tom seemed distracted, fiddled with something on his desk, and was silent for a spell. Galen itched at his temple, and a few moments later, Tom reflexively did the same thing, while staring at his desk the entire time. Then his captain raised his eyes to make contact. "Galen, I know this Pierce thing seems enticing, and it really is a tempting coincidence that we have a connection between the two women. But it could be just that— a coincidence. I said it before, and it bears repeating—it always must be a relative or someone she's really close to. My money's on either the husband or that lover of hers. Make sure that you don't spin your wheels and waste too much time before looking closer into Mike Carlson and trying to locate that asshole in Salem who abused her. And we have to locate the vehicle that ran her over. It looks like it wasn't Carlson's Jeep, so then it must be the asshole's truck."

"OK, I'll refine my, our, investigation. Thanks, Tom," and a knock at Tom's door ended the conversation. Out in the hallway and walking to his office, Galen considered again that his captain was probably right. Tom had overseen more homicides than anyone he'd ever met, and the big-city undercurrent of the New York which Tom had left behind was gradually seeping into this once-mellow West Coast city.

Despite his best intentions after his conversation with Tom, an idea struck Galen as he shut his door, and he was Googling Ithaca, New York newspapers as soon as his computer booted up. He was on the phone with the Ithaca Gazette minutes later.

The person in charge of obituaries in Ithaca sounded eerily similar to Bob Krauss with the Oregon Sentinel—so much so that Galen glanced down at the number he'd dialed just to make sure it was an out-of-state prefix. "Tim Cather, obituaries, how can I help you?"

"Hello Mr. Cather," said Galen. "My name is Galen Young, and I'm a detective with the Portland Oregon Police Bureau. I can email you my credentials right now if you'd like."

"I don't think I'll need them, but it depends on what you want," responded Cather in what Galen now registered as a rather thick New York accent which he didn't have the knowledge to pin down to a more specific place.

"We're investigating a possible homicide, and a person we're interested in has lived in Ithaca in the recent past. My request may be a strange one..." His phone buzzed, indicating an incoming call, but he ignored it. "But I'm hoping you can help. Our local paper has printed the obituaries of two individuals where the original submission has been altered in an unexpected manner."

"Altered how?" asked Cather.

"Well, in each case, it looks like someone called in identifying themself as a family member and added a single sentence to the original obituary. Our local newspaper has no problems with over-the-phone changes, and so these weren't flagged as suspicious until later. I was wondering if these sorts of changes were common in your paper?"

"Most certainly," said Cather. "Grieving family members are understandably under considerable emotional strain and often request corrections over the phone."

Exactly like Krauss, thought Galen. "Then I'm wondering if you can do me a favor. Can you run a search in your obituaries for the period spanning 2011 to 2016? I'm looking for a single sentence in any of them that goes something like, 'so-and-so spent time with a new or recent special friend who loved her dearly.' Here, I'll read the two examples from our newspaper obits." And he quoted the two additions.

"Sure," came the immediate reply when he'd finished. Galen had expected some hemming and hawing, needs for clarification, or further justification, and so he was momentarily taken aback. Then Cather clarified, "Just as long as this doesn't turn into a bring-me-a-brick problem."

"Sorry?"

"You know. You ask me to bring you a brick, so I bring you one. Then you say, 'No, I was thinking of one a little longer.' I find a longer one, and you say, 'No, something a little redder.' I find a redder one, and you say, 'Something a little heavier.' And so on, until I get stuck in an endless loop, all because you weren't clear enough in the first place."

Galen thought for a moment. "I'm sorry, I don't know how to be more specific than that because the wording might change, but it should include the words 'new or recent', and 'special or dear', and 'loved or adored', all in a single sentence. Does that help?"

"Yeah, I think I get it, and depending on what I find, I might be able to expand a little on the key words. It might take me an hour or so, but I got... I have nothing else on my plate right now."

"Thanks so much, Mr. Cather," said Galen. "Do you need anything else from me?"

"Nope. Like I say, I know the kind of thing you're asking. I started here in '14, and for some reason this is starting to sound kind of familiar. I'll get back to you, and if I come up empty, we can go from there—but not forever. How does that sound?"

"Great," said the detective, making sure that Cather had his phone number and email address.

At almost the same moment he hung up from this call, his phone rang again, and he saw that it was Monty. Answering rather brusquely, Galen said, "Monty, I told you..." envisioning another ruined school project.

"But Gramps, this really is important! Mom's been moved to the big hospital—to OHSU!"

Galen could hear the desperation in his grandson's voice. "Take it easy, Bud. That means she's in good hands. What exactly did you hear?"

"Gram just called and said that Coffee Creek called her to let her know. She tried to reach you, but you were busy and she wanted to make sure that one of the two of us knew as soon as possible. She said that Mom reached the point where she couldn't breathe very well on her own, and so they moved her to OHSU this morning. But—can't breathe on her own? That's like totally serious!" Galen could hear that Monty's own breath was catching as he spoke. "Gramp! What if something happens to her? What if she dies?" And then the choking turned into huge sobs.

"Hey, Monty. Your Mom is young, she's strong, and she's a fighter. We talked about this. She's going to pull through. These are all just precautions to make sure that they stay ahead of it." However, in his own mind he was thinking, *Oh, no, not the ventilator, this could be bad.* "Look, do you want me to come home? Are you doing all right?"

Monty had regained some composure at this point and murmured, "No, it's OK. Gram is coming over to pick me up in a few minutes. She said I can Zoom classes from her house as well as from here. She said she has a light day, and you can pick me up after."

"That's good of her, Monty. I'll swing by right after work. And don't worry, your mom is going to be OK."

He heard a thin voice saying, "Yeah," as Monty hung up.

This is not good, thought Galen as he realized that Beth was now going to be even more isolated in a hospital ward than she was at the Coffee Creek Correctional Facility, if that was even possible. From what he'd heard, absolutely no visitations were allowed in any hospital, and that it was only through the graces of the nurses and the time available to them that any contact was possible at all. He sank back in his chair to let this all sink in and was in the same position forty-five minutes later.

His phone pulled him back from memories of Beth's childhood, and those extremely difficult teen and post-graduation years they'd had with her.

"Yes, hello, Mr. Cather," he said, recognizing the number he'd called what he now realized to have been only a relatively short time before as it came up on the screen.

"Hi, Detective Young," said the Ithaca Gazette obituary page editor. "I think I found what you're looking for."

"Really?" Galen snapped out of the lingering fog of his memories. "Similar wording?"

"I think so. I did a keyword search, and found one for sure, and maybe two other obituaries of women that fit the phrasing you gave me. I can email you the obits if you like."

"That would be fantastic," said Galen while trying to maintain an even tone. "This might be stretching it, but is there any way to know if those phrases were added after the original was submitted?"

"Hang on a sec," said Cather, "I'll check." A few minutes later he was back. "Yes, definitely for two of them, and possibly for the third. The third one had so many changes over the course of a few days, that it's hard to tell, and we don't have the original for that one anymore."

"Thank you, Mr. Cather. Can you tell me anything about the women? I'd be interested in how they died?"

"I thought you might ask that and looked them up. One died here in Ithaca in a pedestrian accident—a hit-and-run. No one was ever charged. The two others died out of town. One was snowboarding at Greek Peak near here and they found her off-run with a broken neck. It looked like she ran into a tree. The last obit had a sentence with similar wording to the others, but the woman drowned while on a vacation in Cancun."

A hit and run, Galen was thinking when he said, "You're amazing, Mr. Cather. Yes, please send me those obituaries, and any additional information you picked up. I can ask your local police for more details about the deaths if I need them. You've been a tremendous help."

"Anytime," said Cather as they ended the conversation.

The email arrived minutes later, and Galen scanned each of the obituary notices for that single sentence that was out of place.

...Gail is survived by her husband, Derek, her brothers Robert and Dale, her mother Samantha, and her aunt Grace. She is also survived by her community of friends and the loyal customers of her flower shop 'Gail's Flowers and Fancies.' She will be sorely missed by all, but has always said that we will meet again on the other side. Her love embraced all whom she met, and a recent special someone was humbled to be included within her innermost circle and share time with her.

...In the end it is appropriate that Trish was doing the thing she loved most, and her snowboarding squad will miss her dearly. Her 'Greek' geeks and the crew at WICB have both expressed that they will not be the same without her. Nor will a new admirer she leaves behind as their friendship was just beginning. She is survived by her parents Karen and Bob, and by her fiancé Ray Haversham.

...It was Sarah's lifelong dream to escape the brutal winters of Ithaca and relax in the tropical warmth of Mexico. Her MS was in the early stages, and she wanted to enjoy life and travelling to the fullest before nature took its course. All accounts were that she had a grand time in

Cancun, and she even wrote that she was thinking of moving there, if it was possible. With the love and support of a new, loving friend, she lifted her wings and flew to new possibilities, and it is tragic that her dreams could not be fully realized.

Galen spent the next half-hour verifying the police reports from the incidents, and then thought about what he'd read. *How odd. I can see a vehicular homicide being possible for Gail Jacobs if someone meant her harm, but the snowboarding accident, and a drowning in faraway Cancun hardly seem like foul play. All of these sentences were added while Pierce was in Ithaca, but did he make the changes? What did he have to do with these women's deaths?*

Pierce was back in the interview room a few hours later. Often the second police interrogation was enough to rattle anyone, and nervousness, hostility, or fear began to subtly betray its presence in the suspect. If the detainee was guilty, mistakes began to be made and backpedaling on previous statements occurred. Pierce showed no outward signs of concern as Galen entered the room and registered the interview.

"Mr. Pierce, I must tell you that you're becoming a person of interest to us." Again, the raised eyebrows to which Galen explained, "We've heard from both the police and your previous place of employment in Ithaca. Three women met with accidents, odd changes were made to each of their obituaries, and they were all patients of yours. Add those three to the two recent deaths here, and I'd have to say that I see a definite pattern emerging."

Pierce splayed his long fingers out across the tabletop in a placating gesture, almost as if he were preparing to massage the rigid surface. "I don't know what obituary changes you're referring to, Detective, but I'd say that it's not unusual at all for patients to die in the course of one's professional career. You see, I treat six to ten people per day, and so meet with hundreds of different people each year. I'm sure you'd find the same numbers for anyone in my profession. It's not uncommon at all."

"It's odd that you say you're unfamiliar with the changes in wording I just referred to. Cross-checks of obituaries reveal very few with the type of phrasing I'm talking about, and those we did find were from the periods you were residing in either Ithaca or Portland. Here, let me read them, and see if they sound familiar," as he pulled a sheet from a folder and read paragraphs from the five obituaries.

Pierce said nothing, staring straight ahead, but Galen could detect a slight change, just the smallest hint of what he took to be worry. "There's another little matter of the woman, Trish Mathers, the one who died in a snowboarding accident. It seems she was one of those who filed sexual harassment charges against you in 2012. She claimed you were getting a little too personal on the massage table."

Pierce opened his mouth to say something, but closed it and stared now at the tabletop.

"You see, there is a pattern. There's more between you and these women than just your healing them. And now we're going to dig deeper, which means your life is about to get disrupted. We're going to subpoena your phone records, your email accounts, and get search warrants for your home and your place of work," said Galen, hoping like hell that the justice arm would support his arguments.

Still with little change in his demeanor, Pierce slowly met Galen's eyes and said, predictably to Galen, "I want to see an attorney."

Galen met immediately afterwards with Tom and a representative of the District Attorney's Office, and they were able to hold Pierce overnight to make sure that he couldn't destroy potential evidence before the searches could be implemented.

CHAPTER 37.

DINNER WAS a solemn affair, much of which was destined to become leftovers. The boys were emotionally drained by the news of their mother and eventually drifted off to a half-hearted video game which didn't last, and Ryan soon retreated to his bedroom. Monty was listlessly watching the television, and Galen was about to rouse him for the trip back to their apartment when his phone rang. He recognized the number of the East Precinct. "Young here," he answered.

"Detective Young, this is Officer Douglas from the East Precinct. I was told you would want to hear about this shooting."

He had Galen's attention. "Who was shot and where?"

"Mike Carlson was fired upon in his home. The address is…"

"Yes, thank you, Officer Douglas. I've been there several times. Was there a fatality?"

"Not if he pulls through there wasn't, but it looks pretty bad."

"Ambulance?"

"They're leaving just now."

"OK, I'll be there as soon as I can." *Now who would want to shoot Mike Carlson? Any connection with Erin?* Galen thought as he ended the call.

Jan had gone to lie down, her back feeling somewhat better than on the previous evening. He poked his head into the bedroom they once shared and told her about the call he'd just received. She and the boys had no problem with him leaving while Monty spent the night in his old bedroom. There was none of the enthusiasm previously displayed by Monty, and Galen worried that the day's news about his mother might send him into another deep funk.

The detective was radioed a status report about the shooting victim on his way to the scene. Mike Carlson had apparently been shot in the back with a high-powered rifle as he sat in his living room watching a show on TV. Galen learned that the wound was dramatic, but that the initial assessment from the ER classified it as critical but non-life threatening, and Carlson should pull through if this was the case.

Galen's presence at the residence on SE 112th wasn't absolutely necessary, but he felt that he needed to be there to help evaluate the scene and stay alert for any possible connection with Erin's hit and run, given the two now obvious assaults on the couple. Three patrol cars and the forensics van were crammed into tight spaces in the driveway, but he was able to squeeze into a spot recently vacated by the ambulance in front of the small car port.

It was cool enough that he could see his breath, and that cold swept into the house through the shattered front picture window. He didn't recognize any of those on the scene, and so introduced himself. Patrolman Douglas walked him through what had happened. "It appears that Mr. Carlson was watching TV," and he gestured to the shattered LCD panel once contained by the intact big-screen frame, "when someone fired at least two high-powered rounds through the front window at him." Galen noticed that Erin's display of crystals was standing as before, but littered with bits of broken glass and plastic. "We know they were from a high-powered rifle because the two slugs we've found so far were embedded in the far wall of the next room." He walked to the doorway on the right which led to a guest bedroom where two forensics officers were at work extracting the second round and searching for any additional evidence. "They say they aren't sure if the bullet that hit Mr. Carlson is one of these two, or if it followed a different trajectory. Officers Diggs and Wright are interviewing the neighbors up and down the road, but there's not much to go on. The nearest neighbor thought he heard some shots and a roaring engine, but everything seemed normal when he looked outside. He was curious, but a little scared, he said, and walked across the street to at least check on Mr. Carlson's house. That's when he saw the shattered window, and he was the one who called it in when he got closer and found Mr. Carlson on the couch." Galen and Douglas walked back out to the road to view the house from the shooter's perspective, and the detective was surprised to notice the orange cat curled again on the hood of his still-warm car. When he approached it on their way back into the house, the cat skittered away under the Honda Civic, but when he looked out later it was back curled over the cooling engine compartment.

Galen spent the next two hours interviewing Ralph Owsley, 67, the neighbor who'd discovered Carlson, questioning two other neighbors, gathering as much detail as possible from the forensics team, and chatting with Diggs and Wright about what they'd learned.

The patrolmen had departed, and he was finally leaving the forensics unit to finish their work at 1:00 a.m. He was just about to turn onto the steep road and head toward home when he braked. Something was bothering him, but he couldn't put his finger on it. It was pitch black, the road was deserted, and his mind went back to the earlier days of the Carlson case. *Something about the car,* he thought and then killed the engine, reached into his glove box for a flashlight, and walked back toward the house. He didn't want a loose end to keep bugging him when he tried to sleep tonight, and the recollection that Mike Carlson had expected his wife to drive to a nearby dog park rather than walk along the dangerous road was enough to do just that. *Why hadn't she driven, given the terrible weather conditions?* he wondered. He wanted to see if the car had been disabled or was undriveable in any obvious way, such as having suffered a flat tire.

The orange cat was nowhere to be seen as Galen walked down the slight incline toward the lower carport to have a look at the Civic—just to put his mind at ease. This extra parking space was tucked in under a portion of the house and wasn't completely shielded from the rain, wind, and debris. Wet pine needles and leaves stuck heavily to the exposed left side of the car. The silver sedan was an older model but appeared to be in decent shape, as would be expected with a husband in the auto business.

There was plenty of room to do a quick pass around the Honda and Galen found that the tires were new and fully inflated on the left side. As he rounded the front, his flashlight illuminated the cracked right headlight. He leaned in closer, and there was a slight dent in the right front bumper and a slight pucker of the right hood, too. This side had been better sheltered from the rain, and a faint dull red smear, along with possible shiny fabric were both visible on the right bumper and front panel.

Erin Carlson had been found in the last deep ditch on the right side of the road before her home. The hit-and-run just down the street had been routinely investigated with the usual pictures, measurements, and forensics examination of the scene. The autopsy had revealed no evidence of the vehicle involved, and responding officers had dutifully checked the only obvious car that had been recently used—the Jeep driven by Erin's husband.

If only there'd been a reason to look at Erin's own car, thought Galen as he headed back into the house. *Forensics is going to have a long night.*

He blearily made out the display as he swiped futilely several times to answer the call, finally having his fingers register on the screen. 5:30 a.m.

"Detective Young?" came the youngish voice. "Dispatch here. We were told by patrol that you'd need this information. The Carlson's residence on SE 112th is on fire. I have no details on the extent of the damage yet, but the fire department is on the scene."

"Thanks for the call," said Galen replying on autopilot as he disconnected. He felt disconnected himself, and it took a while for his brain to engage. *I really am getting too old for this job,* he thought as he rolled out of bed and plodded into the kitchen to make a large pot of coffee.

It was only after two mugs of strong caffeine and under the pounding stream of the shower that he was finally able to begin processing the call and what he knew. *Forensic results aren't back yet, but I'm betting that Erin was hit by her own car. Carlson has an alibi for the time, he says he'd expected her to use it to get to the dog park, and he himself was shot last night. Pierce has all the markings of being behind Erin's death, but he's been in custody since yesterday afternoon, so he couldn't have shot Carlson. Now the Carlson's house is on fire? What the hell is going on?* He let the shower run as hot as he could stand it before turning it off. As he opened the shower door and stepped out in a cloud of steam he thought, *Yeah, the Captain was probably right—either the husband or the lover. The husband is in the hospital, and I definitely need to talk to him again. But most importantly—who was Erin's goddamn lover?*

Galen tried the phone route rather than an in-person visit to get an update on the fire and was eventually put in touch with the Powellhurst Station Fire Chief, Wendy Smythe. "Yes,

Detective," she responded after Galen identified himself, "I'm at the scene of the blaze as we speak."

"How bad is it?" asked Galen.

"We have it nearly under control, but the front half of the structure is pretty heavily damaged. I think the house is going to be a total loss—it was going hot when we arrived."

"Do you know how it started?"

"Funny you should ask," she said. "I'm going to call in the fire inspectors on this one. It looks to me like a car was set ablaze to the left of the structure and, with some help, the flames made it into the house. I don't know if it was the gas in the car's tank, or something else, but a neighbor described several small explosions before he saw the flames from his porch."

"I was there last night, and the sounds he heard probably weren't any windows in the house being blown out, because they'd already been shattered by a couple of bullets."

"Interesting," responded Chief Smythe.

"Isn't it?" asked Galen. "How is the car?"

"What car?" she asked. "Nothing but a melted shell."

Thank God forensics was there last night, thought Galen as he wished Smythe luck with the aftermath.

Chapter 38.

"**How's Carlson?**" asked Tom later that morning after Galen briefed them on his visit to the house the previous evening, and the subsequent call about the early morning fire.

"The hospital says he's stable and that the bullet did some damage since it hit a scapula and went through a lung, but it did pass clean through the body. His surgery went well, and luckily, no major vessels were hit," said Galen.

"Well, that's good news, for him, but bad news for his wife's hit-and-run case. I was banking on him being the culprit."

"I'm not convinced that he's in the clear for killing his wife, though," said Galen. "Forensics isn't back yet, but the right side of that Civic sure looked like it had been in a hit-and-run to me." He lifted his coffee cup and saw that his hand was shaking slightly. *Not enough sleep and too much caffeine,* he thought, but it still bothered him to see a tremble in his hand. "I mean, who else could have driven his wife's car other than him? There were reportedly only two sets of keys—one was discovered in her coat pocket, and one Forensics found in a dish on the Carlson's kitchen counter. I think his alibi needs some further verification before we rule him out."

"But why was he shot then?" asked Jenkins. "Maybe someone has a vendetta against the family?"

"Or only against him—because, like I said, it looks like she was hit by her own car," replied Galen.

"So that means that Pierce is off the hook?" asked Cushing.

Galen's jangled brain was done with coffee, and he pushed the cup away, regardless of whether it was still half-full or not. "Well, that's something I don't get either. Pierce has links to five women's deaths, and I still think he's hiding something. He could easily be in the frame, and he has priors of sexual harassment. Just because someone shot Carlson while Pierce was in custody doesn't mean he didn't have anything to do with Erin's and those other cases."

"So, you want your cake and eat it, too?" asked Cushing with a smile.

"Yeah," Galen grinned back. "But I want even more. I want to find that ex-lover and see where he plays into all of this."

"So... that narrows things down considerably," deadpanned Pembrook.

"Galen, I have keys to my sister's place," broke in Cushing, "and I think that most siblings do, especially if they're as close as Erin and Jodi were. I'd bet that both Jodi and Glenn Knowles have keys to the Carlson's house, and vice versa. Now, I'm not saying they have the motive, but they probably have the means to enter the house and access the car keys, too."

"Good point, Deb," said Tom. "Let's make sure we keep our options as wide open as possible on this case. Galen, you might want to have another word with the pair of them."

Galen nodded while thinking that his captain had just contradicted himself by reaching beyond the husband and lover as suspects and mentally added those interviews to his to-do list. "I'm expecting preliminary forensics results from the Civic this afternoon, and hopefully also something from the search of Pierce's home. How about if we meet again late afternoon to cover the findings?"

They agreed to this, and also decided to hold Pierce for another day to give him time to contemplate how their investigation might impact his future, also keeping the window open for results from the search subpoenas to come in.

Galen drove to Jan's house, as he now thought of it, for a quick lunch. He wanted to see how the boys were doing after yesterday's news about their mother. Jan was evidently still at work based on the empty space in the driveway. He rapped on the door and entered to a sudden quiet after hearing "Thanks a lot!" from Monty. No music, no banter, no TV—just Ryan in the kitchen busy making egg salad sandwiches, and Monty pointedly fuming at his phone.

"What's up, guys?" he asked as he walked over to Ryan who was shaking his head.

"I keep telling him it's no use, but he keeps hounding them," said Ryan.

"Hounding who?"

"Oh, Monty keeps trying to get through to..." began Ryan.

"Mom!" yelled Monty, completing the sentence for him.

Galen turned to Monty, and it was now obvious that yesterday's grief had seeded today's outrage.

"They won't let me talk to Mom!" he nearly screamed. "I'm her son, aren't I?"

Galen walked over to be near, but not enter, his grandson's personal space on the couch. He put his hands in his pockets to show that he was relaxed, and then said, "Yes, you are, Monty."

"Then why can't I talk to her!?"

"I can think of several reasons, and I'm sure that you can, too. Remember, your mom isn't the only patient in the hospital. I've read that it's nearly impossible for families to be able to contact their loved ones because the hospitals are overwhelmed just trying to keep people alive. They have to work extra hours. They don't even have time to do their other normal tasks." Galen paused. "And another reason is that your mom probably can't talk right now."

"She could if they let me call her," Monty's voice was beginning to sound less ferocious.

"Monty, you know she's on a ventilator, right?" The boy nodded. "And do you know what intubation is?" Now a shake of the head.

"I do," said Ryan from the kitchen.

Galen stood sideways and gave a sweep of his arm for his older grandson to enlighten his younger.

"It's how they ventilate someone, Monty," said Ryan as he walked toward them with a mayo-covered knife in one hand. "They can't just put a mask on someone and expect the air to get into the lungs. This sounds gross, but they have to stick a tube through your mouth and down into your windpipe, so that the machine can do the breathing for you. There's no way that someone on a ventilator can talk, and they need to stay quiet and sleep so that their body can do the best that it can to heal and fight the virus."

Wow, thought Galen with respect. *Ryan really is growing into a young adult.*

This explanation from his brother knocked Monty back into the couch, and Ryan plonked himself down beside him. "That's what I kept trying to tell you, doofus."

Monty's emotions had run their course, and he had no reserves left. Tears formed in his eyes, but he didn't cry—just tightly folded his arms across his chest and stared for a long moment at the blank TV screen.

Galen waited till then to reach down and give him a squeeze on his shoulder. "We're all wondering and worried just like you, Bud. You're not alone in this. We just have to help each other get through this waiting and see when she is able to breathe on her own again."

Monty looked up and began, "But, what if..." when Galen cut him off with his hand up.

"But nothing, she will."

Over the soggiest egg salad sandwiches Galen had ever eaten, they chatted at the kitchen counter as they ate, and the boys seemed pretty much back to normal. He waited until both were logged into their afternoon classes before he hurried back to the office.

The forensics report on the Carlson's Honda Civic arrived soon after lunch.

Galen read the email enclosure from Brenda Rigby, their head forensics specialist: *2014 Honda Civic, VIN 1HGE8144XL1123485, silver four-door sedan with black interior. Good condition overall, with no apparent previous accidents. Interior: Pine needles on floor mats matching those found on the property. Some hairs on driver's seat that appear to match those of the deceased, under process. Multiple dog hairs throughout the vehicle. Dog chew rope and leash on rear seat. Several sales slips from Joann's Fabrics and WINCO found in seat-side compartment along with two bags of M&Ms. Glove box—registration, local and Oregon maps, insurance details. The entire driver's area appears to have been wiped clean of all prints and dirt. Traces of bleach found, along with a discarded Clorox wipe on the passenger floor mat. Exterior: Good condition with few scratches overall. New tires. Right front side: broken headlight and turn signal lamps, small dent in fender, creasing of hood and upper right panel. Red substance confirmed to be blood and matching the O Positive type of Erin Carlson. Two shreds of fabric that match the raincoat and pants worn by the deceased on initial inspection. Several long hairs under the right windshield wipers which match those of the deceased in color and length, under process.*

His current vision of a burned-out hulk didn't match the description, and he thought again how lucky they'd been to process the car before it was set afire. *And someone knew that that Civic was the evidence proving Erin was killed with her own car*, thought Galen. *Why wait so long to get rid of the car? Why park it back in its spot in the first place?*

His phone rang a few moments later.

"Hey, Galen, this is Stan," said Jenkins.

"Yeah, hey Stan," answered Galen. "You met Brenda over at Pierce's place? Anything show up?"

"Oh, I'd say so," came back Jenkins. "I can see now why Pierce had some sexual harassment charges filed against him. We can't exactly arrest the guy for pornography, but it gets pretty damn close."

"What do you mean, Stan?"

"Well, his phone was locked, but luckily his home computer wasn't. Andy from IT has had easy access into some of the folders. I'd say that Pierce was mixing business with pleasure."

Galen left his question hanging, but Jenkins answered it.

"There are dozens, or maybe hundreds, of image files in a couple of folders here. You'd have to ask Pierce, but from the looks of them, we're guessing that he took pictures of his clients from his phone while their faces were buried down in the massage table. Some are fairly graphic."

"Can you tell who they are?" asked Galen immediately trying to find links with the five women. "Any faces or identifying marks?"

"On a quick skim through, I'd say no. But we'll have Andy and IT see if they notice anything on closer inspection."

"Thanks, Stan. I think this is convincing enough that I need to have another interview with Pierce."

"OK, and Galen?" asked Jenkins. "There might be more, but several of the files are password protected. Just so you know."

"Thanks, Stan. This should be enough, but more is always better."

Pierce's demeanor was completely changed from the one on display in Galen's previous meetings with him. Sitting next to his attorney, he looked like a schoolboy being called before the principal, and another night in detention hadn't helped his now-baggy eyes and greasy ponytail in the slightest.

"Detective…" began Pierce's attorney.

"Young, Galen Young," said Galen as he activated the interview program and gave the specifics for persons present, time, and place.

"Detective Young," continued the attorney when all was ready. "I'm Sharon Quinn. I've had an opportunity to consult with my client, and he's had time to consider the gravity of the possible charges that may be filed against him. He says that there has been a huge misunderstanding, and that he's willing to discuss some of the details surrounding his relationships with the women in question. I'll be monitoring the conversation, and of course, advising my client should he begin to say things that are open to interpretation."

Galen acknowledged that he understood, and then turned his attention to Pierce. "Mr. Pierce, my primary focus is on Erin Carlson who was recently run down by a car. However, you appear to be linked to several other women who met with accidents in two states. We've gained access to your computer and have found multiple pictures of..."

"I can explain!" said Pierce, with pleading eyes. His once straight frame was now stooped, and his previously calm hands had become jumping mice.

"Pictures of your clients in various stages of undress—obviously taken without their knowledge," Galen made sure to state for the record. "Two vehicular assaults on your clients point to murder." And he let this hang in the air.

Pierce's eyes skittered between the detective and the attorney, and then he clenched his fists and squeezed his eyelids shut. As if envisioning his former self, Pierce slowly straightened and let his hands calmly unfold onto the table surface. Galen was afraid that the man was going to settle back into total denial and waited to see if he needed to bring more pressure to bear. It wasn't necessary.

"There's been a misunderstanding," he began. "Yes, I've engaged in questionable practices, but I've done nothing that comes even close to murder." Both Galen and Quinn sat poised to listen and to intervene, if necessary, but both for different reasons. Pierce closed his eyes again and exhaled slowly, but forcefully. He took several cleansing breaths, and then met

Galen's gaze. "Detective, I'm in a unique line of work. In your job, you talk with your colleagues and suspects, but can never develop any rapport that approaches the level that I can with my clients, being able to have deep conversations, and be in very close physical contact with them. There is nothing more special on the planet than this... calling.

"I come to my sessions to love my clients, and they come to love me. We develop a bond that is indescribable. With my hands I'm able to push deep into their bodies and relieve them from pain and blockages. And in our conversations, I'm able to relieve them of many of the burdens they carry that cause these tensions. It is a symbiotic relationship."

Parasitic, came to Galen's mind as he nodded in an outward display of understanding for Pierce to continue.

"Do you have any water?" asked Pierce, and they took a momentary break while water was brought in, and Pierce gathered his thoughts.

"I know you think I had something to do with what happened to those poor women, but all I did was to tell the truth afterwards."

Now it was Galen's turn to pull his head back and raise his eyebrows.

"I loved them, but I just couldn't let the world think that they were squeaky clean after they died."

"What do you mean, Mr. Pierce?" asked Galen. "Did you have anything to do with their deaths?"

"No! That's what I'm telling you. Their deaths each touched me deeply, but at the same time I felt I couldn't just stay silent after they passed."

"So, the obituaries?"

Pierce nodded. "Sarah Thomas and I were an item. I treated her for the pain of multiple sclerosis, and she really responded to the therapy. We talked on the phone and went out for coffee, although even that was getting difficult for her. I was crushed when I found that she'd drowned, especially since I was the one who recommended the healing properties of the warm mineral salt waters of the ocean."

Pierce gulped some more bottled water and took a moment before he continued. "I phoned in that addition to the obituary because I knew that no one else appreciated how close we were, and how special she was to me. It was the only chance for me to make my feelings known. And it was so easy to do.

"And then that damn Trish. Maybe it was a rebound relationship on my part. I know she said I went too far in showing my affection for her, but I could tell that she really felt something, too. After that restraining order, I found out that she was cheating on me. She had another boyfriend that she never even told me about. Anyway, I wasn't allowed to get anywhere near her, and then I heard about her accident. The whole town was in mourning, and I was too, but I realized that people didn't see the side of her that I knew. They didn't know that she cheated behind my back. So, I called in that sentence to let people know that there was someone else involved with her. She wasn't an angel."

Galen glanced over at Quinn. She appeared to be OK with the interview so far, and so Galen prodded. "And the other obituaries?"

Pierce stared at him as if not understanding the question at first, still caught up in memories of Sarah Thomas or Trish Mathers. He blinked his eyes, and Galen could see him gather himself. "I became close with all of them, but, of course, never as close as I was with Sarah. The thing is, during our intimate conversations in our sessions, I found out that each of them had had, or was about to enter into an affair. I couldn't let the world think that these women were perfect, and so I decided to add to their obituaries to show that there was someone else in their lives who no one else knew about. It wasn't me they stepped out with, but the world had to know that they were cheaters. Others just had to know. How could I let their secrets die with them?"

"Secrets die with people every day," said Galen. "Why, for example, change the obituary of Erin Carlson?"

Pierce leaned forward, eager to explain. "My therapy was working on Erin. Her knots and misalignment were nearly back to normal and, in our talks, I was getting her to be happier with her marriage—which was the true root cause of all her tension. Then I noticed that the tension was back, and she let slip that she'd met this guy online, basically destroying all the progress that we'd achieved. She was going to ruin her marriage. She must have sensed my disapproval and suddenly quit her sessions with me. When I'd heard she'd died, I had the obituary editor read to me what he'd received, and just like I thought—it was all a glowing life summary. Her husband just had to know about her affair if he didn't already. The world had to know."

The pain in Galen's jaw erupted, and he dug furiously at it with his left hand. Pierce took this as an indication that the detective wasn't buying his story.

"Honestly, Detective! You have to believe me—I only did it for their own good!"

Galen terminated the interview and found that he didn't care. Pierce was a deluded creep, but he had nothing to do with his case.

The silence of the empty elevator was a welcome relief from what he'd just been listening to. *Here Pierce's change of the obituary led to us finding that Erin's death wasn't an accident, and yet the wacko had nothing to do with it at all,* Galen thought as the door whisked open on his floor. He found himself trying to grasp the mental landscape someone like Brandon Pierce wandered through as he walked down the straight hallway to his office.

Chapter 39.

In order to satisfy himself that Erin's husband had nothing to do with her murder, Galen decided to stop by the hospital and interview Mike Carlson who was now out of the ICU and had been transferred to a critical care unit in the Adventist Health Portland Hospital. As he donned the disposable one-piece suit and N95 mask, he found himself thinking that he would go through ten times this much trouble just to be at Beth's side and let her know that her family was there. The last report had been tepid at best, and the medical staff at OHSU were making no promises.

"How are you feeling, Mr. Carlson?" began Galen, a little formally.

Mike Carlson was gasping for breath and operating at half his normal vocal volume, but he was still as cocky as ever. "Not as bad as I expected for my first gunshot wound, but I wouldn't want to have another." Galen was about to provide his sympathy when Carlson burst out, "They told me someone burned down my fucking house! What are you doing here—you need to catch that fucker that shot me and torched my place!"

"We're working on that, and your case has our full attention, believe me. Do you have any suggestions as to who might have wished to kill you?"

Carlson's eyes turned blank, and he slowly shook his head. Galen could see that he was haunted by just how close he'd come to being extinguished by some unknown assailant.

"We're not only interested in who shot you, but we're also very interested in your wife's car. You might have been told that the fire started there?"

"Yeah, and that was a total surprise. But what does where it started have to do with anything for fuck's sake?"

"Well, we're thinking it might have quite a lot to do with you, Mr. Carlson." The patient stared back at him in expectation. "You see, we found dents on her car that are consistent with a collision, blood samples that match your late wife's, and fabric swatches that match the rain pants and raincoat she was wearing on the night she was hit."

Carlson's expression had become one of utter disbelief, and Galen took mental note that it didn't appear to be a put-on. "Wha... wha..." he began and stopped open mouthed, gasping for breath. "That... That's fucking impossible! Are you telling me that she was run over by her own car?"

"Yes," replied Galen calmly. "I guess I'm telling you exactly that."

"How could she do it?" Carlson asked, taking a moment to try and piece it all together. "Hey, wait a minute. You're saying that I killed my wife with her own car? No fucking way! I was at work, like I fucking told you! Two of my guys were at the shop to prove it!" He took several more deep breaths and then asked reflexively, "But, how could she run herself over?" Galen knew that he was sedated, but waited to see where his logic might take him. "No," continued Carlson weakly shaking his head. "Somebody must have driven her… Or, or she parked the car and then somebody stole it and she had to walk home, and then they ran her down." Carlson had now worked himself into a lather. "Or they drove with her and then threw her out of the car!"

Galen motioned for him to calm down, handed him the cup with ice water at his bedside, and let him decompress for a minute. The detective then said, "Or the simplest explanation is that she went for a walk, you got into her car and drove to a likely spot, and then ran over your wife with her own car, because you discovered she was having an affair."

He watched Carlson's eyes bulge. "I told you! She wasn't having a fucking affair!" he wheezed as best he could. "I was at work—how could I run her over?" He was desperate. "I had no reason to kill my wife, I loved her, and we'd been happily together until she decided she needed a break. That's no reason for murder!"

They had reached a stalemate, and there was no further progress in the interview, especially since Carlson had passed out in front of the detective.

CHAPTER 40.

GALEN HAD just finished his late afternoon report detailing his interview with Brandon Pierce when Jenkins slapped the table with the flat of his hand and startled them. "I think he does have something to do with the case!" he declared, as all those around the small conference table turned to him.

"How's that, Stan?" asked Tom. "Galen's impression was that the man was a creep, but not a killer."

"No, he's not the killer, but he set all of this in motion. We wouldn't be sitting around this table having this conversation if he hadn't added that one little sentence to Erin Carlson's obituary."

There were stares around the table.

"It just occurred to me while Galen was talking," Jenkins continued. "What Pierce put in the obituary was an acknowledgement that Erin Carlson had an affair. If it wasn't there no one would have noticed anything suspicious about Carlson's death. But, what Pierce published was a motive. What if someone—the person who killed Carlson—didn't want that bit of info to go public?" They all processed this as he continued. "Picture this: Erin Carlson's death looks like an accident—an unfortunate hit-and-run, so there's no heat from us and whoever did it is walking away scot-free. But then the perp reads the obituary and sees this glaring sentence pointing the finger right at him—or her, and he thinks that might make us just a little suspicious, which it did. Then he or she sees a need to cover up evidence or eliminate anyone who might know about the affair."

"Oh, God, you're right," said Galen, wishing he'd seen this sooner. "He needs to silence the other person who knew about the affair—thinking that Mike Carlson was aware of it and wrote the obit to rub his face in it. So, then Erin's killer tries to murder Mike... and comes back later to destroy the evidence on the car since he figures we'll definitely be on to him now."

"Galen..." began Tom.

"I know, Captain, you were right. We have to find the man who Erin had an affair with. I'd place him high on our suspect list."

"But I thought we had nothing to go on," said Pembrook.

"No. We don't Michael," said Galen slightly irritated, but then covered with the first thing that came to his mind, "but we're like the Mounties, we always get our man."

While they were groaning and Jenkins was asking Galen exactly which generation he was from, Tom broke in, "This case is a priority now. Galen, talk to the sister and her husband again and get any details you can—or a confession would be even better. Michael, you get with forensics on the ammunition used to shoot Carlson and follow info about the rifle model and any leads on sales of that make that you can—try Salem first. Stan, reinterview the neighbors both about the shooting and the fire. Deb... you go through Erin Carlson's phone and computer records and see if you can find anything about the guy she was seeing. Galen, after you talk to the sister, maybe you should head to Salem and talk to, who was it in charge down there?"

"Blowers," said Galen.

"Yeah, Blowers. And try the liquor distributors again. Come on, people, we have to find something on this guy."

CHAPTER 41.

GALEN PLUNKED himself down in front of John, a glimmer of the last of the day's sun doing nothing to improve his mood. "Hey, John," he said as he signaled for the server to bring him the beer he knew he would only sip at.

"Hi, Galen!" said John, looking up from his crossword and obviously feeling much better about the day than was the detective. "You're not looking too chipper this evening. It's not Beth, is it?"

"It's always Beth, John. She's still on the ventilator and we still don't know which way this is headed."

John looked back in sympathy. "I'm sorry, Galen—of course you'd be down about it."

"But that's not really why I'm so bummed out tonight. I was heading home when I realized there was some news I should pass on to you. And it's just further confirmation that there's no justice in this world. Here I am a policeman where justice is the backbone of my job, and yet I have to accept that as a fact."

"I agree—there isn't any, but why do you say that?"

"You're not going to like this, John," Galen stated glumly.

"Hit me with your best shot," smiled John as the server set a Harp lager in front of Galen who thanked her and took an exploratory sip.

"Gary Rockney has denied any connection with Jason Perkowski or with Robert Armlin's kidnapping. He says that Perkowski acted alone, and that the timing of the whole thing was just a coincidence. He says that the 'alleged' payments from Ortiz to Perkowski were because she and Perkowski were having an affair, which is just wild. I know deep down that he'll plead not guilty to any charges, and he knows that we have no concrete evidence to link him to Robert's abduction. Except for those pictures."

"Pictures?" asked John "What pictures?"

"I think I said before. Rockney had taken some photos of Perkowski together with Armlin, and used them as leverage, through Ortiz, to keep Armlin alive. Now he claims he never took those pictures, and that it was Ortiz who was the photographer. The problem is, we don't have the original source, only the copies found on Ortiz's phone."

"But he sent them to her?"

Galen nodded.

"And the messages have disappeared?"

Galen nodded again. He then shook his head in disgust and stared hard at a large knot in the wood table. "The thing is, I can see him even now concocting some story where he was the one who actually tried to save Robert from the clutches of Perkowski. There's no honor among thieves, and there's no justice for them either."

"I totally agree," said John more adamantly.

"What?" asked an amazed Galen as he lifted his glass to hold it up against his left temple. He found that something cold on the left side of his face could help ease the torment that had sprung back to life. "I thought you'd believe in some higher moral principle guiding us."

John shook his head with a bemused smile on his face and took a big gulp of his Guinness. "Nope. I used to be the same as you, Galen—I thought that life was supposed to be fair. But people get away with shit all around us, and never pay for it—ever. I was all in with John Lennon when he said, 'Instant Karma's gonna get you, it's gonna knock you right in the head,' but not anymore."

Galen, being in the justice line of work, just stared at him, waiting to hear John's rant.

"There is no justice. It's just a concept we cling to because we can't stand for the guilty not to pay. The Hindu's believe in Karma, but I think it's because they saw injustices happening all around them, so they expected payback must be deferred to a later life. They kind of passed the buck. We Westerners think that justice must come at the Pearly Gates, or at least most of us do. But what if there isn't a Judgement Day? What if there's no reincarnation either—just asking?

"Think about it. We aren't even capable of taking responsibility for our own actions. Everyone pleads not guilty even though there are witnesses, or the crime's been recorded on viral videos. So, no one is looking for justice for themselves—we won't even admit to our own smallest transgressions. 'Don't look at me, I didn't do it.' And then all of the attorneys who defend all of the obviously guilty cases? They're not looking for justice at all, they're looking at job security. They see justice

as a process rather than an end in itself. No matter what the
guy did, they want their guy to win. They want him to make
it through the process rather than face some moral judgement.

"All of these famous or wealthy people who literally get
away with murder, fraud, rape, deceit, and just plain ugliness—
they're never going to pay. Not in this life, not at the Pearly
Gates, not in the next life. They just walk—proving that there
is no justice. It's just something that in our guts we feel ought
to happen because we have this concept of fairness that doesn't
play out in the real world."

John picked up his nearly empty glass and then plonked it
down dramatically on the wood table like a gavel. "And that's
what I have to say about that," he grinned.

"John," said Galen, torn between chugging his beer and
pushing it away. "To misquote *Dirty Harry*, you just went
ahead and didn't make my day."

Chapter 42.

Galen was exhausted when he pulled up in front of the sad, soggy house, although to him right now, the entire world dripped like drenched moss, so it was probably just his own take on the wet scene. The rain had been unrelenting on the way down to Tualatin, but the other drivers had acted as if it was just another pleasant, clear day on I-5 South—racing above the speed limit only to slam on their brakes as things collapsed to a crawl, and then speeding up and repeating. He'd tried to keep up, and to slow down in time, but old wet brakes made it trickier than it needed to be. He didn't know if it was his age, the rain, or trying to peer through a filmy windscreen futilely swept by aged wipers, that had completely drained him. *If I'm no longer going to be with Jan, why am I still in this frigging job?* he wondered as visions of arid Pendleton and his brother's place in sparsely populated, mountainous Joseph, Oregon swam through his head. But he knew why he was hanging on as long as he had. He wanted to help keep the bad guys off the streets or find the lost and missing no matter where he was, lack of eventual justice be damned.

He'd called ahead, so that Jodi was expecting him, and he raced from his car to the front porch as quickly as he could—with his wet trousers already limiting his mobility by the time he was rapping on the door. There was no Bobby there to greet him, and Jodi wasn't shushing Galen when she let him in. "Hi, Detective," said Jodi as she hurried to shut the door to the wind and rain following right behind him. Noticing his expectant look, she said, "Glenn took him to work for the day. Mike said that he liked the diversion his nephew provided after Erin died and he even set up a small cot in the office for Bobby to nap on." She reached for Galen's drenched coat and hung it in the short entryway, continuing, "Mike's still in the hospital, but I told Glenn that I needed a break from that kid or I was going to go absolutely nuts," concluding with a sad smile.

Galen followed her back into the small, cluttered living room in which he'd interviewed Erin weeks before and took a seat on the same couch she'd snuggled Bobby on that occasion.

"Coffee?" offered Jodi.

"No, thanks," said Galen, "I think it's starting to fry my nerves, so I'm trying to cut back."

"Tea, then? Or maybe juice?"

"No thanks, I'm fine. The reason I dropped by is to ask if you recall anything else that Erin might have told you about her stay in Salem. At first, I was interested in a description of the man that she stayed with, but now I need to know anything at all that might lead us to the guy. Any details, big or small, about her stay there would helpful. Really, anything, because we have very little to go on at the moment."

Jodi frowned slightly and sat perched on the edge of her chair. "Erin was pretty tight-lipped about the whole thing, as if she wanted to just keep it all in the past and move on. Plus, she was feeling super guilty about having stepped out on Mike. Just a sec, I just gotta have some coffee," as she rose and retreated to the kitchen only to return a few moments later, cup in hand. Once re-settled, she continued, "And to tell the truth, I wasn't the most receptive to my own sister being an adulteress in the first place, and I gave her a pretty hard time about it. When it comes down to it, Glenn and Mike are tight—like brothers. So, she probably kept mum about anything specific because she knew I'd get upset, and maybe tell Glenn. We worked through our issues, but by that time she was ready to return to Mike."

Galen nodded in understanding, but laid his hands open in front of her. "Honestly, Jodi, even a trip to the grocery store might help us at this point."

Jodi took a sip of coffee, cradled the mug in both hands, and then started to think back. "OK, here goes. He never had kids. She was playing with Bobby when she let that slip. She said she knew he didn't because he told her that when she said she didn't have any kids herself, but that she absolutely adored Bobby. She also mentioned that he lived on the edge of a shabby neighborhood and was obsessive about locking things up and always complained about the 'low-lifes' in the houses up the street. Let's see. I already told you that he had two trucks..." She looked out into some distance beyond the enclosed room, "Oh, and one time she said that she thought it was funny that he was a liquor distributor because they still went to the store several times while she was there to buy whiskey and beer. He would go to work most days, but never said a thing about it when he got home. They never went far or explored the area, and even though she'd asked about the sights to see, he always wanted to stick close to home—there was always some game he just had to watch."

Galen could tell that that was about it. "I assume she was excited to meet him, drove down with the possibility that she'd never see Mike again. Anything about that?"

"Nope, that emotional part is what she kept to herself—except with having enough of the guy's attitude and rowdiness. She said that he was abusive and kind of thick—that's what she called him—'a thickheaded redneck.'"

"Did they go anywhere besides the store?"

"No..." she was quiet for a moment. "Actually, Detective, I just lied—there was something else that I haven't mentioned."

Galen looked at her questioningly and she shook her head. "Erin made me swear to never tell a soul, because it was about how bad things got for her in the end. But, now that she's gone and I really want that guy to pay for treating her so badly, I don't see the harm.

"Erin said that about the time that she and what's-his-name started having real problems and she was thinking of leaving him and going back to Mike, she'd lost her car keys. She said she kind of panicked and looked everywhere for them because she was starting to feel trapped, but they'd disappeared. She said that she and the guy got into a big fight because he insisted that she didn't need her keys anymore—anyway he had his trucks. She said that she was going to leave him and threatened to go to the police if he tried to stop her, and that's the first time he hit her. The next morning, he was like all apologetic, and he took her to the nearest Honda dealership to have a new set made. She said they laughed afterwards, because when they got back to his place, they found her old key under a table mat. But then he lit into her for being so stupid as to lose her key in plain sight and beat her again. The next day as she was getting ready to leave, she couldn't find the replacement that she was sure she'd put in her purse, but luckily she'd kept the original in her bra."

Jodi was concluding the story, "Erin realized what a bad decision she'd made, and that's when she..." while the detective was thinking, *Ah, another key was made, and the lover might have kept it. And—whoever made the replacement for them saw both Erin and her partner together.* When he tuned back in to Jodi, she was saying, "... need to know, but twice there's been a silver pickup parked across the street. Our neighbor was worried about it and called it in to the police the second time, but it was gone before they got here. Brady, the neighbor who called, says that he thinks the driver was watching our houses. There have been a lot of burglaries in our area lately."

Galen absently made a note of this and said, "It's probably nothing, but make sure you call the police if that truck comes around again."

The rain continued for the entire drive south to Salem on I-5, but at least the cars began to spread out half-way to the state's capitol, turning his knuckles back to pink from white. He'd already convinced himself that the alternate route home would take more time, but that he'd take 99W on the return trip and pass through McMinnville and Newberg. He liked that route better than I-5 anyway—99W was only two lanes and passed through small towns, but most importantly, the pace was much more in keeping with his driving and windshield wiper speeds.

Tom had told him that it might be better to let Blowers and the Salem Police Department make inquiries at the car dealerships, but Galen had insisted that he was only forty-minutes away and wanted to learn first-hand whether anyone at the main showrooms remembered Erin and her friend. Tom had reluctantly agreed, but had reminded his detective, "Don't forget, this is not our jurisdiction, and I don't want any complaints coming back from either a concerned citizen or from the Salem PD that we've overstepped our bounds." Galen had assured him that he'd connect with Blowers, which he did immediately following the conversation, and then began punching in the location of the Honda dealership Blowers had suggested for him to contact.

Honda of Salem was perhaps the city's largest seller, and he felt conspicuous pulling his dull, dented car into a parking spot alongside a row of sleek new models. Ignoring the salesman who greeted him at the door, he followed the sign straight to the Service Department. "Can I help you?" asked Tim, as indicated by the name embroidered on the chest of his red polo shirt.

Galen flashed his badge, and stated, "I'm interested in someone who had a key made between August 21st and September 7th. A Ms. Erin Carlson had apparently lost the original and had a new one cut to replace it. Can you tell me if that was done here?"

"I should be able to help with that," said Tim. "Let me check our records." He spent some time at the Service Department computer and then turned from the screen. "Yes, Ms. Carlson had a duplicate issued on September 6th. Do you need anything else?" in a voice showing he wondered why he was being bothered with such a mundane request.

"Yes." Galen now adopted a manner that breathed officiousness, but not enough to be especially overbearing. "What we are really interested in is the person who accompanied her. Were you the individual who cut the key?"

"Well, actually, we program them," said Tim.

After a wilting stare from Galen, Tim thought back. "I'm not sure, we have quite a few replacements made every week and that was a little while ago. It was either Aaron or me who helped her."

Galen awoke his phone and thumbed through his photos until he found the official scan of Erin Carlson's picture. He pivoted the screen so that Tim could see the image.

"Yeah, I remember her. I did make that key. She laughed a lot about how she couldn't believe she could lose her key in such a small house, and she said they'd looked everywhere for it. She was pretty embarrassed about the whole situation—not just losing the key, but having to come in for the replacement, too. As I remember, her husband seemed more than a little miffed about the whole thing."

"Do you remember his name?"

"Her husband's name? Must be the same as his wife's—Mr. Carlson? ... oh, it was Carl Carlson. I remember it as the kind of doubled-up name you wouldn't want to be stuck with?"

"Carl? How do you know his name was Carl? Did his wife call him that?"

Tim thought about how he did happen to know Mr. Carlson's first name. "No... Pat called him that. Our supervisor was walking back into the service area, and said something like 'Hey, Carl! Poker on Wednesday—right?' And I especially remember Carl giving him back one of those big ol' two-fisted thumbs-ups," miming the exchange.

"Right, then, where's Pat?" asked Galen immediately.

"Back in the garage, I think," said Tim, looking around to make sure his boss wasn't in the immediate Service reception area.

Galen thanked him, followed the direction Tim was pointing, and went off to find Pat. The rain was pounding on the roof, and the streetlights were triggered by the dark gray skies outside. The shop lights were bright enough, but Galen felt like the full sun was shining down on him as Pat began to speak from a great height. The man must have been 6'9" if he was an inch, and he bore great news.

"Sure, I know Carl," after Galen had asked about the man he'd apparently played poker with on Wednesday nights. "We've been pals for years. He's part of our Wednesday poker night, and the Seahawks gang. Why do you want to know?" As before, Galen had flashed his badge, and seemed to be accepted as a local authority.

"What can you tell me about Carl? I don't even know his last name." Pat was suddenly playing defense as betrayed by his changing expression and arms-crossed posture. Galen needed to reassure him that this was no big deal. "He came in a while back with his new girlfriend to get a key made and..." he thought quickly, "she's been laying very low since then—I'm trying to find her because her relatives are worried sick about her."

"That was his girlfriend? He never mentioned her... must have worried about our razzing him about it. He sure does go through the ladies, though."

"And, so, what's Carl's last name, and what can you tell me about him?"

"Sanders, Carl Sanders. He works at Lowes, and, as you can gather, is a bit of a gambler and a sports nut. We go hunting and fishing every year—elk up past Bend, and steelhead on the Deschutes."

"Lowes? That's funny, I'd gathered that he's a liquor distributor here," said Galen.

Pat stared down at him. "How'd you hear that?" he asked and then answered himself. "Of course, you're the police." He shook his head. "No, Carl's been working at Lowes for probably three years now. As you no doubt already know, he had his distributor's license revoked and got fired from his warehouse for selling to rummies out of the back of his truck."

Galen nodded seriously as if he did know this. "That was a real shame. I'd really like to talk to him in person and see if he can help us find his missing friend. Would you know where he is right now?"

Pat checked his watch. "Like I said, he works at Lowes, so that's probably where you'll find him."

"Thank you, Pat, you've been most helpful."

Back in his sedan, the windows began to fog up, the smell of mildew had returned with a vengeance, and the rain created a din as he made some phone calls. Cursing himself for once that he didn't carry a Bureau-issued tablet, he first reached Detective Cushing. "Hi, Deb. Are you in the office?"

"Yeah, Galen, what's up?"

"I found the name of Erin Carlson's boyfriend in Salem. He's Carl Sanders. Could you do me a favor and run a quick check on him?"

"Sure, just a sec." There was a pause. "And that's 'Carl' with a 'C' and not a 'K'?"

"Yeah, try with a 'C' first," and he then waited while she consulted her computer. He suddenly wondered why he'd called Cushing—not that he didn't want her to be involved. He could have called Jenkins, Pembrook, or Andy in IT, but he'd chosen Deb. She was the detective who seemed to be most like a partner to him, but now he worried that she'd see his constant inquiries as treating her like a personal secretary. *Ah, jeez,* he thought, *I'm going to have to make sure I explain that that's not the reason I call... sometime.*

"OK," began Cushing. "This is probably him. Carl L. Sanders is a 39-year-old male, of course, born in San Diego, CA, 5'11", weighs 220, brown hair, brown eyes, and lives at 2428 Claude St. near 24th in Salem. He graduated from high school in San Diego, joined the Navy and was honorably discharged in 2007. He's held several jobs in Oregon, the most recent three being in Salem. There was some trouble in his previous job, and he's now employed as a cashier at Lowes. The trouble he got into was..." she searched for a moment, "Oh, here. He was a partner in a wholesale liquor distributorship for six years, but got busted for selling to non-retailers. No jail time, but a reprimand, and loss of his license. Also, on the books he has two assault charges in the last five years, and three sexual harassments are on file."

"Thanks, Deb, I really appreciate your researching this for me. I promise to join the twenty-first century and get a tablet soon."

"Now, Galen. Don't go telling stories," she chuckled. Then more seriously, "He sounds like the kind of guy that Erin Carlson described. Where are you?"

"I'm in Salem, and I..."

"Galen, don't act without authority down there!" Cushing interrupted.

"Don't worry, I won't. I checked in with the locals. I'm going to brief the captain, and then call Blowers with the SPD and let him handle it. I just wanted to know more about Sanders before I did. Besides, I'm way too old to play the rogue cop."

"Ya think?" she laughed as she ended the call.

Next, he called Tom. "Hey, Captain, I'm fairly sure we've discovered the ID of the man who Erin Carlson stayed with in Salem. His name is Carl Sanders. As Jodi said, he and Erin did go together to have a replacement key made, at Honda of Salem. Luckily, one of the service personnel was a friend of his and was able to provide us with his name. Cushing has just given me all the details we have on file for him," and he read off the particulars from his notepad.

"What is it with you and keys lately?" asked Tom.

"Yeah, I was wondering the same thing," thinking that Tom's wife, Carol, would probably have an esoteric explanation readily at hand.

"OK, Galen, check in with Salem PD and see if they need any further help. If they do, you can stick around down there, otherwise I want you back in the city. They can handle this Sanders, and they're probably already familiar with him anyway by the sounds of it."

"Will do, Captain," said Galen. He was next on the phone with Blowers and the Salem Police Department.

After Galen relayed what he'd discovered, he asked if they had any more on Sanders. "Let me check here, Galen," responded Blowers. Even above the pounding rain, Galen could hear the clicking of computer keys. "Yeah, Sanders is known to us. We have a recent sexual harassment claim against him from a co-worker at the Lowes where he works, and he makes complaints about street people loitering near his house on a regular basis. One of those homeless claimed he brandished a gun at him about a month ago, but there was no way to prove the allegation. I'll have some of the boys bring him in for a talk. Why don't you come on over to HQ here and you can join us?"

As suggested, Galen hung out at the Salem Police Department building, but after two hours, they still had no luck in finding Sanders, either at home, or at Lowes. His manager had said that Sanders had taken sudden sick leave earlier that afternoon. Patrolmen had interviewed his co-workers at the store and had tracked down a few of his friends to see if they had heard from him lately, also checking out his usual hangouts, with no luck.

"Galen, I'm guessing that his friend, Pat Owens at the Honda dealership, tipped him off that we were interested in him and that he's laying low for now. We have an APB out for his silver F-150 that's missing from in front of his house, and we've alerted all of the local hotels and motels to be on the lookout." Blowers then became more serious. "You know, I don't think you can help us anymore by sticking around. We can let you know if he turns up or if anything else develops."

Galen could take the subtle hint that toes were now being stepped on. He was going to add, "We didn't even know who we were looking for until I suggested we ask at Honda dealerships," but smiled instead in reply. "Yeah, thanks Todd, I appreciate your efforts," without saying how much he wanted to be part of cracking this case.

Blowers could see how keen Galen was to aid where he could, but his own desire for autonomy took precedence. "We'll let you know if Sanders turns up," shaking Galen's hand, in effect showing him to the door.

CHAPTER 43.

THE RAIN hadn't eased in the slightest, but Galen still enjoyed the more leisurely pace and what he could make out of the scenery on the drive up 99W. He'd taken a small detour for a quick cruise down SE 3rd that served as Main Street in McMinnville, and then stopped for gas before resuming his drive north. *This is the sort of place we should have moved to instead of Portland,* he thought, enjoying the atmosphere of the area. *Quieter, and still in easy driving distance to Beth at Coffee Creek.* He wasn't keen on a town that was too artsy-fartsy, but McMinnville seemed to be doing a good job of meshing the older architecture of a once-aging downtown with a more vibrant array of businesses. Plus, it was surrounded by open fields in the flatlands and boasted wineries in the hills to the west. *Maybe, when I finally retire. Jan... Jan can stay in the clutches of the city for all I care now.*

He was more than halfway between Newberg and Tualatin when he reflexively glanced to the east. Situated a little over a mile away was the Coffee Creek Correctional Facility. If this was a normal visiting day, he would have swung over to spend some time with Beth, but nothing was normal now, and Beth was struggling under a ventilator at OHSU in the heart of Portland. *Christ, I hope she's OK,* thought Galen, *but the sad part is, she'll end up back in Coffee Creek once she sur-*

vives this. If she survives this. He braked suddenly as he hadn't noticed the car slowing ahead, returning his concentration to his driving, and making it home in one piece to his daughter's youngest son.

The highway was skirting Tualatin when he realized he was only blocks away from Jodi Knowles' house. Now that he knew Erin's boyfriend's name, he wanted to see if Jodi recognized the name Carl Sanders.

This time, Bobby answered the door. He seemed almost bored to see the wet detective on the other side when he finally got the latch open. He went running off on tiptoes with no word, and Galen was left to shout a gentle, "Hello?" after him. Jodi peeked around the corner from the living room where a program was audible from the TV.

"I thought I heard something," she smiled. "Come on in, Galen," as he donned his mask and balked at tracking water in on his wet shoes. "Glenn's in the kitchen fixing himself a snack. He dropped Bobby off early because he said that a non-napping toddler just wasn't cutting it. I guess Bobby's been fussy all day without his mom." She swung her arm in a circle doubly hard to signal that wet shoes weren't a problem and so he followed her once again into their living room.

Not bothering to sit, Galen said, "Jodi, I'm on my way back from Salem, and we've learned the identity of the man Erin was seeing there. Does the name Carl Sanders ring a bell? Did Erin ever mention him?"

Jodi shook her head. "Nope, she never mentioned that name to me."

"We've just discovered who he was this morning, but he seems to be aware of this, and is avoiding his normal haunts. The Salem police are on the lookout for him, but so far, nothing. We now believe he may have been involved in your sister's death. And..." thinking of Sanders' missing silver truck, "if you should happen to see that truck your neighbor was worried about—a silver Ford F-150—show up outside again, call the police or me immediately. Please. You see, Erin might not have told you much about Sanders, but she might have told him a great deal about you." He didn't want to worry her with his new suspicion that Sanders wasn't only interested in getting rid of Mike Carlson. Sanders might also suspect that Jodi had been aware of the affair and that she'd been the one to add that fateful sentence to her sister's obituary.

"That pickup hasn't been here since Brady across the street called about it the other day," said Jodi with a worried expression. "Glenn said that if he was home when that guy came around again, he was going to go after him with a tire iron. Like I said, there have been some break-ins in the area recently, and the neighbors are on the lookout. Anyone suspicious loitering on our street should be noticed."

"Hello, Detective, I thought I heard someone," said Glenn Knowles as he rounded the corner into the living room, a plate of nachos in hand. "What suspicious person should be noticed?"

Galen again described the truck, why it was of interest, and that the police should be notified if it was seen in the neighborhood.

"Well, that bastard!" said Glenn. "If he does come around here, he's going to regret it."

"Let me stress that I'm urging you not to confront him. Make sure that you call the local police instead—that's what they're trained for."

Glenn grumbled but nodded his head, and Galen left them after receiving another assurance that they would alert the police of any sightings.

The dark, close clouds provided no relief from the rain as Galen dashed back to his sedan, pants soaking again, and slammed the driver's door shut. The interior predictably fogged up immediately after he started the engine, and he sat for a minute, giving the blower time to fight off the condensation. Even so, he could make out the unrelenting drops splattering the street and glimpse the gutters along the curbsides, now running like rivers. Despite the downpour, one thing was becoming clear, however. Carl Sanders had driven to the Carlson's house, used Erin's own car to run her down, read the revealing obituary, and tried to kill Erin's husband thinking that Mike could link him with her murder. Sanders had also tried to destroy any possible remaining evidence by setting fire to the car. And now it was possible that he had some intention of silencing Jodi.

Galen spoke with Daniels at the Tualatin Police Department and gave him the details about Sanders along with a description of his truck. He requested that the department add some extra patrols in the area, and, if possible, place a car on lookout at Jodi's house during the evenings.

His windscreen finally cleared as he finished the call and started home. Wipers slashing madly, he had only driven four blocks from the Knowles' home when his phone buzzed. Galen was surprised to see it was Jodi. "Hi, Jodi, did I leave something there?"

"No, Galen. I think he's back—that silver truck just pulled up across the street."

"Jodi, I'll be right there," said the detective, immediately turning at the next intersection. "As soon as you hang up, call the police—and you and Glenn stay away from your windows. I'll be right there," he repeated and hung up.

The silver truck's windows were tinted nearly black, but Galen could see two things simultaneously as he approached from the opposite direction: that the driver's window on the F-150 parked across from the Knowles' house was edging down, and that their front door had opened and Glenn Knowles was stepping onto the stoop. What appeared to be a gun barrel was just emerging as the truck's window slid down, and then he thought he could see the gun buck, though he was still too far away to be certain or to hear anything other than the rain pounding on his roof. Glenn appeared to give a start as it did so. Galen was just slowing near the house and paying close attention to the truck when he glanced in the direction of the Knowles' and was shocked to see Glenn now kneeling on the sidewalk.

He floored it for the last few yards and then skidded his car to a stop between the house and the truck, relieved to see Jodi helping Glenn back inside just as he heard the second shot above the rain's constant din. He was now focused solely on the truck and prayed that Jodi and her husband were all right behind him. The shifting barrel betrayed that the driver of the truck was now, as a mirror image, focused solely on him. Galen had his gun out and was just unlatching the safety belt when the window beside him exploded, glass shards biting into his face. He instinctively got one shot off and then threw himself sideways to straddle the center console and the passenger seat, struggling for a moment with the seat belt that he was now partially laying upon. Finally extracting himself, he heard the truck door slam and another shot tore across his back and into his left shoulder as he was reaching for the passenger door handle, his left arm suddenly no longer responding to his commands.

Galen let his gun rest for a moment on the seat as he unlatched and flung the passenger door open with his right hand. The next bullet nicked his head, but to him it felt like he'd been hit with a hammer. Things swam for a moment, but he knew he might have mere seconds left to act. With an effort, he heaved himself forward across the console on his stomach, managing to get his head and shoulders out of the passenger door. He thought about pushing himself free with one more lunge, but knew that Sanders was nearly at the car. Settling for halfway out, he leaned forward, bumping his head against the curb on the way, so that he was looking upside down under the car, now able to see Sanders' feet and the reflection of his legs in the dimpled water that covered the street. Wrestling his right arm into position under the car while the gutter water splashed against his head, Galen fired four quick shots without being able to aim as well as he hoped.

It was as if a heavy mist had seeped inside him—fogging his brain as well. He closed his eyes and the racing gutter stream sloshed around his upper head, soothing the searing tear the bullet had made, and filling one ear to deafness. As he breathed through his mouth, he found himself to be vaguely thankful that at least he wasn't drowning. He was sure he could hear several things with his other ear: the rain pounding on the hood of his car; the screams of a man as if he had two shattered ankles; the wail and whoop of fast approaching sirens; and the voice of a woman gently calling his name as she began to hold his head away from the rushing gutter.

Chapter 44.

"Oh, Galen, thank God," said Jan as he came to.

His head was killing him, and he felt like he was still swimming underwater. However, he knew where he was and, surprisingly, he found that he could remember many things—the arrival of the ambulances, the shelter of an umbrella as they loaded a handcuffed Carl Sanders into an ambulance with two accompanying officers, his own ambulance ride to a local hospital, and the quick transfer to OHSU which was closer to home, but most memories after that were fuzzy.

"Hi, Jan," he said with a raspiness that surprised him. *Oh, the tubes during surgery,* he thought. "Where are the boys?"

"I have a friend looking after them," said a masked Jan. "No one under 18 is allowed into the hospital unless they're patients themselves."

"And how are they?"

"Better now. Monty nearly went catatonic when we heard about your shooting—especially since we still don't know about his mother. Ryan stepped up as the man in the house and helped his brother through it until we finally heard that you were going to be OK."

Galen noticed that Jan hadn't mentioned Beth by name, and nodded which caused the room to spin for a moment. When the ensuing feeling of nausea passed, he asked. "How long have I been out?"

"I don't know. They said they stabilized you last night, and then they had you into surgery the first thing this morning."

He couldn't see anything that had been repaired, but his left arm was strapped down. "Do you know what they did?"

"You'd better ask the doctor when he comes around. They said some bones were broken, and that there was some minor lung damage, but that you should heal well."

Galen coughed, giving him a strong hint as to where the damage was. "Water?"

Jan reached for a cup with a straw and held it up to her husband's lips. Galen took a couple of sips and felt an immediate soothing of his throat. He drank some more.

"OHSU, right?" he asked. Jan nodded. "How's Beth?"

"They said that she's not getting any worse, and that that's really good news. They're not sure when she'll be off a ventilator, but expect it to be fairly soon."

Galen sighed in relief. What a strange world. He was in the same hospital complex as his daughter, but unable to see her. And he was suffering from a gunshot wound to the shoulder just like Mike Carlson who had received one during Sander's first attack.

"What are we going to do, Galen?" asked Jan. "If I have the boys to look after, that will be hard enough—but to take care of you, too?" She suddenly softened. "I mean, of course I'll..." Just then the doctor swept aside the hanging curtains, and she stopped.

"Good afternoon, Mr. Young," said the youngish, to Galen, doctor. "How are you feeling?"

Galen gave himself a quick evaluation. "Still a little dopey, and I have a pounding headache."

"Yes, you were lucky there—if the angle of that bullet had been any steeper, it might have entered the skull. As it was, it glanced enough to give you a small concussion, but you should be OK from that after a few days. There might be some more pain to come. We used a nerve block on your shoulder during surgery, and that might take a day or so to wear off. The procedure went well, and your prognosis is good." At Galen's raised eyebrows he continued. "That bullet, unfortunately didn't glance off your scapula but went into and through it, angled, and then hit your clavicle which was also severely fractured. There was damage to your left pleura, and the concussive force has bruised your left lung, but both of these will heal soon. You will need to keep your left shoulder immobilized for six weeks at a minimum in order for both bones to heal. We've done our best, but you might find that you won't have the same range of motion as you now have on your right side when all is said and done."

"How long will I be here?"

"We'd like to keep you for a few days just to make sure that there's no internal bleeding anywhere that we haven't caught and watch for brain swelling. We don't expect either of these, but we want to have you under observation, just in case. After that, you'll be free to go home, but nothing strenuous for at least another week."

Galen thanked him and caught a look of concern mixed with exasperation on Jan's face as the curtains swished closed behind him.

Tom stopped by the next morning. "How are you feeling, Galen?" he asked as he stepped into the quiet room with four solid walls which Galen had been moved to.

"Much better, Tom. Sorry I was so out of it when you dropped by yesterday."

"That's OK. It looked like you could use the meds."

Galen nodded, without a resulting feeling of nausea, and asked, "Are Jodi and Glenn all right?"

Tom smiled reassuringly. "Yes. A bullet just grazed Knowles' thigh and he's already out of the hospital and ready to go back to work. Another round hit the lintel just above the door and missed them both."

Galen smiled back in relief. "And Sanders?"

"You're quite a shot from upside down, you know that? Three bullets in the ankle and lower leg on the left, and one in an ankle on the right. He wasn't going anywhere." Tom took a seat next to the bed. "He used a pistol to attack you, but we also found the rifle he used on Mike Carlson, and ballistics has matched it with the rounds found in Carlson's house."

"Have you talked to him?"

"Cushing has and is back in with him this afternoon," affirmed Tom. "No confession on killing Erin Carlson yet, but we expect one to come soon. When Deb asked him why the shooting at the Knowles' house, he confessed that the obituary had set him off—which was basically an admission that he killed Erin and that he was the one who shot Mike. We, of course, need more formal interviews, but Deb thinks that he'll come around given all of the evidence against him."

"Yeah, but if he has good attorneys, we don't have anything solid to connect him to actually running down Erin Carlson, other than his subsequent actions."

"We'll see what a jury says?" asked Tom as they both lapsed into silence.

CHAPTER 45.

AMELIA HAD wanted to help Monty with his saxophone playing and had joined him in easy duets by accompanying him on the French horn. Ryan had wanted what Amelia wanted, and so had added his acoustic guitar to the mix. The trio had worked up a quirky set, but Galen never tired of hearing any of the tunes they played.

It was an odd ensemble of instruments, and the sound emanating from the trio was even stranger, but Galen enjoyed the music. He'd asked before, and so he knew that what he was hearing at the moment was a rendition of a song he was previously unfamiliar with—'Hallelujah' by Leonard Cohen. This, to him, was much better than the cacophony of the ragtag garage band that Ryan had begun practicing with recently in fits and starts.

After the shooting, it was obviously impossible for him to maintain the apartment and care for Monty since he was now the one in need of TLC, so the pair had temporarily moved back in under the familiar roof with Jan and Ryan.

Jan returned home and busied herself with putting away groceries and staging things for dinner. As the practice concluded and the boys and Amelia were stashing their instruments, Jan asked if they would mind preparing the meal she had in mind. There was no fuss, and soon clattering utensils and laughter came from the kitchen as they began to assemble a pan of enchiladas.

"How are you doing, Galen?" asked Jan as she entered the living room and sat beside him on the couch. He was propped up in an awkward position to keep the pressure off his back and shoulder, and she patted some of the bolsters to keep them in place.

"Much better, Jan," said Galen. "I didn't need any pain-killers today other than the Tylenol I was taking before this happened."

"That's good to hear."

"Yeah," he replied. "The only downside is that the painkillers gave me a break from the shingles, too, and now I'm feeling them again like they're on steroids." He awkwardly reached up to scratch his left temple with his right hand. "So, same old, same old."

"At least the headaches are gone."

Galen had the feeling that all of this was just small talk leading up to something, and sure enough, Jan's face became more serious.

"Galen, I was called by the Governor's Office today, and after that I received a call from the Department of Corrections."

Oh, no, thought Galen. *Something's happened to Beth, and this can't be good.* He straightened himself up as much as possible and then asked, "It's Beth, isn't it?" Beth had been in a touch-and-go situation at OHSU and had seemed to be turning a corner. The last report had been that she was beginning to breath on her own but needed oxygen at nights. Still, they expected long-lasting impacts to her respiratory and nervous systems, and to anticipate memory issues for some time to come. They had all been cautiously optimistic and waiting on pins and needles for more news.

Jan nodded, but didn't appear to be devastated by what she had to say, which Galen took as a continuation of the poor relationship his wife had with their daughter. Then she almost smiled. "The Governor's Office said that they've been selectively pardoning inmates who've served more than half of their sentences and who've been severely impacted by the virus. They were letting me know that Beth is a candidate for early release and may not have to return to Coffee Creek if she survives, which they now expect her to."

Galen couldn't immediately respond. It was as if he himself had been freed from life-support, too.

CHAPTER 46.

TWO WEEKS later, Galen was back in the apartment. Jan had tried her best, but was becoming increasingly irritable by the day and so he had decided to make the move earlier than expected. After several arguments, Galen had finally divined that Jan's main source of stress was the thought of having Beth living under the same roof with her again. It had seemed at first that his wife had softened her stance about her daughter given the severity of Beth's illness, but Jan remained convinced that Beth had sinned beyond redemption, even if she was being released from her earthly prison.

Jan had lapsed into her silent treatment, the boys were on edge, and Galen had had enough. So, after a soul-bearing heart-to-heart one evening, the pair had finally decided that the best and only solution would be for them to divorce. This would separate funds and allow Galen to find a small house that he, Beth, and the boys could live in until Beth was able to manage on her own. Jan had refused to sell the house she was in, but had agreed on a home equity loan equal to Galen's share.

Galen hated the thought of finding another house in Portland, but realized that it would be something he could leave for Beth and his grandsons if she liked it and was some-day back on her feet. He knew that after retirement, he himself would need and want to move further inland to quieter and more wide-open spaces.

There was a thump at the basement door and the hiking duo tromped in, red-faced and smiling. Galen slowly rose from the couch and walked over to the kitchen to greet them.

"Hi, Gramps!" said Monty as he threw his small backpack down next to the jumbled row of shoes and boots at the door. "Have you ever been up the trail above Multnomah Falls? It's totally awesome up there. They even have a platform you can like stand on and look all the way down to the visitor's center. We even hiked further up and followed the stream to some rad rocks with another little waterfall."

"Nope, I've never been," Galen lied. "I hope you took some pictures."

"Duh," said Monty as he opened the snack drawer in the kitchen. "Want some, Carol?" he asked while holding out a bag of Cheez-it's toward his friend.

"No thanks, Munchmaster," replied Carol which brought a huge smile to the boy's face. Turning with a grin of her own to Galen, she said, "Detective, the next time we go on a hike we'll need a whole box of Clif bars," to which Monty exploded in laughter.

"It's on the list," said Galen to Carol's back as she turned and closed the door behind her on her way up the outside steps —which struck him as a rather abrupt, if not rude, action.

"Speaking of groceries," she said as she returned with both arms full. "I spied the list on the counter when I picked up this rascal, and we stopped by Albertsons and got most of it."

"What?" asked a shocked Galen. "You didn't have to do this, Carol. Jan stops by and does our shopping, for now."

"Yeah, but we wanted to. So, there," in a kidding childlike voice.

"Well, I really appreciate it. How much did it come to? I'll go get the checkbook."

She handed him the receipt, and he left the kitchen to hunt up the checks. Monty was busy building a sandwich, and Carol patted him on the shoulder as she passed him, following Galen into the living room.

"Say, Galen?" asked Carol as he fumbled one-handed with the checkbook at a side-table. She reached over and held the book open with her long fingers while he wrote out the amount. "Tom and I were wondering if Monty could stay with us one night this weekend, if you don't need him. We were thinking we could drive to the coast and spend some time at Cannon Beach, and maybe find a trail to explore."

Galen turned from writing the check to see Monty standing behind her with mouth full, furiously bobbing his head, a thick sandwich grasped firmly between both hands.

Chapter 47.

"**You're looking** better every day, Galen," said John as he held the door open for his friend to enter. It was getting too cold for them to meet outside at the pub, so John had started asking the detective over to his home on Kearny St. for an occasional beer after work. Galen still had his left arm wrapped up and in a sling, but he was much more mobile, the back of his head was now unbandaged, and the cuts on his face and neck now just faint red lines.

"Thanks, John," said Galen as he slipped off his shoes and took the offered seat. "And I feel much better too. I only have a few more weeks before I can chuck this damn sling."

John gave him a pat on the good arm and asked, "The usual?" as he ducked into the small adjoining kitchen to fetch them some ales. Galen knew he needn't reply and sank back in his newly accustomed seat—a worn cozy chair upholstered with the image of a faded green Chinese dragon. He loved this living room—dark but warm, heavy curtains sometimes thrown open, stacks of books and newspapers, gas fire in the small stone fireplace, and a few fine-art prints mixed in with sixties era posters on the walls—the eclectic furnishings of a contented bachelor.

"Try this," as John set a pint glass on the one open space remaining at the side-table. "It's a new Irish ale from Ecliptic Brewing."

"Thanks, John," said Galen, hoisting the glass and toasting his friend as he took a welcome sip. "Hmm, not bad."

"There's more—I've really taken a shine to it."

The pair sat and caught up on events since they'd last visited. The conversation turned, as it often did, to Robert Armlin, since he had been John Doherty's dearest friend. As they were warmed by the fire and the ale, John slid into a philosophical mood, staring quietly into the flames. After several minutes of comfortable silence between them, John asked, "Do you know that song, *Carrickfergus*, Galen?"

"I don't think so. Sounds Irish?"

"Yeah, an old tune, and it just came to me as I was sitting here. There's this verse that goes..." and John started singing in a low raspy voice:

> *My childhood days bring back sad reflections*
> *Of happy times I spent so long ago*
> *My boyhood friends and my own relations*
> *Have all passed on now like melting snow.*

Ah, this is going to get sad, thought Galen in preparation when John had finished.

But his friend surprised him in a way. "You know, I'm reaching that same point in my life now. No family, since my brother passed last year, and now Robert..." He took a deep breath and looked up at the ceiling, as if trying to halt some tears that may have been coming, but for once they never appeared. "Anyway, maybe Bob's death has made me more aware of my own mortality than I already was."

Galen slowly shook his head in sympathy. "Sorry, John. This has been an even tougher year for you than I thought."

"Yeah, it has. But while I was thinking about that song, I realized that it's the same for almost everybody my age who's still around. And it ain't going to get better for any of us, so dwelling on it isn't going to be any help at all, now is it? All we can do is keep the memories of those before us alive, and hope to God that someone does the same for us one day.

"So, and this has been on my mind for quite a while—I want to do something to celebrate Bob in a way that I think he would have appreciated." Galen was about to ask what that was when John continued, "I approached Emma with my idea, and she's already wholly on board. I want to compile his greatest editorials into a book and add my perspective on them— how prophetic he could be, or how much things have changed since he posited something—for the better or worse. Sort of a social memoir-slash-commentary. Emma has even agreed to edit it and has offered to write some commentary, too. She's actually excited about it."

"What a great idea," said Galen as they talked about the possibilities and then lapsed again into their own musings while enjoying the fire. He cradled his left arm in his right—his very personal reminder of his recent brush with death, and his thoughts wandered from the close of Robert's life to what remained in his own: his impending divorce, retirement, and the future of his daughter and her sons. After his shooting these had seemed overwhelming, but now he knew he could deal with them, even as his emotions still ranged from trepidation to relief. In his mind, he was suddenly back in the Pendleton high country looking across the scrub brush at a distant, towering thunderstorm making its way toward a place that desperately needed the rain.

"Do you want another?" snapped him out of his revery as John rose from his seat and headed for the kitchen. "Let's toast to the new book!"

Acknowledgements

I want to thank Lynn Ate for her suggestions and time spent in editing, and Jessica Hatch of Hatch Editorial Services for an editorial assessment that pointed me in new and better directions. The beta readers at Entrada Publishing also provided most welcome comments about the very rough first draft.

ABOUT THE AUTHOR

David Ackley grew up in Fairbanks, Alaska and raised a family in Juneau. His professional career in Alaska included both fisheries biometrics and management positions with the state and federal governments. He has earned Master's degrees in Chinese Language and Literature (Wisconsin), and in Fisheries Science (Alaska). David is now retired and living in northern Idaho, where he began a small business in lutherie – building guitars, Irish bouzoukis, and ukuleles (www.dastringedinstruments.com). The lutherie business has flagged somewhat while he gets some stories out of his head. Please visit the Rain and Breeze Books website, www.rainandbreeze.com, for more information about David and his books.